D0283566

A Second Chance Summer

Book One of the
Coming Back to Cornwall
series

Katharine E. Smith

HEDDON PUBLISHING

www.heddonpublishing.com
www.facebook.com/heddonpublishing
@PublishHeddon

Katharine E. Smith is a writer, editor and publisher.

An avid reader of contemporary writers such as Kate Atkinson, David Nicholls and Anne Tyler, Katharine's aim is to write books she would like to read herself. She has four novels to her name, and one non-fiction guide, written with fellow indie authors in mind.

Katharine runs Heddon Publishing from her home in Shropshire, which she shares with her husband and their two children.

For my friends.
Life would be a lot less fun without you.

A Second Chance Summer

BACK

It's hot in the club and the bassline of the music shudders through the floorboards as I sway almost imperceptibly in time with the beat, enjoying the feeling of hands on my hips, warm breath on my not-quite sunburned shoulders.

I lean back. His kiss slides along, from the straps of my sundress, up my neck, stopping just shy of my earlobe, where he whispers my name.

Just as he's moving his hands around my waist, the alarm begins to sound and I turn in a panic, to see... not beautiful, golden Sam but short, middle-aged Jason Wilberforce, my boss from World of Stationery, where I have worked for six years. I gasp, and try to push him away and, as in all good stories, I wake up to realise it's only a dream.

Sadly for me, I am no longer eighteen and my beautiful, golden Sam is long since lost to me. A summer romance, as everyone told me it was destined to be.

But, as I start to come round, blinking sore eyes and cursing my alarm clock, I also take in the light – that special, unmistakeable light, and the sounds from outside.

The seagulls calling from the roof above my dormer window.

The street sweeper, making its rounds, preparing the town for another influx of visitors strewing the streets with chip wrappers; dropped ice creams which no amount of accompanying child's tears will wash away; carelessly discarded beer bottles. It all gets swept up, only to be replaced like-for-like, every single day.

Garden birds and their songs add a sweetness to the morning; unfailingly cheerful and seeming to sing for the sheer joy of another day dawning.

And just there, if I listen carefully - try to strain my hearing past this immediate cacophony - the constant, comforting - exciting - sound of the sea.

I am back, in my beloved Cornwall, exactly where I was ten years ago, in that summer of Sam. This is the county that calls to me when I am away from it; rugged and wild, exciting and exotic. The place which makes me feel alive.

Julie, my best friend, my companion that first summer so long ago, is also back; tucked away in the room next to mine, just a thin wall separating us. We're both twenty-eight now and a lot has happened in ten years but we've given ourselves another summer and we are both determined to make the most of it.

1

Unfortunately, in order to secure our places in Cornwall this summer, both Julie and I have had to take on two jobs each. My first, which I am busily readying myself for, is as a breakfast waitress. The very same job I had ten years ago, when I'd just finished my A-Levels. In the intervening years, I've accidentally established a career in sales, and I have to say I've become pretty good at it. Over the years I learned the full range of stationery products my firm had to offer, and I established good relationships with many of the long-term clients. However, it hasn't made me happy – despite the OK pay and the regular incentives. And I am pretty sure that Jason Wilberforce (he of the wandering hands and mouth from my dream) would not be able to make me happy, either.

Julie, meanwhile, has just come out of a long-term relationship. She was due to be getting married next year, to Gabe, who I really like. I personally think they are well suited, but she says she just isn't ready for it: "We've lived together three years and already all the domestic chores have fallen to me. I'm cooking every night, picking up his dirty pants from the bathroom floor, reminding him when it's his mum's birthday. I just... I feel trapped. I don't like it. It's not me."

So she left him. She left him a note, which I think was pretty cowardly of her, but I suppose at least it wasn't a text message, and went to her mum's. It was while she was there, just a few short weeks ago, that she called me up with this ridiculous idea that we could re-live our golden summer, as we'd taken to calling it. I'd laughed before I'd realised she was serious.

"Come on, Julie, you and Gabe will be back together by the end of the week. You're meant to be together."

"Hmm."

"You love him!"

"I'm not sure how much that has got to do with anything anymore. I don't think he loves me."

"Of course he bloody loves you!"

"Then why does he expect me to do everything? It used to be that he told me he loved me every day. Now, more often than not, he's asking me what's for tea."

She had me there. And in honesty, having got nowhere near the moving-in stage of a relationship, never mind getting engaged, and certainly never mind getting married, I could see her point. It didn't sound like much fun.

Sure, I did everything around my flat, but then there was only me there. I could eat what I wanted, watch what I wanted on TV, put on whatever music I liked, leave the washing-up for the next day or clean the place from top to bottom (although admittedly this only happened very occasionally) in the knowledge that nobody was going to come and mess it up – or, if anybody did, it would be me. Sometimes one of my parents would let themselves in when I was at work, if they knew I was having a hard week, and leave a freshly-cooked meal, or give the flat a good clean, but that was a very occasional treat and I certainly never asked them to do it.

For the last few years, I have been settled, self-sufficient, and my life has run to a timetable: 9-5 office job (sometimes working later if a particular contract necessitates it), Pilates on a Monday, running club on a Wednesday, after-work drinks on a Friday, and a well-earned lie-in on Saturdays and Sundays, with perhaps a lazy meander around the shops, or a meal out, or an evening at a friend's house. Sunday lunch at my parents' and maybe a walk out on the Malverns or in the Wyre Forest, to 'blow the cobwebs away' as Dad always says. It has been all very comfortable. And very predictable. But now friends are getting settled, trying out being grown-up (or so it seems to me), getting engaged, even talking about having children! Julie, as she well knew, had caught me at the exact right moment to persuade me to try something new.

"OK, OK."

"OK, we're going to Cornwall?"

"No, OK, I get it. I take your point. But you can't just ring me and say 'Let's go to Cornwall' and expect me to drop everything."

"Why not?"

"I've got a job…"

"… which you hate," Julie supplied.

"I've got a flat…"

"… which you could easily rent out. Really, really easily. In fact, Lee's looking for somewhere at the moment. That would make things easy."

Lee is Julie's older brother. OK, that was one solution and I'd known Lee since he was thirteen and we were eleven, so I knew I could trust him. Renting to him should be easy. But I wasn't going to capitulate, just like that.

"I go to Pilates…" I tried, lamely.

"I'm pretty sure they've got Pilates in Cornwall."

"I've got a notice period at work…"

"Yep, so if you hand in your notice tomorrow, we could

be heading off in a month's time. Just ready for the start of the season. I've spoken to Bea and she's happy to have us both back at the Sail Loft. You as breakfast waitress and morning receptionist, me as breakfast chef. That means we've got our evenings – except for the odd one when Bea needs me to cover."

"You've spoken to Bea?"

Bea Danson is the owner of the Sail Loft Hotel, where both Julie and I had worked that golden summer. We'd kept in touch very loosely over the years; Christmas cards, mainly. Bea had been lovely to work for and, judging by some of the stories which the other seasonal workers had to offer, this was quite unusual.

"What?"

"You've spoken to Bea? Without even asking me first?"

"Well, yeah. I mean, I could have spoken to you first but I knew if I did you'd come up with a load of reasons not to do it. So I've spoken to her, and she's got jobs for us. And David can rent us our old rooms again."

David, Bea's younger brother, had previously let us rent his attic rooms – which were tiny and had a pokey kitchen with a two-ring hob, and a small, hot bathroom with a porthole window, but were right in the centre of town - for a very reasonable price. We'd really fallen on our feet, for two fresh-faced teenagers down from the Midlands. But was it possible that ten years later we could relive the experience and be as happy as we were back then?

"I'll call you back," I said.

Within twelve hours, I'd handed my notice in at work. Jason's face had fallen. "But you're our best salesperson. Nobody knows our range like you do. Nobody else has stayed here as long as you."

The last sentence was the nail in the coffin.

"What if we call it a sabbatical?" he'd asked. "You have a break for a few months and come back to us after you've had your little summer holiday."

Call it what you like, I'd thought. It isn't that Jason is an unpleasant man; he is perfectly nice but sometimes I think he lives for work, and that he was sizing me up to follow in his footsteps. He sometimes called me his number two, which would have the rest of the office snorting with laughter, but he never seemed to notice. I felt a sudden, strong urgency within me; a need to escape, and a resistance to having my life mapped out for me in such a way. Maybe the predictability of everything had been niggling away at me for a while. Julie knew this and seized on this opportunity, which works for both of us – as long as she really does want to split up with Gabe. Oh well, there's no going back now, for me at least.

Twenty-four hours later, I'd agreed a rental contract with Lee for three months, which more than covered my mortgage. I'd spoken to David about the rooms, and to Bea about the job(s), just to double check that these arrangements were as firm as Julie was suggesting. Not that I don't trust my friend, but she and I are at other ends of the spectrum when it comes to needing reliability. Luckily, both David and Bea sounded happy to hear from me and I must admit, after I'd spoken to them, I felt a slow wave roll right through me, washing away a certain greyness and replacing it with nerves, and excitement. It seemed that Julie was to be trusted after all. And from that point on, until the day we left, I couldn't stop looking at photos of Cornwall online, checking out the webcam footage from the harbour. I just could not wait.

Thirty-one days later, I was rammed into a car with Julie and about a hundred over-full bags and cases, Radio 1 on full blast as we merrily headed down the M5, ignoring the fact that the sky was full of grey, low-hanging clouds and starting to weep great fat tears onto our windscreen. It clearly wouldn't be able to hold back much longer. We didn't care. We were off to Cornwall.

We had to park a few streets away from David's house as it is on one of those charming but inconveniently slim streets in the centre of the town. We decided to go and say hello before bringing in any of our luggage.

"You're here!" David exclaimed and he insisted on giving us a proper Cornish cream tea first (we couldn't bring ourselves to tell him we stopped at a McDonald's just half an hour earlier) before helping us bring all our bags into the house and up the stairs.

It felt like nothing had changed in the flat since our last visit. Even the vague smell of washing powder and furniture polish seemed reminiscent of those days. The rooms were spotlessly clean, and looked spacious with bare shelves and just a bed, chair and chest of drawers, but as soon as we'd dragged all our bags up and started to try and sort out places for clothes, books, computers, they seemed to shrink. But they also started to feel like home. David says he's had a few lodgers come and go over the years, but he doesn't really need the money and he says that, depending on the people, it can be easier to keep the rooms empty.

"It must be a bit annoying, having people running up and down your stairs," I said to him on my third, increasingly breathless and red-faced trip. We share

David's front door, traipsing through the shady, dark hallway and straight up two flights of stairs, to get to our rooms.

"Oh, it's OK with you two – I did have a guy one year who kept bringing different girls back, though, and that got a bit annoying. And noisy, on occasion. Also, it's giving strangers access to my house. I don't know who they are, they might want to nick something. Or they might take a fancy to me while I'm asleep. Who could blame them?"

"Well, indeed," I laughed. "You're safe with me and Julie, though. No offence."

"None taken! Anyway, I'm often at Martin's these days so you and Julie have got the place to yourselves a lot of the time. You can use my garden if you want to, and my kitchen if you need something a bit more substantial than the one upstairs."

**

Now we have a few days to just acclimatise, as Julie calls it, during which we meander around town, drinking too much most nights, and revisiting all our old haunts. Although the town hasn't changed very much in some ways; the harbour remains the same and the twisty, turny streets – which are not open to negotiation – are exactly as they were, it seems as though new houses and blocks of 'luxury apartments' have been squeezed in wherever there was an iota of space. And many of the old shops and restaurants appear to have had a facelift; replacing old, weathered wood and aging, worn carpets with shiny chrome and expensive black tiles. Hoffs, the nightclub where Jason and I (I can't help an involuntary shudder at those words) had been in that dream, and which featured sticky carpets and sweat-dripping ceilings, is now a posh-looking fish restaurant. Despite all of this, as I walk the streets and beaches each day, I feel increasingly like I am back home.

After a few days, I am also acclimatising to a new kind of work – or at least one which I thought I'd left behind long ago. I get dressed in the flat; white blouse and black skirt, sensible flat shoes, and hurry with Julie along the early morning streets to the Sail Loft.

Bea is waiting for us and greets us with the most enormous hugs. She doesn't seem to have aged a day in ten years. I am touched by her warmth for she must have had different staff each year since we were last here but she seems genuinely happy to see us, and I am instantly at ease with her. Once my first shift is done, I have my own breakfast (cooked by Julie), change into a dark blue skirt and light blue shirt, and I'm transformed into the hotel receptionist. The work is not exactly challenging and I can feel my inner voice screaming at me about taking a major backwards step in my career (maybe that's my dad's voice I can hear, come to think of it – he's a great one for security and stability, so I guess I've inherited my steady side from him) but I am really enjoying it.

Mostly, the customers are lovely people – but of course there are the ones who just love to complain, about anything and everything. Toast is too hot/too cold; there's a small (invisible) mark on a spoon; the eggs aren't runny/are runny; the bacon is greasy/too crispy/not crispy enough; somebody's finished the orange juice and it hasn't been refilled. I learned ten years ago to try and spot these types as they entered the breakfast room. It would seem that I haven't lost that skill.

Now that I'm on reception, I have a whole new list of complaints to compile: the sand hasn't been washed from the shower by the chambermaid; the teabags haven't been replenished; there's a layer of dust on the TV; the seagulls are too noisy.

For the most part, though, people are lovely. You generally get people at their best when they're on holiday. I keep a few notes about the more eccentric characters, though; they're good fodder for the book I intend to write one day.

What I have noticed is that I'm more tired than I used to be when I was eighteen. And I wouldn't say that at twenty-eight I'm exactly ancient. But I am sure Julie and I used to be out at pubs/clubs/beach parties till about 3am most mornings and still be bright and breezy into work. We'd rest in the afternoons, ready to begin it all again. Now I feel like if I fall asleep in the afternoon, I won't wake up again until the next morning. Instead, I try and go for a run along the cliff paths, which is bloody hard work, especially now the days are getting hotter. I'll cool off and ease my muscles with a swim in the sea, which is my ultimate luxury and one of the main draws for me to this place. I have dreamed for so long of living here and I'm sure that if I could, I'd swim in the sea nearly every day, and I'd still be doing so when I was ninety. There is magic in the air in Cornwall, I swear.

2

Since we've been here, Julie really does appear determined to re-live that first golden summer, in every way. Even now we're working, she wants to be out almost every night. Although Hoffs is long-gone, there are now three clubs in town to choose from: Shapes, Nico's and Ecuabar. Shapes is a bit more music-driven and a 'proper' club, with visiting DJs and live acts, and all-nighters at the weekends. Nico's is typically cheesy – your average 'cattle market' - and Ecuabar fancies itself a cut above, with a VIP area and expensive cocktails. We have been to all three but there is no way we can afford to go to Ecuabar very often, and Shapes is also a bit pricey although I much prefer the music there. Nico's is definitely playing to the tourist crowd, with happy hours every night, 2-4-1 cocktails, Ladies Night (can you believe anywhere still does that?) on a Thursday and karaoke on a Wednesday.

Somehow we always seem to end up in there, swaying back to the flat in the early morning, and getting back up again just after five. It's not surprising I'm tired.

The other thing Julie is determined to re-live is going on the pull. I'm not kidding; she must have got off with four different men already, and it's only week two.

She laughs when I mention this. "Making up for lost time, aren't I?"

I can't help but think of Gabe and how he would feel about this. Julie doesn't know but he came to see me, the night before we left. I'd just got back to Mum and Dad's, after making sure I'd cleared the flat for Lee, and there was Gabe, sitting in his car.

I spotted him before he saw me; he was gazing into the distance and he looked so sad. I knocked on his window and he jumped then opened his door, smiling at me.

"Hi Alice, I'm sorry to just turn up like this."

"That's alright!" I said, giving him a hug. "You could have knocked on Mum and Dad's door, you know."

"I didn't want to disturb them," he said, "and I'm not sure where I'm welcome anymore. I'm not sure…"

His voice drifted away and I waited a moment for him to finish his sentence but it seemed he couldn't.

"You're not sure of anything much?" I suggested.

He nodded and his eyes filled with tears. I put my hand on his and pulled him towards Mum and Dad's. "Gabe's here!" I called, pushing him up the stairs as I knew he wouldn't want them to see him crying.

"Alright, love!" Dad's distracted, TV-watching voice drifted back.

Gabe and I sat quietly for a while and he pulled himself together, which I could see was an effort.

"Look after her, will you, Alice?" he asked, his brown eyes fixing mine.

"Of course I will," I said. "And I'm sorry, Gabe."

"Don't be!" He laughed without any humour. "I messed up. I just… got lazy, I suppose. I should have known not to do that with Julie. You know what she's like; strong, wild… it's what I love about her."

I couldn't help but agree, internally at least. I'd been amazed when Julie had moved in with Gabe, and more so

13

when they'd got engaged, because although she was rarely out of a relationship, I hadn't ever imagined her really settling down. But I could see he was good for her. However, I think he dropped the ball if what she's told me is true, and what he said seemed to back it up.

Gabe didn't stay long but I promised I'd keep in touch with him while we were away. "I don't want to know what she's up to," he'd smiled sadly, "I just need to know she's OK."

I gave him a hug.

"Don't tell her I've been to see you, please, Alice. She'll think I'm trying to get to her through you. I'm not, I promise."

I think Julie probably just needs to blow off steam. She is careful to make sure it's tourists that she targets, so that she doesn't get a reputation around town.

"Why aren't you getting stuck in, anyway?" she's asked me.

The answer is, I just don't feel like it. Unlike Julie, I don't think I have anything to prove to anyone. I've had a few boyfriends over the years since we were last here but I've learned to be cautious since Geoff.

I got together with Geoff a few months after the golden summer, after I accepted that Sam and I were not meant to be, after all. It was probably a rebound thing and Geoff was so different to Sam but he was so intense. After three dates, he wanted to be with me every night, and when he realised I loved Cornwall so much, he said he'd quit his job and we could move down here. Well, I knew I wanted to move down here, but I found it a bit unnerving that he was ready to pack everything in for somebody he really hardly knew. He had a good job, and a place to live, and seemed really well set-up. He changed his mind about Cornwall after a few months, anyway, but I carried on dreaming.

In the early days, Geoff would bring me flowers, chocolates, bottles of wine. He had a nice car and took me out to the countryside for walks, evening meals at nice pubs, that kind of thing. On paper, I guess it all looked good. He seemed the romantic type and was very attentive. Only for me, he was too attentive. I was, after all, only nineteen. He was twenty-three, which seemed very grown-up back then. I could tell Mum and Dad had their doubts but somehow I stayed with Geoff for well over a year. It doesn't sound long now but it felt like ages. When I did finally gather the nerve to tell him it was over, it was awful. He sobbed, and sobbed, then sobbed some more. He asked what he could do differently. He said he was going to ask me to marry him.

I was in my second year at university. Getting married was the last thing on my mind. I also knew that I still harboured thoughts of Sam, which confirmed that Geoff was not the right person for me. Geoff's sorrow quickly turned to anger but I had made up my mind and I knew I had to stay strong.

Now I'm back here, I can't help but think of Sam and he is on my mind every day. It seems like every corner I turn, a memory floats up. The wall where he was sitting when he'd pulled me to him, and kissed me on our first proper date, when he'd tried unsuccessfully to teach me to surf then bought me chips and tea, in polystyrene containers. Somehow, nothing had ever tasted so good.

In the evening, we'd walked for some time then we had stopped at this wall. Sam smelled of the sea, and smoke from the bonfire down on the beach. I can even remember what he was wearing; a dark-blue hoodie, which was soft to the touch, and a pair of knee-length shorts, which hung gently from his frame and revealed his blonde-haired, tanned legs. His arms reached inside my zip-up jacket, and encircled my waist. Gently, he reeled me in.

Sam's eyes were brilliant blue (I concede I have maybe embellished my memories but this is how I see them in my mind) and his hair was wavy; neither long, nor short, dark-blond. A typical Cornish surfer, I suppose. But one of the funniest, kindest people I had ever, and have ever, met.

I do keep wondering what would happen if I bumped into him but I know he was itching to leave Cornwall – strange though that may seem to me. He had laughed when I said I wanted to move here.

"Oh yeah? Going to open a beach café?"

I'd blushed a little as, in my teenage mind, that was exactly what I was going to do. It was going to be amazing. Julie and I had already discussed the idea.

"Go surfing every day?" He'd pushed his point a little further.

"Erm…"

"Ah, I know, it would be amazing, but I've seen so many of those businesses come and go. Seriously, Cornwall might be beautiful but there's fuck-all for folk to do and fuck-all money 'less you're a second-home-owner from the Home Counties."

That was me put straight.

I wonder what he has ended up doing. His dream was to work in wildlife conservation but he hadn't been too hopeful that he would be able to follow it. And anyway, people change. When I was eighteen, I didn't know what I wanted to do – maybe work for a charity, or work with animals - but I did know I didn't want to work in an office. I ended up selling stationery. Could Sam be working in the City, in London? I just couldn't put him in a suit and tie, somehow.

Maybe a super-cool digital designer based somewhere like Bristol, or Brighton.

I knew where his Auntie Lou lived – or at least where she had lived ten years ago – but it is a little way out of town and I had never met her so I couldn't just happen to be passing and pop in to say hello. And the flat above the fancy dress shop, where Sam sometimes stayed with his mate Christian, looks like it's no longer lived in. But anyway, Sam is not why I'm here. He's just a happy memory from this place. I am not about to become a stalker. I am not Geoff.

So far, whenever Julie cops off with somebody, I've taken it as a chance to actually go to bed a bit earlier. I make sure she is OK, and happy, but I can't just stand around like a lemon while she's got her tongue down some bloke's throat. I ask her to text me when she's heading home, and I wait up to make sure she's safe, even though she tells me I don't need to.

I'm not exactly averse to some romance if it should come my way, but I am not interested in pointless, drunken snogs. Besides which, I haven't seen anybody with whom I'd like to share a pointless, drunken snog.

Tonight, as it's Saturday, it's extra-busy everywhere. There are rumours of a party on the beach and I'm quite keen to go. I used to love those parties: music pumping out of somebody's speakers; fires crackling, the heat sending the air wavy; the sound of the sea rushing across the sand towards us, trying but failing to find us; retreating in the darkness.

This is the kind of evening when I could be tempted into a kiss, I suppose. There's something far more romantic and exciting about a beach party than a heaving, too-hot club.

Julie and I have both had an afternoon snooze, in preparation. Tomorrow, Sunday, is our day off, so we don't have to think about getting up early. I am really looking forward to lying in my bed, reading all morning, maybe having a little doze, listening to the gulls, and the people passing by on the street below.

We drink a gin & tonic in my room, Julie mucking about with some new glittery make-up she's bought. I have gone light on the make-up, with a little bit of mascara and eye-liner. I feel like my skin's already caught the Cornish sun and I leave it bare. I'm wearing a FatFace tunic, with some shorts underneath and a hoodie I bought here ten years ago zipped over the top. The other thing I love about beach parties is that there is no pressure to dress up. Quite the opposite, in fact. I'm very happy to dress down.

Julie is in cut-offs, with a hooded vest top. Her dark, curly hair is loose down her back and she's bought a silver anklet which sets off her dark-skinned legs beautifully. She is stunning, Julie, and I always tell her that she really doesn't need make-up but she never believes me.

"Fancy another?" she asks me, sucking an ice cube from her empty glass.

I laugh, and gulp my own drink down. "Why not?" I feel that familiar excitement of a night out, followed by a day off. I feel suddenly, headily, free. I hug Julie.

"What's that for?"

"Just… this. I'm so happy. What a great idea. Thank

you, for making me do this."

"That's OK! Thanks for coming with me. I don't know what I'd have done if you'd said no. Probably have gone back to Gabe."

"You wouldn't… would you?" I don't like to think that I'm behind them being apart. I want to tell her about him coming to see me, but he asked me not to. And really, what good would it do to tell her? It would just make her feel worse about things.

"Nah! But I don't suppose I'd be here. I do kind of miss him, but I'm too angry at him to miss him too much."

"Well… I hope he's OK. I do like him, you know that. But you've got to do what's right for you." I consider telling her about his visit the night before we came down here but I don't see what good it will do any of us.

Julie nods, and pours an extra dash of gin into her drink. "You're right. I have. To freedom!"

She clinks her glass against mine; a tad too vigorously, I think, as some of my drink sloshes over the side, onto my bare legs.

"Freedom," I agree.

Beach party, here we come!

The streets and the pubs are busy as we walk through town; people are crowded onto and around the tables outside the Mainbrace.

"Stop for one for some Dutch courage?" Julie asks.

I would normally say we've already had enough Dutch courage, especially given that our bags each hold plenty of ready-mixed gin & tonic (this would have been cider ten years ago; maybe I have changed more than I thought) but I'm filled with excitement and nerves and another drink doesn't seem like a bad idea. "Go on, then!"

We push our way inside, and I take in the warmth of the pub; its atmosphere – there is a mixture of locals and holiday-makers, chatting and laughing. This is one pub where anyone and everyone can feel welcome. Julie edges her way steadily to the bar, and I keep close behind. The crowd seems to part for Julie and admiring glances are cast her way but she doesn't notice. In her wake, I'm looking around surreptitiously. No matter how hard I pretend otherwise, I'm keeping an eye out for Sam.

Julie turns suddenly. "You're definitely going to bump into him this summer, I can feel it."

"What? Who?" I ask, unconvincingly.

"Don't give me that!" She grins. "You two were in lurve, properly. I know you're looking for Sam."

She turns abruptly at the sound of the barman's voice, and I can tell from his reaction that she is giving him her most winning smile. "What's it to be, my love?"

"We'll have two G&Ts please, barman."

"I'm guessing you two ladies don't need slimline tonic?"

Smooth.

"Too right. Full fat tonic for us, please."

"Here you go," the barman smiles at us both, wiping the bar with a small towel before he places the bottles and glasses in front of us. "What are you two up to tonight, then?"

"Beach party," Julie says as I hear a guy behind us muttering that he's dying of thirst.

"That right, eh? Well, don't forget us, if you get a bit cold down the beach."

"We won't!" Julie scoops up both glasses and bottles, and flashes a winning smile at the very thirsty man behind, before sashaying through the waiting drinkers with me once more following on.

We take the drinks outside and lean against the pub garden wall. I am happy to just rest here for a while and watch the boats bobbing in the harbour. I always used to love watching them as the night slowly seeped into the daytime, bringing moonlight and mystery.

"He was cute!" Julie says.

I roll my eyes. "Who was?"

"That barman."

"If you say so."

"Come on, you miserable bugger, lighten up! He was cute. And charming."

"Charming... or slimy - *I don't suppose you ladies need slimline tonics* – how many times a night do you think he says that?"

"Well, I liked him!"

"You like everyone."

"Do not!" Julie nudges me in the ribs and we both break into laughter.

Despite her tendency to cop off with a different bloke every other night, I am really loving having all this time with her. It's just like it used to be. We have known each other since we started secondary school, so we've done all our growing up together. Periods, bras, first kisses, first sex... first ex... We know each other without having to explain ourselves or make excuses. I've missed her since she's been with Gabe. I decide to tell her.

"Have you really?" she asks.

"Yes, of course I have, you wally. I mean, I was always really happy that you two were happy. And you know I liked... *like* Gabe a lot. I wasn't jealous, and you never made me feel like a gooseberry or anything but, you know, when people settle down together, things inevitably change. They have to. I totally understand."

"Well, you don't have to worry about that now!" Julie clinks her glass against mine.

"You do miss him, though?"

Her face softens, and saddens a little. "Yes, of course I do. How could I not? And I still love him, really. But I'm not sure that's enough."

"Have you heard from him?"

"Not much, not these last couple of weeks, but that's probably my fault," she admits. "I went to see him the day before we travelled down here and told him I didn't want him to get in touch for a while. I think I was a bit of a bitch, really."

I think again of his visit to me. I guess that followed whatever Julie said to him.

"Why don't you give him a ring?"

"I will, I suppose. Someday soon. But not tonight. Come on," Julie pulls on her determined and happy expression, "drink up, we've a party to go to."

I had half wondered if we might stick out like sore thumbs on the beach – if everybody else would be eighteen and we'd look like old fogies. I needn't have worried. By the time we reach the beachside road, the light is fading, highlighting the bright swipes of orange and pink across the sky, above the setting sun. Occasional vapour trails criss-cross the colours, gradually vanishing as the planes which expelled them disappear across the ocean.

I am gripped by excitement at the sight of the beach, which appears to be hosting not one but four parties – each with a fire at the centre, each competing for the title of Loudest Music.

I want to laugh aloud. I feel like I'm eighteen again.

I don't. I'm not.

Julie and I look at each other. Where to begin? Both suddenly swept by the same inspiration, we pull off our shoes on the sandy pavement, which is still warm from the heat of the day. We each take hold of the other's hand and we run down the slipway, onto the sand, laughing as our feet sink into the soft, white grains. We nearly run headlong into a man with a crate of beers under his arm. "Steady on, girls!" he grins.

Girls! He called us girls. Maybe we're not so old. We remain holding hands as we wander tentatively towards the closest fire. Here, the party-goers are, if anything, older than us – and much, much younger. There are families with kids, who dart about round the fire, not quite ignoring their parents' pleas to be careful. There are coolboxes, and disposable barbecues. Picnic blankets, and plastic cups and plates. These are organised people. This is not for us.

I smile at a little girl who goes to hide behind my legs, and stop for a moment while the boy chasing her tries to make up his mind if it's OK to carry on while she's hiding behind a stranger. I grin at him and move quickly out of the way. He pounces, and the girl giggles. "Sorry!" I say to her and Julie and I walk on.

The next party is the opposite. This is what I had feared; teenagers, some of whom are already too drunk to walk and talk sensibly, some of whom are clearly smoking drugs and making no effort to hide the fact, and a couple of whom are getting intimately acquainted in the sand, with little regard for anyone else on the beach. Julie and I glance at each other and swiftly move on.

"I'm starting to feel like Goldilocks!" I say. "The first party was too old, the second party was too young… and the third party was just…"

My words come to a halt, as do my steps, because there, at the edge of the crowd of the third party is Sam. My Sam. He is ten years older, he is slightly broader, and his hair a little shorter, but I'd recognise him anywhere.

3

"Quick!" I grab Julie, and pull her away.

"What are you doing?" she asks. "I thought you were going to say that party was just right."

"It's Sam!" I hiss, daring a quick glance in his direction to check if he's noticed me, but he is deep in conversation with one of his mates.

"Sam? *Your* Sam?" Julie asks.

Ridiculous to call him this, I know, when I was only with him for three months at the most, and that was ten years ago. But both Julie and I know that, so far, Sam has been the love of my life. Geoff knew it, too. He found out somehow and I don't think it helped in terms of his feeling insecure, and becoming increasingly possessive – but I know that was his nature and that if hadn't been Sam, it would have been something else that triggered it. I tried to convince Geoff that it was over with Sam; just a summer romance, a teenage fling, but he wouldn't believe me.

And he was right not to. When I look back, I may have thought about Sam if not every day then every week, for these last ten years. And I worry that makes me a bit mad. But isn't love meant to be a kind of madness?

Still, I am shocked at my reaction to seeing him now. I really feel like I'm eighteen again. I should be acting much more mature than this. But I can't. I don't know what to do or where to put myself so I drag Julie away and we move on to the next party, which really isn't the right one for us and also ruins the Goldilocks simile. As far as I recall, there were no heavy metallers in that story. But here they are, dressed in full leather jackets on the beach, on one of the hottest evenings of the year. Playing thrash metal from an old-school stereo. The only hope is that the sand will get into it and put a stop to the noise.

Still, they are nice enough, and friendly, despite looking quite surprised to see us joining them. A thin girl with bleached blonde hair and a ring through her lip is looking at us suspiciously but I give her my best smile as I wait for my thumping heart to calm down and she just shrugs.

I sit on the sand and Julie, having little choice, joins me. She reaches into her bag for her drink. I can't believe she's brought her gin & tonic in a National Trust flask. It's not going to help us fit in round here.

"Mum gave it to me!" she exclaims defensively. "Anyway, just wait and see how nice and chilled my drink is, compared to yours."

I take a slug of it. She's right. And I'm pretty sure I detect a hint of lemon, too. "You could have put a Metallica sticker over the oak leaves."

"I'll just say it's ironic," Julie says as she pulls two plastic wine glasses from her bag.

"Oh my... I think you're looking for the first party," I say.

"Ah, shuddup. I didn't co-habit for three years without picking up some middle-aged tendencies," she says, splashing drink into both cups. We clash them together then put them to our lips. As the gin does its job, even the metal seems mellower, somehow. We remain on the outskirts of the group, watching as the sun gradually disappears from view over the headland. I cast occasional glances to the next party along, trying to see Sam again. As the night gets darker, the figures become even harder to tell apart, and silhouettes merge with the shadows which the flames throw out. I am torn between going over; finding him and just saying hello - like what happened between us was no big deal, and like I don't still dream of him from time to time – and staying here, with my new heavy metal friends, pretending I'd never seen him.

Julie makes the decision for me, though. Three drinks in, my words are slurring slightly, and so is my vision.

"The flames look soft, don't they?" I say to Julie.

"What are you wittering about, woman?" she asks. She tips her flask upside down to check it's empty, running her finger round the rim and sucking it to get the last few drops. "Right, I'm afraid I can't stay here any longer. That guy over there – don't look, the big one, with the tattoos and the Popeye forearms - keeps looking at us, and I think he's got designs on you, or me, or both of us. I also need to hear some proper music. Now."

With that, she drags me to my feet and, despite my protests, I find myself being propelled back towards the next party along. The one with Sam.

"Oh, I don't know, I'm not ready…"

"Don't be such a wimp!" she says. "This is just a bloke you had a knock around with when you were eighteen. You've built him up into this idea in your mind, put him on a pedestal. You need to see him, otherwise you'll never move on. He could be a total tosser by now."

"Yeah, you're right!" I say. "OK. OK. I can do this. Stop, though."

I get my bottle of drink out of my bag. I take a swig. It's warm. I pass it to Julie. "Told you the flask's much better," she says, wiping her mouth on the back of her arm. Nevertheless, she takes another big swig.

I start to tiptoe exaggeratedly towards the party.

"I'm not sure that tiptoeing really works on sand, you know," I hear an amused voice just to my left. A voice I'd know anywhere. I turn. I try to look cool.

"Sam!" I say. "What are you doing…" I squeal as my foot finds no ground beneath it and I fall inelegantly into a hole some kid must have dug earlier in the day.

Shit. Maybe if I stay here he won't realise it's me.

"Hi, Sam," I hear Julie say. Damn her. She and Sam both reach down to help me up. He is laughing and I am trying to push the hair out of my eyes, the sand off my clothes.

"Julie?" He is saying. "No way! And Alice… oh my god, I can't believe it's you. Although the way you fell into that hole just then, I should have known straightaway."

He's laughing at me, and now I'm laughing as well. My clumsiness has broken the ice. "Oh my god," he says again. "Are you two here for long?"

"The summer," I say.

"No way!"

"You've said that already," I answer more sharply than I mean to.

"I guess I probably have. I just can't believe it's you."

"You said that, too." I speak a bit more softly this time.

"Yep, well… look, don't go anywhere, OK? I'll be back."

Woah. Be still my beating heart. I collapse into the sand, and Julie sits next to me. "So, I guess he still remembers you," she says and nudges me.

I just smile and, shaking slightly, take another giant swig of warm gin & tonic.

4

I can't sit still while Sam is gone. Julie smiles at me. "Calm down, will you? You nearly knocked my drink over then!"

"Sorry," I smile, slightly shame-faced. Surely I should be better at dealing with these things by now? The butterflies in my stomach say otherwise.

Out on the sea, the lights of a boat bob up and down as it ploughs its way determinedly through the waves, heading for the harbour in the next little inlet.

"I can't believe it!" A loud voice breaks my reverie and I turn to be enveloped in a huge, bear-like hug.

"Luke!" I exclaim, and I'm delighted to see Sam's best friend drawing back from me, his smile as big as I remembered. The beard is new, though. The hug is not the only bear-like thing about him.

"You haven't forgotten us, then?" Luke is still grinning. He was another big part of that golden summer; the four of us used to hang out all the time, and he turns now to Julie to give her the same all-encompassing treatment. I feel a bit more relaxed.

"Well, well, well, couldn't keep away, eh? Change your mind about me?" He nudges Julie.

"You guessed it," she smiles.

Luke did have a thing for Julie back then but she wasn't really interested. He was a lovely bloke but I guess at eighteen he hadn't fully grown into his body. He was tall and a bit ungainly, and a bit overweight. From what I can make out in the dark, however, he fits his body perfectly now – or it fits him.

He squeezes in between us. "Room for a little'un?" He puts an arm round each of our shoulders. "A rose between two thorns."

"G & T?" I ask, and feel embarrassed suddenly – like a townie. It was always cider or beer back then.

"Great," Luke certainly doesn't seem to mind, and takes a swig. "Urgh, that's warm!"

"Sorry, we should have saved some in Julie's National Trust flask."

"Oh, nice. Gone up in the world, have we?"

"Not really," I admit. "In fact, we're back at the Sail Loft. Julie's a proper chef now, though."

"That right?" he asks her.

"Yeah, I've been doing it for years now."

"You always said you were going to be a chef," Luke says. "Well done."

"How about you, Luke?" I ask. "Did you make it as a champion surfer?"

His turn to be embarrassed now. "Nah. Fact, I only get to do it when I'm back for weekends."

"You don't live round here anymore?"

"No, I live in London now."

"London!" I exclaim.

"Yeah, I'm a software developer."

"Bloody hell, I didn't see that coming."

"Yeah, well after you girls left us, I sat my A-Levels again, changed all my options, went to uni in Bristol, and moved to London with a job."

"Well, that's great!"

"I guess. It hasn't changed me, though." Luke grins again.

I'm so happy to see him, but I want to ask him about Sam. I can't, though. I don't want Luke thinking I'm still pining after his friend, even if I am.

"Are you back for long?" I ask instead.

"Two weeks, this time. Ma's been poorly, and Dad needs a break. I don't really like being away while she's ill, see, but not much I can do about it."

"Well, I'm glad you've kept your accent!" I say, then for fear of sounding flippant, quickly add, "I hope your Mum's OK?"

"Not really. S'cancer. She's not going to get better."

"Oh."

"I'm so sorry, Luke," Julie says. "She's a lovely lady."

May, Luke's mum, used to tolerate us hanging out in the old garage at the end of their garden, which we'd do if the weather wasn't good. There was a darts board in there, and an old TV, and a fridge full of beer and Coke. She used to bring us sandwiches sometimes, and would always try to 'feed us up'.

"Yep. She is," he sighs, and his large frame slumps.

"I bet she's glad you're back to see her," I offer.

"And your dad," Julie adds.

"Yeah. I don't know. I think I might be back a fair bit this summer, I really don't know how much longer she's got. So you might be seeing a bit more of me!" He puts his smile back on, "Good news for you, eh, Julie? You might just be in with a chance."

"I'll bear that in mind," she says. Something in her cool, flirty tone makes me look sharply towards her but it's hard to see her expression in the dark.

31

We sit and catch up on each other's news. Luke's not saying too much but I have a feeling he's been very successful. He's certainly not showing off but in describing life in London it's clear he owns his flat there, and has a pretty good social life.

I'm sad to think of his mum. I don't know many people our age who have lost a parent and I can't imagine how it feels to know that your mum is going to die. I feel like Luke needs to have fun tonight, though. It gives me something to think about other than Sam – for a while. I still can't help wondering where he's got to.

Passing the bottle between us, it's not long before the drink is all gone.

"I'll go grab us some more," Luke says, "Don't move."

"We won't," I say. I edge back up to Julie.

"He hasn't changed a bit!" I say.

"I wouldn't say that," she replies, "did you feel those muscles? And he's a successful IT guy now!"

I look at her. "So you're saying…"

"Well, I wouldn't say no…"

"Well, bloody hell!" I exclaim. "That would never have happened ten years ago!"

"A lot's changed since then."

"Yes, it has," I say, "but just bear in mind, he's not a holiday-maker, and you swore you were only going to go after tourists."

"Yeah, I suppose…"

"And his mum's ill, you need to be careful."

"OK!" she snaps. "I'm not talking about anything major. I was just saying, he's a bit different now. And I wouldn't say no…"

"Fair enough." Maybe we've both had a bit much to drink and now isn't the time for this conversation. "Don't know where Sam's got to, though."

"No, that's a bit weird, isn't it? I'm sure he'll be back soon, though."

Before long, Luke is back, with a trio of glass bottles clacking together between the fingers of one hand.

"Careful, they're all open, and they're all different, so I don't know who's getting what. Could be beer, could be cider."

He hands them out and we all clash them together, toasting the reunion.

"So good to see you girls again," he says.

That's the second time tonight we've been called girls. I am definitely loving it here.

"Do you know where Sam is..?" I venture, after a slug of what turns out to be strong cider.

"Sammy? He's about somewhere..." Luke answers vaguely. "I know he wants to come and see you. I think he just had to see somebody about something..."

Something about his evasiveness makes me prickle with unease. There is something going on. And why shouldn't there be? I haven't seen Sam in ten years; anything could have happened in that time. Presumably he's had girlfriends, it's perfectly likely that he has one now. He could be married, for all I know. He certainly owes me nothing and yet I feel put-out at the thought he could be with somebody else.

Luke says he's going to have to go soon, as he's promised his dad the 'day off' the next day, and anyway, he doesn't want to waste any of his time with his mum by being hungover. "Will you give me your numbers, though?" he asks. "Maybe we could go out for something to eat the day after tomorrow..?"

"That would be lovely," Julie says, grabbing his phone from him and tapping away at it. "There, I've put in Alice's and my details. I've put a 1 in front of 'Julie' just so I'm number one."

You've got to admire her cheek.

"You've always been number one to me, Julie," Luke laughs and leans in to kiss her on the cheek, then turns to me and does the same.

"I'll see if Sammy can make it, too," he says, "though it depends..."

Depends on what? I want to ask. Instead I say weakly, "That would be nice."

"I don't know where he's got to right now," Luke says. "If you see him, can you tell him I'll ring him tomorrow?"

"Of course," I say, but I have a strong feeling now that we won't be seeing Sam again tonight. The butterflies have gone, and been replaced by a slightly sick feeling. Once Luke has gone, Julie leans back in the sand and I sit holding my knees to my chest. I feel a bit cold, like the cool damp of the sand is seeping into me.

The metallers' party is still going strong but I can see glowing embers a bit further along, where I'm guessing the teenagers have upped sticks to get home in time for curfews. The family party is long-since over and the group we've pinned ourselves on the outskirts of is starting to drift away now, the fire dying down and the bottles all empty. A couple of people move around with bin bags, clearing the detritus.

"The stars are spinning," Julie slurs.

"Then I think that's a sign it's time to head home," I say. I check my phone. "Look, it's only 11.15. An early night!"

I stand unsteadily, and pull her up. We link arms and

34

make our way tentatively across the sand; scared of falling in more holes, and scared that the contents of our stomachs might make an unwelcome reappearance if we make any sudden moves.

I feel strange. Not just because of the drink. I have actually seen the man I think I love – in person – after ten years. I constantly question myself whether I can really love him – or is it just the idea of him? Julie has said maybe it's easier for me to feel like that about Sam because I know I won't see him. I know what she means. I can't deny how I felt when I saw him tonight, and how now I have a huge, stomach-pulling drag of disappointment deep within me. But it was also lovely to see Luke and I'm looking forward to seeing him again in a couple of days' time, with or without Sam.

5

I wake on the Sunday morning to the sound of church bells; normally a joyous experience but today each *clang* seems as though it is occurring within my skull. I didn't think I'd drunk that much but actually, when you add it up: the drinks at the flat, the one in the Mainbrace, the ready-mixed gin & tonic on the beach, topped off by a bottle of strong cider, it's no surprise that I'm feeling this way and, judging by the groans from the room next door, Julie is not faring much better.

I lie still for a while, convinced that if I don't move my head all will be well, but I can't deny the urge to use the bathroom for much longer. Eventually, carefully, I edge my way towards the side of the mattress, tentatively raising myself up and putting my feet on the floor. Then it's all systems go and I make it to the toilet just in time, as the contents of my stomach make an unwelcome bid for freedom. It's been a long time since I've been sick from drink, and I can't say that I've particularly missed it.

"Did we have chips last night?" I call through to Julie, flushing the evidence away, and eyeing myself disgustedly in the mirror.

"Er... I think we might have. Can't talk about food at the moment, though."

My eyes are red, my hair is stuck to my face, and there is

dried dribble on my chin. My tan seems to have all but disappeared. This is not a good look. I head to the kitchen and get two glasses of cold water, taking them in to Julie's room.

"Budge up," I say, sitting on her bed.

"Do I have to?"

"Yes!" I sip at my drink, resting my head against the wall and willing myself to feel better.

"Good night, though, wasn't it?" Julie says.

"I... think so."

"Weird, seeing Sam and Luke again."

"Yep." I keep replaying the scene of bumping into Sam, but there really wasn't much to it. What did he say to me? *I can't believe it's you.* That had seemed fairly promising. That made it sound like he was pleased to see me. But why hadn't he come back? He'd told us to stay put. Maybe he'd just wanted to reunite Luke with Julie.

"Luke was looking fiiine..." Julie croaks.

"Julie," I say warningly.

"What?"

"It's Luke!" I say. "Not some holiday-maker who's going to be gone within the week. And his mum's ill. He's... vulnerable."

"I know, I know. Maybe I can make him feel better?"

"I really don't think you can make up for his mum dying of cancer," I say.

"Alright, I'm just messing about. You're just pissed off because Sam didn't come back."

"So what if I am?"

Now we're both annoyed with each other. These things don't tend to last long, though. "Come on," I say, "we're both hungover, and we need some breakfast. I'm going to jump in the shower and hope that I've seen all I'm going to see of last night's chips."

"OK," Julie says. "I'll wake up properly now." She closes her eyes.

"You're going back to sleep!"

"No, no," she murmurs.

"Well I'm getting up, and I'm going to get some breakfast. You're welcome to join me if you want."

"Yep, just coming…" she is unconvincing. "Sorry about Sam…" she manages to say before she's snoring softly again.

Back in the bathroom, I put some bleach down the toilet to see off any lingering hangover germs. I put the shower on, fast and hot, and soon the room is filled with steam so I open the porthole window, panicking a gull who must have been perching above it. It chatters at me, annoyed.

"Sorry!" I say. I can see the sky is a deep blue and I am longing to be out there. The shower does a great job of seeing off much of my hangover; I am left with a gentle, throbbing headache so I take a couple of Anadin and I go into my room, pulling out a bikini, cut-off shorts, and a wide-necked t-shirt.

My hangover is usurped as I feel engulfed by a rush of love for the summer, and just for being here in this brilliant place. With a bit of time on your hands, you can wander the streets, and there is no option but to feel relaxed. It does help that the majority of people you pass are on holiday and treating their days accordingly. It's just such a contrast to being back home, sitting (or, often, standing) in a packed bus, then joining the streets full of people heading this way and that to sit for a whole day in a stifling, air-conditioned office.

When I've voiced this to people, they tell me I feel that

way in Cornwall because I'm on holiday. And yes, I know they're right to some extent – but actually, I'm not fully on holiday. I am working. It's a different kind of work, and it's certainly less well-paid, but the pay-off for me is just being here.

I have a spring in my step as I wander out of David's dark, cool hallway and into the fresh sunshine of the street. Families wander along, parents hand-in-hand with children. Of course it is not all perfect. There is a mum trying to calm her toddler down about something or other and he is having none of it. They are standing in a shop doorway. She has a bag at her feet, with a plastic spade protruding from it, and a picnic bag on her back. He hits her and she looks thoroughly flustered. I try to offer a sympathetic smile but she doesn't see me. Further along the street, a young girl is telling her dad that he's *so* mean and he is gently explaining to her that he can't just buy her a surfboard, that they cost lots of money and anyway, she can't surf. She shouts at him that yes, she can surf. If she just had a board she could show him. I have the feeling he is losing his cool but is aware of the people passing by.

Still, for the most part, people are happy – and I know these things are the stuff of everyday family life. They will be sorted out and forgotten in minutes, arguments disintegrating and dissolving in a day of freedom, sunshine and sea air. I feel lucky, though, being unencumbered as I walk along the cobbled street that leads down to the harbour. I know a great place where I can get my breakfast and sit and people-watch.

However, as I approach Joe's, I see this is not going to be possible. It is packed, and the tables outside are all taken. I walk past one where a couple sit reading a paper. They have a golden retriever, who rises and sniffs at my feet as I stand looking at the menu. It seems that the price structure has changed somewhat in ten years; in fact, the whole place looks different; dark, cool and stylish, with a contrived surf-shack feel that just doesn't seem authentic, somehow, and some kind of Ibiza-style club music playing on the sound system.

I'm in no hurry, although I think that the sooner I eat, the more quickly I will see off the last of this hangover. As all the places around the harbour are more upmarket now (for 'upmarket' read 'expensive'), I move into the rabbit warren of narrow streets, and make my way to the same beach where we spent last night.

As I turn the corner and the vast stretch of sand reveals itself, I am hit by a blast of cold, salty wind, straight in from the sea. There are numerous surfers making the most of the open, unsheltered water, and it looks like a different beach. I am impressed that there is little, if any, litter from the parties; the only real sign of them the circles of rocks which encased the fires.

I buy a fried-egg sandwich, a large latte, and a freshly-squeezed orange juice from the much more reasonably priced shack on the beach. Taking off my sandals, I wander along to the cluster of rocks which protrude from the middle of the beach at low tide. I carefully climb up, trying not to spill my drinks, and feeling the rough surface scratching against my bare skin. Once atop the largest rock, I pull my hoodie on against the chill of the sea breeze and settle down to watch the surfers, draining my orange juice cup in seconds. The fresh, sharp juice and pulp invigorate me and I feel myself coming to life. I sit a little straighter and unwrap my egg sandwich, eating it guardedly against the scavenging gulls, who would think nothing of taking it clean out of my hand if they could.

Soon, I am feeling human once more and I can sip my coffee leisurely, enjoying the luxury of time and space and fresh sea air. In my bag I have a beach towel and a change of underwear and in a while I might head round to the more sheltered beach on the other side of town for a swim but right now I am happy here. I can't even be bothered to read my book. I can just lean back against my jagged seat, using my hoodie to soften the surface, and observe.

There are families out for a Sunday morning walk; children in swimsuits, bikinis, or nothing at all, splashing in and out of the waves. Couples walking hand-in-hand along the shoreline. Determined, experienced surfers far out where the waves start to form; less confident novices trying to catch already-broken waves closer to the shore.

I let my mind wander back once more to the meeting with Sam. I can't believe I saw him like that. I know I've been looking out for him but I really did think he would be long-since gone, he was always so adamant there was nothing to stay for in Cornwall. Maybe he's just back visiting, like Luke? I smile at the thought of Sam's friend; despite his evident success, and his beard, he hasn't changed at all. He's one of the friendliest, most open people I have ever met. I'm so sorry for him and his family that they are having such a hard time. Maybe he will be able to throw some light on the Sam situation; well, undoubtedly he will, if I can summon up the courage to ask him. Or maybe Sam will come out with us for dinner tomorrow night, like Luke suggested. I can't tell if that idea excites or scares me. Probably both.

I just hope Julie steers clear of Luke. He's in a vulnerable position at the moment and actually, for all her bravado, so is she, so soon after her break-up with Gabe.

However, it is none of my business, really. We're all adults now, or at least doing a reasonably good job of pretending to be.

I put the wrapper from my sandwich into my now-empty coffee cup and pull my hoodie up so it half-obscures my eyes. Despite the coffee, and the sharpness of the juice, I feel tired again. Maybe there's time for a little snooze.

6

I am rudely awakened by a sudden drenching. I sit up quickly, pushing seaweed out of my face, to the sound of a little girl saying, "I am so sorry. I slipped. I'm really sorry."

It takes me a moment to collect myself, and come round enough to say it's fine, although I'm not yet sure if that is the correct answer.

"Are you OK?" The girl looks about nine years old, though to be fair I am no expert, and she's peering at me from under the rim of a wide-brimmed, yellow sun hat. I'm convinced by her look of concern that she really is sorry and it was a genuine mistake.

"It's OK," I say, "really!"

I smile and she looks relieved. I see the figure of a woman, laden down with bags, running along the beach towards us.

"Oh my god!" she pants, out of breath, as she gets to us. "What happened? Sophie, what did you do?" She looks from me to the girl, and the girl and I both burst out laughing.

"I think she decided I needed waking up," I say. "The tide's coming in, after all. She probably saved my life."

Sophie gives me a grateful smile. "That's it."

"Sophie..." her mum says in a warning tone, but she's grinning. "I said to wait for me before you started rock climbing. Honestly," she turns to me, "she doesn't listen to a word I say."

"No harm done," I say, "really. And I probably really did need to wake up. I hadn't actually planned to fall asleep in the first place. Do you happen to know what the time is?"

The woman, who, with a full face of make-up, is looking very glamorous for an afternoon on the beach, looks at her phone. "It's just after twelve."

"Wow, then honestly, I think it's a good thing that you woke me!"

"Well, thank you, for being so understanding." I'd say she is a little older than me. She has a proper Cornish accent, and bare, tanned arms and long legs, one of which is on display through the gap in her sarong. I notice her perfectly painted toenails. I want to curl my toes under so she can't see the chipped mess my own nails have become; I haven't bothered to redo them since coming down here.

"Can I get you a cup of tea or coffee to say sorry?" she asks.

I'm about to say no when I think, actually, I'd love one. "That would be great. Yes, please. Can I have a cup of tea?"

"Of course! Sophie, you come with me and we'll bring this lady a cup of tea back."

"Will you watch my bucket for me? There's a crab in there."

In that case, I'm grateful that the whole contents weren't emptied over me. "Of course."

"Thanks!" The girl skips off with her mum, and I allow myself to wake up a little more in my own time. They return with not just a cup of tea, but a KitKat.

"Thank you so much!" I say.

"It's no problem," Sophie's mum says. "Sorry again!"

She takes Sophie's hand, and they wander off towards the rocks at the far end of the sand. "See you later!" Sophie waves at me and I wave back.

A sip of my tea scalds my mouth. It's much too hot to drink and it will be for some time. I decide there is only one thing for it. I must swim. There is a gap between the surfers and I decide to take the plunge right here and now. I peel off my clothes, feeling slightly self-conscious in my bikini but I chastise myself for being so silly. Who cares? Half the people here are dressed as shiny seals, in their wetsuits. Nevertheless, I shove my clothes into my bag and I tuck it into a hollow on the rocks. I'm not planning to swim for long and I will keep an eye on it from the water. I don't think it looks particularly nickable, anyway.

The water is so cold but I suppress a shriek, pressing determinedly in until the waves are pushing over my shoulders and I may as well take the plunge. I duck my head under the water and bring it back out again, shaking the salty sting from my eyes. I laugh out loud. There is nothing like this feeling; nothing. And although I know how beautiful it is swimming in the warm waters of the Indian Ocean, for example, there is something about this biting Cornish sea which brings me to life. It makes me want to jump for joy. However, I have appearances to keep up so I restrain myself, instead dashing back and forth in short, sharp bursts of front crawl, and occasionally plummeting under the waves then slowing down to a more relaxed breast stroke. I stay in the water far longer than I meant to but I think that seeing as I'm here, and my body's acclimatised, I might as well make the most of it.

I lie on my back for a while, my ears submerged in the

water, so my view is of the sky and the fast-moving, barely-there clouds. This is one of my favourite things to do. Shutting out the world and listening to the bubbling voice of the sea. A seagull comes into view and is as soon gone from sight. I know there are surfers nearby so I need to be careful; I really don't fancy getting run over by some over-enthusiastic surf dude and their board, but just for a few moments it is just me, the sea and the sky. It is bliss.

Soon enough, I right myself, and think of my cup of tea getting cold. And the KitKat! I am suddenly ravenously hungry. I half-reluctantly swim to shore, moving as gracefully as I can onto my feet and splashing through the shallows, where the water seems far warmer now. I watch the rainbow of sea spray caught in the sun's lights, with each kick of my feet. I remember this from my childhood. I love the feeling of it now just as much as I did then.

I head off to the rocks to dry, noting that the tide is much further in already. It's moving fast now. I allow myself to dry on the rock while I drink my tea, although it is disappointingly much cooler than I had hoped. The KitKat does not disappoint, though.

Then I gather up my things and I pull my clothes on over my still-damp bikini. I can't be bothered to change properly; once I'm in a more sheltered spot the sun will soon have me dry. I'm thinking what to do, trudging each footstep carefully through the sand, when I feel a tug on my top.

"Look what I found now!" It is Sophie, the little girl who half-drenched me earlier.

I smile. She is very sweet, though I don't think I'd have been half as forward at her age – or any age. And I'm surprised her mum doesn't mind her just accosting strangers like this. But I can see her mum a little way away, talking earnestly into her phone, and seemingly not paying attention to what her daughter is doing.

"What is it?" I ask, peering into the bucket.

"This," she says proudly, "is a starfish."

"No way!" I am genuinely impressed, and I let her prod around in the bucket until she finds what she's looking for. She gently lifts it, on its shell bed, from the water, for me to have a quick look. "Can't keep it out of the water too long," she says, "and I have to put it back before I go. Dad says whatever I catch, I have to put back."

"I totally agree," I say, and take a look at the tiny star-shaped creature. It's beautiful. And tiny. Its dark skin is patterned with cream and orange shapes, which look like tiny stars themselves.

"It's a Asterina phylactica," says Sophie.

"Is that right?"

"Yep," she places it back in the bucket.

I notice her mum, who has finished her phone conversation, looking round the beach, and I wave to get her attention. I really don't want her thinking I am trying to steal her daughter. She comes jogging up, still managing to look lovely as she does. No accidental falling into a hole for her. "Oh, hi again," she says as she recognises me.

"Hi," I say, trying to look as harmless and non-child-stealer-like as possible.

"Sophie, I said to just stay still," she admonishes the girl.

"Yeah, but you were on the phone for ages," Sophie rolls her eyes. "Anyway, I saw…"

She looks at me, obviously expecting me to fill in the rest of the sentence.

"Alice," I oblige.

"Alice over here, and I knew she'd like the starfish."

"Sorry!" Sophie's mum says to me again.

"It's fine," I reassure her, "I do like the starfish." I smile at Sophie.

"See?" Sophie looks triumphantly to her mum. "Was that Dad on the phone?"

"Yeah, he's just coming into town now. We should go and meet him, I guess." Sophie's mum turns to me. "Are you on holiday here?"

"No, well not really. I'm... working for the summer. Seasonal work, you know." I feel suddenly embarrassed, like I am far too old to be doing summer work.

"Oh, OK," Sophie's mum doesn't seem bothered.

"I mean, I'm on a, I suppose a career break."

"Well, good for you. I've been on a few of them myself!" she smiles. "Well, you might be interested in this class I've just set up. Pilates. On Monday nights, at the church hall."

"Really?" I say. "That sounds great. I was looking for a Pilates class, believe it or not. Or at least I was going to look for one. I've only been here a couple of weeks, to be honest, I hadn't quite got round to it."

"Brilliant! Well, that's sorted, then. Here, let me give you a card. In fact, would you mind taking a few? Handing them round, maybe at work?"

"Oh, OK. Sure." I don't see a problem in doing that but I can see where Sophie gets her forwardness from.

She hands me a few A5-sized cards. 'KC's Pilates, 6-7pm'. "And can you fill in one of these forms for me, so I know if you've got any medical requirements?"

"Of course, shall I bring it with me tomorrow?"

"You could just do it now, if you like."

Wow. Talk about closing a sale. Jason Wilberforce would love this woman.

"Sure..." I say. I did want to do Pilates, after all. And anyway, even if I fill in the form, it doesn't mean I have to go to the class. I don't really like feeling pushed into things, but maybe this is one of those fortuitous meetings; I wanted a Pilates class, and one has come to me without me having to put in any effort.

As I fill in the form, I can feel Sophie getting restless. "We need to go and meet Dad," she's saying.

"Look, I can bring this tomorrow..." I start to say.

"No, no, don't worry. Sophie, you go and put the seahorse back in the rocks... look, the tide's up to the ones in the middle of the beach now."

I look and see that the spot where I had fallen asleep is now being licked by the waves. I shiver at the thought I could still be asleep there. That would be a bit of a shock.

"It's a starfish!" Sophie thunders and storms off to put her exciting find back where it belongs. I suppress a smile. I hurry up filling in the form; I don't want to be the cause of a family argument.

"There you go," I say.

Casey, as I guess she is, smiles widely. "Brilliant. See you tomorrow!"

"I guess you will."

7

When I get back to the flat on Sunday, it's early evening. After leaving the beach, I'd gone for a long walk along the coastal path and I'd gone quite a bit further than I'd originally intended. It was too beautiful to leave; so many tiny wildflowers, tucked in amongst the waving grasses and spiky gorse. Each time I reached a curve in the path, where I could have turned back, I'd look around the headland and see more of the dry track stretching ahead, and think to myself I would go just to the next turning. It was only hunger that made me turn back.

By the time I get home, Julie has gone out. The thought of having the flat to myself for a while is a welcome one; although being here with Julie is loads of fun, I guess that having got used to my own space back home, it is nice to have the luxury of some peace and quiet. I make myself some sandwiches and eat them on the decking outside the back door. Even though David says he doesn't mind, I don't like doing this when he is here; it feels intrusive and like I am taking advantage of his generosity. He's been over at Martin's, on the other side of the estuary, all weekend though, so it's a perfect opportunity to soak up a few more rays. A gull sits on the wall at the end of the garden, hopping slowly from foot to foot, clearly trying to decide whether or not to make a move on my food. I give it my best stare and keep it at bay.

When I go in, there is still no Julie. It's only early, though. I have a shower, dry my hair, and put the TV on. Before long, I am asleep, and dreaming strange dreams. Sophie, the girl from the beach, is with me, and we're trying to carry this huge bucket of water but its flimsy plastic handle is breaking. Then I'm by a fire, and then there is Sam. I had a feeling he'd appear tonight. How could he not, when he's been on my mind all day? "Stay there, I'll be right back," he says, but I remain alone, sitting on a wet, rain-soaked beach, just waiting.

Julie is already up in the morning, when I shuffle into the kitchen. She hands me a cup of tea. "Drink me."

"Thanks, Julie." I take the tea into the shower – which Julie thinks is a weird thing to do – and come out of the bathroom feeling like a different person. I must have slept a long time last night, and I think it did me a lot of good, despite the weird dreams.

"So where did you get to yesterday?" I ask her, as we hurry along the quiet streets to the Sail Loft.

"God, well, when I woke up it was like two o'clock! I can't believe I slept so long! I was starving, so I went out. I did text you, didn't you get my text?"

"I didn't check my phone," I admit. "I was trying to escape my hangover. I reckon I fell asleep about eight last night, though!"

"Well, you probably needed it." Julie smiles at me. She looks really happy. The sea air must be agreeing with her. "Are you still up for going out tonight, with Luke?"

"Yes, of course, it was really good to see him again, wasn't it?" I don't mention the fact that he suggested Sam might come. "Oh, and I found out about a Pilates class,

51

which is at six, so maybe we can arrange to meet Luke after that. Have you heard from him?"

"Oh, he texted yesterday. Maybe you need to check your phone! He's going to pick us up about eight, take us to some place along the estuary."

"Oh, OK. Perfect," I'm not bothered that they've made these arrangements without me, in fact I'm quite happy to be organised by somebody else for a bit. I wonder if Sam will be joining us. I can't bear to think about it. It's not until I'm standing in the hotel dining room, ready for the first guests of the day, that I realise Julie didn't answer my question about where she was last night.

Work passes quickly; there's a full complement of guests, and all arrive in the dining room within half an hour of each other. I'm just grateful there are no room service requests to deal with. They are luckily few and far between, and usually couples on honeymoon, or second honeymoon. I find the whole thing a bit awkward, to be honest. The ruffled bed covers, the closed curtains, the guests in their nightwear (or, worse, under the covers). Maybe it's my fault; I should try to stop my mind wandering.

By the time we've cleared the dining room after breakfast, and Julie and I have eaten, there is reception duty to do while Julie oversees the tidying of the kitchen and planning for the following day. I don't really believe Bea needs a receptionist; it's not a large hotel, so it's rarely hugely busy, but I try to make myself useful doing other things, like stock-takes, ordering stationery, etc. I think Bea just can't be bothered to do it all herself anymore, as she did when we were first here. She's worked extremely hard to get to this point so I don't blame her for wanting to take it a little bit easier. As she always tells me, the stress of just owning a business like this is more than enough for anyone. "It all hinges on a good summer, and guests can cancel any time up to a week in advance. And they will, believe me, if the weather's awful. People believe they need some sunshine on their holidays and to be fair, that's probably true. Then there's all the overheads, looking after the building, there's always redecorating to do, insurance to pay… the list's never-ending."

Lunchtime soon swings around and Julie and I head back to the flat then down to the beach for a lazy afternoon reading and swimming. I can't deny, I love this life. I work from six till one, with not much of a break, really, but that's a seven-hour day, and it means I have all afternoon and evening off.

It seems to be agreeing with Julie, too. She is so happy and it seems to me that she is calmer than she has been for some time. I eye her from behind my sunglasses; she's lying propped against her bag and rolled-up towel, reading *Emma*. She has a small smile around her mouth, and her eyes are heavy-lidded, relaxed; she just looks so… content.

"What you looking at?" she raises her eyebrows at me. Maybe I'm not being quite as subtle as I'd thought.

"Just you," I smile. "You look happy."

"I am happy."

"And you're really OK… about Gabe, I mean?"

A little furrow passes over her brow, like one of the tiny clouds scudding across the sky. "Yeah. I mean, I do miss him, as a person, you know that. But I really don't miss that life. God, Alice, it drove me mad. Really, really mad. I thought things were meant to have changed for our generation. I thought he'd be different to my dad."

"Well, he was probably brought up by a mum who did everything for him," I say. "He may be progressive, and talented, and politically active; all those things. But when he gets home he still wants to be looked after."

Julie snorts. "Like a little boy."

"Yes, I guess so." I feel a bit bad talking about Gabe like this, but I also feel angry that he let the side down so badly, and let Julie down.

"I called him yesterday," she says, "but he didn't answer."

"Well, he's probably angry at the moment. Give him a bit of time. It'll be OK."

"I hope so."

"Anyway, what I was saying was how happy you look! I didn't mean to bring the mood down!" I grin. "Fancy a swim?"

"Definitely!"

We tuck our books away and lay our towels over our bags then run into the sea.

I can't convince Julie to come to Pilates with me. She says she's going to have a bath instead. "Fair enough," I say. "In that case, I'll come back, have a quick shower, and should be ready for eight."

There are not many people at the hall but I guess Casey's just getting started.

"Hi!" I say to her, and she gives me that wide, open smile which she shares with Sophie.

"Thanks for coming!" she says enthusiastically.

"It's no problem, in fact I've been looking forward to it. How's Sophie?"

"Oh, she's good, had a long day at school today, and gymnastics after. She's with her dad now."

"I thought she might come to your class," I joke.

"No, no, she's not really old enough," Casey answers seriously.

"No, I suppose not," I agree.

"OK, well I guess this is it."

I look round at the four other people in the hall and I feel sorry for Casey, and determined to try and get Julie to come next week. Maybe Bea will come; and David. I feel bad, thinking of the fliers I said I'd hand out, scrunched up at the bottom of my bag.

"Don't worry, we'll soon get the word round," I say, looking at my fellow group members for support. One of them smiles but the others look away.

Casey, her voice echoing round the large, airy hall, soon has us spine-rolling, doing the hundreds, and the oyster, and I think she's pretty good at this. Because there are not many of us, she is able to look at us all carefully and help us tweak our positions. She clearly takes it very seriously and I can see, as she is dressed in leggings and a vest, that it seems to have paid off for her. "You're a good advert for this," I say at the end of the class, gesturing to her physique, and she smiles while I go red, thinking it sounds like I'm coming on to her.

"Thanks! And thanks for coming, I really appreciate it."

"No problem. I'll drag my friend along next week if I can, and see if I can muster up some other people, too."

"That would be great."

"Say hi to Sophie for me."

"I will."

8

My hopes for Sam joining us are quickly dashed when Luke picks us up. He pulls his car up outside David's house, hazard lights flashing, and I can already see he is alone.

"Sam sends his apologies, he had a prior appointment tonight," Luke says vaguely.

"No worries," says Julie, confidently pulling back the front seat so I can climb into the low-slung back of the car, leaving her to sit up front with Luke. I'm struck by her easiness, like this is her car. I wish I had her confidence sometimes.

"Yes, no problem," I mutter, swallowing my disappointment and at the same time experiencing a slight relief.

From the moment we take our seats at dinner, it feels like I've managed to pull up a chair at the table of a couple on a first date. Luke and Julie are clearly so into each other. They are all smiles, and they keep meeting each other's eyes but then hurriedly checking the menus, or asking me a question about Pilates. As if we are all here as equals; three friends just out for a nice meal. It's so unconvincing but I play along. "Maybe you should both come to Pilates next week," I suggest.

"Yeah, I'm up for it," says Julie. "Are you up for it, Luke?"

"I could be persuaded," Luke smiles lazily and I feel Julie shifting next to me.

"Great," I say, determined to ignore whatever is going on here. "Luke, do you think any of your mates will want to come?"

"Erm, maybe," he says. "Get Julie to pass on some details, will you?"

"It's OK, I can send you the details," I say, "I meant to bring some fliers with me."

"No problem." Luke looks back at his menu and Julie looks at hers. I take the chance to have a proper look at Luke. He really has grown into himself, if that doesn't sound too patronising. His big brown eyes, shaded by long lashes, sit comfortably in his well-structured face. Within his thin dark red shirt, his broad shoulders are confidently straight. He doesn't hunch them like some larger people do, as if trying to make themselves less noticeable. And when I say 'larger' I don't mean he's overweight; he's built a bit like a rugby player, only he doesn't play rugby. I remember he was never great at surfing despite his fervent desire to be, and that's probably because of his size, I guess, but I remember he was just starting to take an interest in climbing.

"Are you still climbing, Luke?"

He looks up. "Yeah, I am. I can't believe you remembered that about me!"

"I remember a lot," I say, smiling. "You were just getting into it, I think, when we were here back then."

"Yeah, yeah, that's right... I was. I couldn't ever get the hang of surfing like the other boys. It took a lot for me to admit that. I do mostly indoor stuff now, in London, you

57

know, but it's good to come back here and have a go at some of the cliffs."

I glance at Julie, who is gazing at Luke. Oh god. I'm glad I'd already made up my mind not to interfere anymore because I can tell by the look on her face that there would be absolutely no point.

"You do yoga, as well, don't you, Luke?" she says.

"Yeah, that's right."

I could ask how she knows this but I've already worked out where she was yesterday, or at least who she was with. I don't mention this. I want her to tell me, and in fact I want to know when she is going to tell me. "Well, it's obviously agreeing with you," I say to Luke and he smiles at me, revealing his straight, white teeth.

I hope Julie knows what she is doing.

Luke has brought us to an upmarket, modern restaurant called Cross-Section, which is built up on an old jetty, above the sweeping sands of the estuary. We are seated by a large floor-to-ceiling window, which stretches the whole length of the restaurant, gifting the diners a view of the sun setting and a whole array of seabirds swooping in, gliding gracefully into the shallow water, or strutting about in the shallows looking for their tea.

The nearby door is open and a warm breeze drifts in, occasionally ruffling the tablecloth.

"This place is great," I say to Luke while Julie has excused herself to go to the Ladies. (She actually called it 'the Ladies' – when she'd normally just say 'the bog' or at best 'the loo'. Who does she think she's fooling?)

"It belongs to a mate of mine and Sam's," says Luke, and he seems to jolt slightly at the mention of Sam, like he hadn't quite meant to bring him into the conversation.

"Anyone I know?"

"Do you remember a guy called Christian?"

"Oh yeah, he lived above the fancy dress shop." An image of an auburn-haired, freckly boy comes to mind.

"That's the one. He's done really well. Went off to study under one of those TV chefs – one of the less knobby ones – and came back with a business loan; he's had the whole jetty rebuilt, and the restaurant on top of it. Got his eye on a Michelin star, I think."

"So you and Christian have both done well for yourselves," I say. I can resist no longer. "How about Sam?"

Luke looks at me, and swallows. He really doesn't want to do this, I think, but I have no idea why.

"Sammy?" he says, like he's playing for time.

"Yes, Sam."

"Well, let's see. He still lives round here. Works over at Falmouth now. Facilities, or something."

This really surprises me. "But he was so adamant he was going to leave here. He was going to be a..." I quickly revise my sentence so it doesn't sound like I remember every little detail about Sam; I'm not keen to reveal my obsession, "I'm sure he wanted to be a scientist of some kind; a conservationist, I'm sure?"

I know full well that was what Sam wanted to be. He always loved the sea, and the wildlife, and he thought he might be able to go and work abroad somewhere. He'd thought about marine biology, or zoology. He would retire to Cornwall, he said, or maybe come back when he'd made enough money to buy one of the big houses on the leafy road heading out of town, but he wanted to see the world first, and he wanted to make a difference.

"I know, it was always him that was going to get out first

opportunity. I had no intention of leaving, but look at me now. Just shows how little you know when you're eighteen."

"I suppose." I think of myself at eighteen. "You're totally right, in fact. I was absolutely sure I would never be stuck working in an office. I was going to be out there, actually *doing something*. It probably used to drive Mum and Dad mad, seeing as they both work in offices."

"Ha!" says Luke, "I was the same. Scorning them for spending their lives at work, earning money to make sure we had somewhere nice to live, and could afford for me to do stuff like the climbing."

"I guess that's what it's like when you're a teenager." I realise I have changed quite a lot over the last ten years. "So sure that you're going to do things your own way, and not be like your parents. You have no idea what they're giving up for you."

"No," Luke looks sad. "You don't."

"But you know what?" I can see he's thinking of his mum, "My dad says they do it because they want to. And that it's infuriating when your kids are like that, but he reckons he was the same with his parents – that you have to be like that to keep things moving."

"I like the sound of your dad," Luke smiles.

"Yep, he's pretty cool. How is your mum?" I ask, looking him in the eye.

"She's not good, not great. She's on so much pain relief, she's not quite herself anymore; not quite there, even when she's awake."

"I'm sorry," I say quietly. "I remember her very well, she was so good to us when we were here."

"Yeah, that was Mum. *Is* Mum," he corrects himself. "Me and Marie – remember my little sister? - always had

60

friends round, and Mum and Dad have loads of friends, too. It was always busy in our house, full of people, and laughter. It's so fucking quiet now."

I don't know what to say so I put my hand on his and give it a squeeze. I'd wanted to ask him more about Sam but this is clearly not the time.

Julie soon returns, and with her the energy and vitality of the evening. Luke orders a bottle of wine and, as he's driving, leaves almost all of it for me and Julie to drink. "It's on me," he says, and goes red. "I'm not trying to be flash. It's just – it's great to see you two again. Really, really great."

He smiles at both of us but his eyes meet Julie's for just a moment longer. It may be the wine but I am filled with a warmth, for this lovely man; this old friend, who is so kind and generous, and open. I think that even if I never see Sam again, I will be happy that we have met up with Luke. I just hope that Julie knows what she is doing but I know, I know, I must leave it to them to work out whatever is between them.

"To old friends," I raise my glass and they bring theirs to join it.

"What God has joined together, let no man put asunder," says Julie, and we all collapse into giggles.

We work our way through a table full of tapas dishes, and another bottle of wine. As darkness creeps up outside, the seabirds disappear from view, to the safety of the sand dunes and their nests in the rocks nearby. Hundreds of tiny lights come to life on the decking and wooden rails outside and the breeze whispers across my skin. I feel drunk, and full, and happy – but also very aware that

Luke's and Julie's chairs seem to have edged closer together during the evening.

I excuse myself to go to "the *Ladies*", as I say pointedly, grinning at Julie, and when I come back out, I see my friends talking quietly, heads together. Luke leans forward and kisses Julie and I suddenly don't know where to put myself. I can't just walk over to the table and squeeze my chair in between them. Instead, I think I will give them a few more minutes, and I'll take some time for myself, have a look outside. I love the sound of the sea at night, and some fresh air might clear my head a little. I make my way slightly unsteadily between the other tables of diners and out through the wide doors, onto the decking, where I lean against the banister, looking out over the vast, black sea, which is darker than night. The lighthouse across the bay sends sporadic messages my way. I soak it in; the warmth of the night, the calm of this place. And I know it can be wild, and angry, when a storm blows in, but I love that, too. There is nothing we can do to control it, and that appeals to me.

There was a night, that golden summer, when Sam and I were up on the headland looking back at the town; we'd walked along the rocky path for a while, with a picnic, and a bottle of cheap wine, and we'd sat on a rock, just over from the path, with a view to the sea below, where a seal was hanging out, pointing its nose above the water so that it looked like a dark glass bottle bobbing on the waves, then dipping back under and appearing somewhere completely different.

It had been a humid day, the sunshine hazy and the air cloying. At least from our vantage point, the air was a little cooler, the freshness coming from over the sea. However, as we sat and ate, and drank, and kissed, the sky was taken over by a bank of dark, forbidding clouds, and with them came forceful gusts of wind.

"Uh-oh," said Sam, "storm's on the way."

"Wow," I said, marvelling at the speed of the change. I shivered and Sam offered me his jumper; silly eighteen-year-old that I was, I'd come out in shorts and a vest top. I pulled it on, as he rapidly packed our things away and pulled me to my feet. "Come on, can't sit here. They said there might be a storm tonight but I didn't think it'd be this early. Don't want to be sitting here if there's lightning."

Instead of heading back to town, however, Sam headed the other way along the path and I carefully picked my way after him, trying to keep up.

"Where are we going?"

"You'll see."

As he spoke, a low rumbling came from the skies and then, as they say, the heavens opened. I started to worry, after what Sam had said about the lightning. Surely it was safer to be back in town? He pulled me along, though, and up through some of the scratchy gorse. I remember complaining, like a little kid, and him laughing. "It'll be worth it, I promise!"

Then I saw it; a run-down, ramshackle old building, with gaping, glassless windows and a door half hanging off its hinges. "We're not going in there?!"

"That's exactly where we're going!" Sam laughed again.

He held the door back for me to go through and I could see a little fireplace built into the walls.

"Isn't this even more dangerous? What if it falls down?" I asked him.

"Well, it's been here about three hundred years, I reckon, and it hasn't fallen yet." He pulled me to him and

63

our rain-sodden clothes stuck together. "Here," he kissed me, and pulled his jumper off me. "Let's hang this up to dry. I don't reckon we're going anywhere for a while." He hung the jumper off an iron hook in the wall by the fireplace and pulled a towel out of his rucksack, wrapping it round my shoulders. Then he turned me round, to look out of the small windows. As he did so, a crackle of lightning split the sky. "Isn't that view worth the risk?" he whispered. He put his arms around me and briefly rested his head on my shoulder, kissed my neck. The rain was pounding on the roof, dripping through in more than one place. I shivered again as I felt Sam's hands slide under my top.

"Yes," I agreed, "it is."

9

When I go back into the restaurant, Luke and Julie are doing their best to play the innocent, just-good-friends game. Who do they think they're fooling? Well, me, actually – as I don't let on that I've seen them kissing.

"Where did you get to? You OK?" Julie asks, looking slightly concerned.

"Oh yeah, fine thanks… I just went out for a bit of fresh air but it's so lovely out there, I was probably gone a bit longer than planned, sorry. Did I miss anything?" I can't resist this and the sharp, quick look between them doesn't escape my attention.

"Not really… though the waiter did bring these over." Julie pushes a dessert menu in my direction.

"Great!" I say. "Are we all doing this?"

"I'm in," says Luke.

"I'm not sure, I'm trying to be good…" says Julie.

"Trying to be boring, more like!" I say. "Come on, live a little. This is a celebration, of seeing our friend Luke again!"

"She's right," says Luke, "and please don't tell me you're 'trying to be good' or 'watching your figure'. Life is too short." As he says this, his brow creases slightly, and I know he must be thinking of his mum.

"I agree," I say. "It's much too hot for sticky toffee

pudding, even though that sounds lush, so I think I'm going to go for the ice cream sundae. And a coffee. But Luke, I really, really don't expect you to pay for everything."

"We've been through this already," says Luke, "and arguing over the bill is almost as boring as calorie-counting. Now, what are you having, Julie?"

She caves in and orders the chocolate brownie, with cream and ice cream. I'm proud of her. Luke goes for the same as me, and he orders us all a Sambuca.

"Now this takes me back," I say, as he lights the coffee beans on top of the drinks and I watch the blue flames dance across the liquid. We used to drink these in the Beach Bar, the three of us and Sam; we'd buy one or two then sneak a bottle from one of our bags for refills. The strong, aniseed taste is a vivid reminder of those long-ago nights.

Luke only takes a sip of his, then splits the rest between us. "I can't, I'm driving. I just wanted to have a taste, to remember. You two enjoy it, though. Those were happy days, Alice." He smiles.

"They were." I think if it were only Luke and me now, I'd ask about Sam, but I can't with Julie here. Even though she's my best mate. She knows me too well. I want to ask innocently but she knows exactly how loaded any questions are. As much as I know that she's really into Luke.

We are the last diners in the restaurant but I am starting to yawn and Luke says, "We'd best get off. Doctor's coming to see Mum in the morning so I want a good night's sleep, and these lot probably want to get away anyway."

The young waiters and waitresses are busily tidying

everywhere except our table. Probably willing us to leave. I feel their pain.

"Yes, let's go," I say.

Luke helps Julie and I into our cardigans. He really is a gentleman. "Now you two go out to the car, I'll settle up and be right out."

We do as we're told and I slip my arm through Julie's. "Happy?" I ask.

She turns to me, her eyes shining in the light from the restaurant windows. "Very!"

"Good." I say no more.

When we get back to the flat, I invite Luke in but then I make my excuses and say I hadn't realised how late it is. I go to the bathroom, brushing my teeth and listening to Luke and Julie laughing together. Then I bid them goodnight and go to bed, switch off my light and lie in the velvety darkness, my mind a whirl of thoughts and memories.

In the morning, I hear an alarm go off in Julie's room but I check my clock and it's only about 4.30. I can squeeze in just a little more sleep. I hear the click of Julie's door and some murmuring, then very gentle footsteps moving slowly down the stairs. I can't help but smile. It may be against what I think is my better judgement, but it was nice seeing Julie so happy last night.

I hear the sound of the kettle. I try to ignore it, but it's so light outside and my flimsy curtains do a poor job of keeping that light out of my room. I close my eyes, turning my head away from the window, but after a moment there's a little knock on my door. "Can I come in?" Julie whispers.

"Yes…" I may as well just accept I'm awake. She opens

the door slowly, a cup of tea in each hand, and she squeezes into my bed with me.

"And who was that tiptoeing down our staircase?" I raise my eyebrows.

She grins. "Don't be angry… you're not, are you?"

"No, I'm not angry. It's none of my business, anyway."

"But what you said, about him being vulnerable, and me only just splitting up with Gabe…"

"Yes, well that's all true, but what do I know about these things? I'm hardly an expert at relationships, am I?"

"Oh Alice, you bloody should be. You should have dozens of boyfriends."

"Ah, thanks," I smile but I don't want dozens of boyfriends. Just the one will do.

10

Since that night, when Julie isn't working and Luke isn't with his parents, the two of them have been together. I am not surprised. This is Julie. She has always leapt from one relationship to another. Even though she swore that this time was different; that she wanted a real break from all of it, and to just have fun this summer, she has discovered an opportunity she can't resist. And I don't mean to sound cynical. This really might be 'it'. Luke is, after all, lovely. But Gabe is lovely, too. I worry that she's too quick to get over him, but I know it's none of my business. I can just observe, support her, and be there if things go wrong. That's what friends do.

And I don't really mind that she's so tied up so much of the time. It's not like I don't ever see her, and sometimes the three of us hang out together, but to be honest I'm quite happy having some time to myself, too. And I can't deny I'm relieved that our stint of partying every night has been so short-lived.

Still, sometimes I find myself at a bit of a loose end. This afternoon, for example, Luke and Julie have gone over to Sennen Cove. They did ask if I wanted to go, too, but ever since the night at the restaurant, I've had a strong urge to walk the coastal path, find that little shepherd's hut, or whatever it was. Today, the sky is blue, and I have a picnic prepared. A spicy vegetable pasty, a bag of Seabrooks ready salted crisps, an apple, a large bottle of water, and a flask of coffee. Julie bought me a flask of my very own: 'It's not National Trust, you're not quite there yet, but I think it's time', read the note on the bag I found on my bed. It made me smile.

The flask is tartan, and Julie is threatening to buy me a matching blanket for my birthday, so that I can sit on one of the harbourside benches sipping tea from my flask, keeping my legs nice and warm. "Watching the world go by," Julie said in a croaky, old-lady voice. "You're twenty-nine. That's nearly thirty. Time to start slowing down. If you can actually get any slower."

"I'm not twenty-nine yet, you cheeky cow! Anyway, you're only two weeks younger than me!"

We'd been some of the youngest in our year at school and had bonded over this. We also had summer-holiday birthdays, which was great as we never had to go to school on our birthdays but also meant people were often away and our parties were sparsely populated. We'd made a pact early on to always be there for each other's parties, even if it meant having to have them a week before or after our birthdays, if our parents had inconsiderately arranged a family holiday at the wrong time.

She's only teasing about me slowing down but she's right in a way; I've been realising more and more that I've let life become too comfortable. Back home, I would often find I'd be eating the same meal on the same night of the week. Watching boxsets on TV and having lots of early nights. All very comfortable, and comforting, but – despite what my new tartan flask may say about me – I know I am still young. "Life's too short," Luke had said. He may have been talking about missing puddings for the sake of saving a few calories, but it goes much deeper than that. Do I really want to be lying on my deathbed (why do people insist on using this analogy? Is there really any such thing as a deathbed?) and thinking, 'I wish I'd had time to see season seven of *The Good Wife*?'

Actually, I've already seen season seven of *The Good Wife*, but you know what I mean. Coming down to Cornwall is, I hope, the first stage of me shaking things up a bit.

I set off through the town, dodging families looking in fudge shop windows; panting dogs pulling on their leads, desperate for shade or a dip in the sea on the dog-friendly beach; the ever-present dropped ice creams, broken cones sitting sadly atop the melted messes like misplaced party hats.

I push on through the crowds, and along the back of the beach road, until I'm at the gap in the hedge, the unofficial route to the coastal path which saves a few hundred yards of walking up a steep road. This way is a bit scratchier, and involves a steep scramble through the undergrowth, but I'm rewarded at the top with a dramatic view: the town to my right, windows glowing in the sun; the coastal path twisting off to my left, and, straight ahead, the sea. The beautiful body of water stretching on to the horizon and beyond. Calm today, with just the odd white-top breaking here and there. The odd shadow of a cloud skimming lazily across the top. Seabirds swooping and plummeting into the cold depths, sending plumes of bubbles to the surface.

Mixed with the sea air is the aroma of wild garlic and something sweeter; Sam could probably have told me what it was. That was something I loved about him; his unashamed love of nature and wildlife. His eyes would light up when he talked about something he'd found on the beach; he still loved rockpooling, even at the age of eighteen. And his enthusiasm when a pod of dolphins came through the bay was catching, to me at least. Very probably, I was your average love-struck teenager. Whatever Sam had been into, I'd have followed. But I've never quite forgotten his knowledge of, and passion for, the natural world and whenever I watch *Springwatch*, or *Coast*, I think of him. I've even let my imagination wander to the point where I think he might pop up as one of those guest presenters, talking us through some aspect of the world which most people would never even notice. Imagining him in an office somewhere, in a shirt and tie, doesn't ring true, but I guess most of us have to compromise. We've all got to earn a living, somehow. I feel sad for him that he didn't get to fulfil his dream, though.

After catching my breath for a while, I start to walk. I've got sturdy sandals on, which are great for getting over the rockier parts of the path, and I feel confident taking the more challenging routes. I pass other walkers and say hello to them, but I don't stop to chat. I get into my stride and there's a spring in my step; an energy building up in me. This is all so familiar, this path; unlike the town, with its spruced-up bars and restaurants, this has not changed a bit. Year on year, the plants and flowers are renewed, and the families of tiny birds spring new fledglings, ready to learn and grow, eventually nesting in the wind-ravaged trees and deep, thorny bushes, creating families of their own.

I can hear crickets from within the undergrowth.

Butterflies and bees travel busily between the flowers, gathering nectar in the heat of the day. The sun is beating down on my back and I stop to put some sun cream on. Luckily, I'd thought to ask Julie to do my back before she went off to Sennen. I've been left with a clearly distinguishable hand mark on my skin before, when I've tried to do the job myself.

It's not far now, to the little cottage, or shack, or whatever you want to call it. It's silly, but my heart is beginning to thud. I don't know why I feel nervous. Except I do know why. This place is where I fell in love.

I round the corner, see the clifftops falling away in front of me, revealing more sparkling sea and the path stretching on, but this is where I take a detour and where I also wish I'd covered my legs for the walk. The area around the path is well-maintained but thick with plantlife and there are some definite sharp thistles in there. I push through the low-hanging branches of a wind-beaten tree, and there it is. Exactly as it was, only this time baking in the sun. It's smaller than I remembered; did people ever really live in here? Some tiny trailing purple flowers with delicate, soft-looking leaves grow from the stone walls, and I can see that the roof looks a little more holey than it did. I walk up to it slowly; do I dare go in?

Nudging at the door tentatively, it seems fairly stable, so I push it further and go in. It is cool inside, and smells of earth, and damp. There is the fireplace I remember, the hook where Sam hung his jumper that he'd carefully peeled from me; and there are the windows, with just a slight view of the sea now, as the trees and bushes have grown in the intervening years. Holiday agents would describe this place as having a 'sea glimpse'.

I sit on the floor and pour a little coffee from my flask

into its tartan cup. I don't want to stay too long; it feels quite strange being here and I still have that tiny seed of doubt about the safety of the building. But I want to breathe it in, revisit that golden summer, that summer of Sam – when everything seemed straightforward, and obvious, and opportunities were endless.

Before I stupidly let Geoff into my life, with his controlling ways, and the awful things he said and did.

I don't like to think of him. He was the polar opposite of Sam, which is, I suppose, why I agreed to go out with him, but if I'd ever known quite how different he was, I don't think I'd have let it happen. I'd have been better off on my own.

But I push those thoughts away. I was young; Geoff was young, really. I don't suppose either of us really knew what we were doing.

Instead, I think back to that storm; Sam's hands on me, his warmth against my shivering body. His mouth kissing my neck, whispering into my ear, while the thunder crashed and the lightning threw its weight about, below them the sea thrashing wildly and, in the hut, Sam and I moving gently and sweetly together.

I sit for a while, after I've drunk my coffee, on the cold earth floor, thinking about that moment, and I feel tears coming; not for me, now, but for my teenage self. I was so hopeful, and trusting, and I remember being absolutely sure that Sam and I were meant to be together. I was devastated at the end of that summer, when I had to leave, but I had my place at university. My parents would never have forgiven me if I'd given that up for a boy – and rightly so – and I'd never have earned a living down here out of season.

Anyway, Sam promised me that he loved me and we would keep things going. I could come and visit him, and he'd come up to me, too. "I haven't seen enough of the rest of the country," he said.

"I wouldn't bother, to be honest. The industrialised Midlands versus this," I'd gestured to the sea, the cliffs, and the vast expanse of sky.

"It's not always like this," he'd smiled. "But you're right, I'm lucky to be here."

We'd said our goodbyes and Julie and I had trudged onto the train, both in tears, mourning the end of our summer of freedom.

At first, Sam had kept in touch. A lot. I'd had five texts from him before I'd even got home. We talked every night, for about three weeks, and then there was nothing. I rang him but the number seemed to be dead. I realised I had no other way of contacting him, and I could hardly just pop down to Cornwall. I waited, feeling agitated, then worried for him, then angry, then broken-hearted. Mum and Dad were concerned about me, as I lost so much weight, but they just couldn't or wouldn't understand how I could be that way over someone I'd only known such a short time. Eventually, I stopped talking to them about it. And then Geoff came along.

I met him at my cousin Amy's party. The two of them worked together, and he seemed quite nice; grown-up, smart. He liked rugby, and music, and beer. He asked me out and I said no, but he got my number from Amy – who didn't ask me for my permission and I really wish she had – and phoned and texted me, until eventually I gave in and said yes. I should have listened to my gut feeling, but I didn't really have the energy. With Sam on my mind, and in my heart, I let Geoff take me out wherever he wanted to go. We'd go to see bands he liked, rugby matches, to his local. I've already said, he did things by the book: flowers, chocolates, a beautiful bracelet at Christmas. He tried to charm my mum – although I think she saw through him immediately – and bought bottles of expensive whisky for my dad. I knew they still didn't like him but I suppose at least they thought I was getting over Sam. And I was concentrating on my studies – which I was, because Geoff wouldn't let me have a social life outside of seeing him. I hardly even saw Julie while I was with Geoff, unless it was under some strict conditions set by him: it was easier if she had a man on the scene, although Geoff didn't even like me talking to her boyfriends.

He very quickly became jealous, and controlling, telling me what to wear. He was very keen for me to do well at university, and seemed very much the supportive boyfriend in that respect, but he often picked me up after I'd been at the library; giving the impression that he was doing me a favour but in reality he was keeping me from mixing with any other people; particularly any men.

He really lost it with me when we were talking about going on holiday. I suggested Cornwall and he hit the roof. "Do you think I'm stupid? You want to go down there to see that Sam, don't you?"

I was shocked. I didn't think I'd ever mentioned Sam to him. The name pulled at my heartstrings and I wanted to cry but also it pumped some anger into me – anger at Sam for letting me down, and Geoff, for thinking he could tell me what to do.

"No," I shouted, "I do not want to go there to see Sam. I want to go there because I love it. It's somewhere that makes me happy, which is more than can be said for you."

He was immediately apologetic and placating. It seemed like he regretted what he'd said. "I'm sorry, I don't know what came over me. Let's choose somewhere together; somewhere neither of us has ever been. That way we can explore it together, make our own memories. "
We went on an all-inclusive to Greece. And it was on the plane back from that holiday that I first tried to finish with Geoff, but it was another year before he was finally, truly, out of my life.

11

I allow the last drops of coffee to drip from my cup onto the cold earth, then I screw the cup onto the flask, bending slightly to walk through that rickety old doorway, back outside. I'm immediately hit by the warmth and amazed at the difference between the air out here and the more stagnant atmosphere of the ramshackle little building. I'm also struck by the sounds; the birdsong, which I'd barely noticed before, seems to hit me, coming from all around. I recognise the steady chirruping of a blackbird and I wonder if I'm near its nest, but I couldn't tell you which types of birds the other songs belong to; I'd need Sam for that.

I edge my way gently back through the scratchy undergrowth, pushing the branches of the tree out of the way and trying to pick my route carefully. I can see the main coastal path ahead of me now, and the wide open sunshine, waiting to welcome me into its warmth. At the last moment, I don't quite know what happens. Maybe one of my feet has become entangled with a bramble, or I've – yet again – managed to stumble into a hole; either way, I lose my footing and I come bursting, swearing, out of the undergrowth, only my bum on the path, landing with a sore bump and clearly startling the man who has just come up the steep steps that would take me down, and on around the path.

"Shit. Sorry," I say, looking up into the shocked face of Sam. "Oh!" I exclaim, and I feel the blood rush straight up to my face. Great. Last time I saw him, I'd just fallen into a hole in the sand. Now it looks like I'm trying to ambush him.

"Alice? Are you OK?" he asks and I can tell, even though I haven't seen him properly for ten years, and he is doing an admirable job of keeping a straight face, that he is trying not to laugh.

I pull a stray leaf from my hair, and straighten my top, trying to remember that I'm annoyed at him, but it's no use. I am suddenly convulsed with laughter and tears are squeezing from my eyes.

"Are you crying or laughing?" he asks me, still trying to keep that concerned look.

"I'm… laughing…" I say, making myself more comfortable, pulling my knees up and resting my head on them briefly. I look back up at Sam and he's laughing openly now, too.

"I wish you'd seen yourself," he says. "I thought you were going to knock me into the sea!"

"Sorry," I splutter. "Sorry…" I can't form a proper sentence yet. I do feel like I may be in danger of crying but I don't know if it's from the pain which is starting to swell in my ankle, the emotion of seeing Sam again, or the sheer embarrassment of the situation.

"Here." He reaches a hand out, and pulls me to my feet. I stagger a little, and gingerly try to put my right foot on the floor. I yelp.

"Let me have a look," Sam crouches and gently touches my ankle. I wish I'd bothered to shave my legs this morning. "It looks like it might be swelling," he says. "You might have sprained it. Look, lean on me, and we'll head back to town together."

"No, I'll be fine," I say, but I clearly won't be. In seconds, Sam has his arm around my waist and I am leaning into him, using my good foot and limping. I can't believe I'm in such close physical proximity to the man I have dreamed about for so many years; but this isn't quite the situation I'd imagined.

"So… this is weird," he says.

"Yep," I laugh.

"Good job I was there, though, you'd have had to drag yourself back along the path to town otherwise. Could have taken a while."

The image of me slithering along the clifftop path has me laughing helplessly again. We stop for a second.

Sam chuckles. "You always were a classy type."

"I know, a lot of people have commented on my natural grace."

"Not to mention elegance."

I can't quite meet his eye, but I grin, and I elbow him.

"Ow! Come on, let's at least get you to somewhere you can sit down. But I think we need to get a cold compress on that ankle."

There's something about the way he says 'we' that makes my heart jump. I let him take my weight again and together we move along the path. We don't talk much; I'm too busy trying to ignore the pain, but also thinking how soft the hairs on his arms are; how warm he feels, and how strong. Like Luke, he is bulkier than his eighteen-year-old self, but it's nice. He feels solid.

"Think you can get to the Beach Bar?" he asks. "If you can get there, we can use their First Aid kit."

"I'm sure I can," I say, "and then you'll have to let me

buy you a drink to say thank you."

"If you insist," he grins.

I can feel my skin becoming sweaty next to his, from the heat of the day, and the close contact. I guess it's his sweat too. Mingling with mine. I try not to think of it. I really don't think I could walk without his support, and I have to remind myself he is just being kind, looking after me. He is being Sam.

"I was trying to work out which birds I could hear," I say conversationally. "Are you still into all that?" "Oh yeah, I volunteer with the RSPB down at Land's End some weekends. I love it." Sam's voice is slightly gruffer these days, but his Cornish accent is still there; rounding words off as they roll from his mouth.

"Luke said you work over at Falmouth?" I don't want to sound like I've been talking about him, but I need us to be talking; the silence only lends itself to thoughts I shouldn't be thinking.

"Yeah..." he doesn't sound particularly enthusiastic about this; certainly not as much as he did about the birds. "Pays the bills." I take this as an end to that particular line of conversation. We go quiet once more.

"You're back, though?" he says suddenly.

"Yes, well, for the summer at least." I don't know where 'at least' came from; I don't think I'll be able to stay down here any longer than that.

"That's great."

"Yeah, it is, I'm really loving it. Pretending to be eighteen again..."

He laughs quietly, "I wouldn't mind that."

"No, nor me." My mind is whirling; what did he mean by that? Just that being eighteen was great, or is he thinking of that summer, too?

We both go quiet. I listen to the sea, and the steady but slow crunch and slide of our shoes on the path (the sliding sound being my injured foot); try again to distinguish some of the different birdsong. Despite the increasing pain in my ankle, I find that I don't really want this walk to end. Because what happens next? We go to the Beach Bar, bandage my ankle. I buy him a drink, if he'll let me, and then we go our separate ways.

I want to ask him so many things, but I'm scared of the answers, and worried that he'll think it's none of my business. I feel like I should just appreciate this situation as it is, right now.

As we come up to the top of a steep bit of path, a headwind knocks us both slightly, and Sam's arm tightens round my waist. "You OK?"

"Yep," I manage. From here, we can see the beach, and the town spreading out before us. The beach is busy, with small colourful tents and wind-breaks dotted across it. The wind carries the sound of joyful children's voices towards us, as they chase waves in and out on the shoreline. Further out, the slick surfers bide their time, like sharks stalking their prey.

We have to take the official route back, bypassing the steep slope I came up earlier. As we head away from the isolation of the coastal path, and back towards the town, I become increasingly aware of our proximity to each other. Sam doesn't seem bothered, though, and keeps hold of me as we walk down the slipway onto the beach. We don't stop till we get to the bar, where Sam shouts to a guy we can just see in the backroom: "Got your First Aid kit, Andrew? Got a sprained ankle here!"

He sits me on a sandy settee, and makes me put my foot up on the table. I can see the ankle is discoloured, and twice as big as it was earlier. So… stubbly legs and an elephant ankle. This is going well.

"Here," Sam soaks a thick serviette in water from a jug, and wraps it around the offending area. It is immediately soothing.

"Mate," Andrew calls from the bar, "here you go. Want a drink as well?"

Sam looks at me. "I'll have a beer, please," I say, "and this is on me, OK?" I start fishing around in my bag for my purse. "I'll sort it," Sam says firmly, "you can always pay me back later."

I don't protest; I hold the serviette around my ankle and Sam returns with two cold beers, and the First Aid box. He unwraps a bandage and carefully removes the serviette. "That looks nasty, but we'll soon have it back to normal." Skilfully, he wraps the bandage, alternating it around my ankle, then my foot, so it feels firm and secure. He fastens it by tucking the end in. "How's that?" His blue eyes are on mine and I look into them properly for the first time in a while.

"That's great," I say, looking away and taking a hurried sip of my beer. "Thank you."

"It's no problem." He moves to sit next to me on the settee and I fight the urge to lean into him. How is it that after a full ten years, this still feels so familiar, so comfortable; so right?

Both of us are quiet for a while then I say, "So what have you been doing, then?"

He splutters. This was a little joke of ours; born from the way his cousin used to ring him pretty much every day but have nothing to say – instead, putting the onus on Sam to make the conversation. I used to encourage Sam to come up with increasingly outrageous answers.

"Well, let's see… when did we last see each other? Except for the other night?"

"Ten years ago."

"Right, ten years ago. OK, I guess you missed the Circus Years, and my stint as a Blue Peter presenter."

"Oh, yeah, I don't think I saw any of that."

"How about the mission to Mars?"

"Was that you?"

"Yeah, course that was me."

"You've been busy."

"I have, it's true."

We're quiet again. I can't think what to say. The questions are burning away in me, and I want to tell him I've missed him, but I think I might sound a bit mad.

"It doesn't seem like ten years," he says.

"No, not now I'm back here. It feels like I've never been away," I kick myself for the cliché.

"Seems like that to me as well," he says softly.

I dare to look again into his eyes and I think I see a reflection of my feelings there. Maybe the beer's going to my head, and all that sunshine. Or maybe I'm still in shock after that fall.

"Lots more bars here, though, and flash restaurants." Why have I changed the subject?

"Yep, that's true. I guess all that's happened since you left."

"Luke seems to be doing well," I say.

"He is, he's doing great. So gutted about May, though."

"I know, she was always so lovely. Remember when we used to hang out there, that summer? Well, I suppose it wasn't just that summer for you."

"No. No, she was always happy to have us round."

"Did you know Luke and Julie are seeing each other?"

"Yes," Sam grins. "It's great he's got something to smile about. How is Julie?"

"She's the same as ever, really," I say. "We're meant to be reliving our days of freedom! This was her idea, to come back and now she's launched herself into a relationship!"

Sam smiles widely. "That's mates for you." He looks at his watch. "Look, I'm going to have to get going soon. Can I help you get back to your place?"

My stomach sinks. I'd stupidly envisaged us staying for another drink... maybe two... maybe more. Of course, though, he'll have things to do. Maybe he's going to meet a girlfriend. My pride wants to say that I can make it back on my own, but I know that's just stupid. "If you've got time, that would be great. Thank you." I can hear a politeness in my voice; a formality that wasn't there a moment ago. I have to protect myself, though.

"It's no problem." It feels like Sam wants to say more, but he doesn't.

We shout thanks to Andrew, and leave the First Aid box back on the bar, with our empty bottles.

"Want to lean on me again?" Sam asks, and I do, very much, not just because of the pain in my foot.

I hobble along, his arm along my shoulder this time. I can't talk to him like this. Instead, I concentrate on walking, and look straight ahead. Tears are threatening again and I am annoyed at myself.

When we get to David's place, Sam asks if I want him to help me up the stairs but I say no. I can't bear the thought of him coming up there, bringing more memories fluttering down like confetti.

He looks me straight in the eye and for one crazy minute I think he's going to kiss me, but he looks away, down at his watch, and looks worried. "I'd really better go," he says. He squeezes my hand. "I hope that ankle's better soon."

"Thank you, Sam," I say, and I really mean it.

"It's no problem."

I watch as he hurries off along the street; his shoulders are broad under his t-shirt, and his back tapers in neatly. I feel sad, and I wish I'd said more. As I'm about to go in, though, Sam turns round, calls back to me, "You owe me a beer!"

He grins, and is gone, and somewhere in me a little light of optimism pings on.

12

I manage to pull myself up the stairs, shouting hello to David.

"Are you OK?" He appears at his living room doorway. "I thought I could hear some kind of sea monster dragging itself up my staircase. I was about to hide behind the sofa. Ow, that looks painful!"

"I twisted my ankle," I say, "on the coast path."

"And you managed to get back here? That must have taken you all day!"

"It's OK, I had some help."

"Oh yeah? Some hunky surfer, was it?"

"Actually, do you remember Sam?"

"Sam… *your* Sam?"

I can't help but smile, that he remembers Sam, and that even he calls him 'your Sam'. That's me, Julie and David that think that way, at least. If only Sam did, too.

"The very same."

"What… are you two..?"

"No, nothing like that," I hasten my reply. "He just happened to be coming along when I fell."

"And I suppose you fell straight into his arms?"

"No, worse, right at his feet."

David laughs.

"Come in, Alice, why don't you come and rest in here a

bit? I've got a lovely pouffe you can rest your foot on."

"Thank you David, that actually sounds lovely."

I haven't seen much of David since we've been back but he's on annual leave at the moment and Martin's at work so David's been at home a bit more. Last time we were here, he was going through a hard time. He was about my age then, in his late twenties. He and Bea had been through a lot, their parents dying a few years earlier, within months of each other. When David had returned to Cornwall to live, he hadn't found everybody in his home town accepting of his sexuality, or the lifestyle they imagined he'd had living 'upcountry' as a gay man. That's not to say everybody thinks like that but I think some of his old friends gave him a hard time. In honesty, I think he'd struggled even in Bristol, not just with his sexuality but with his stressful job, working for a law firm there.

David had been in three longish relationships in the time he'd been away, all with older men, none of which had worked out particularly well. He had decided to return home when a job came up down here, at a place in Truro, but he had found it hard coming back and I think felt like he'd never find the right man. I'd spent more than one evening comforting him; he'd been drinking quite a lot at that time too, which didn't help matters.

Now, he says, he has the occasional nice glass of wine or whisky, but he's much happier "not being a lush" and since meeting Martin three years ago he's really settled down. He's also been made partner at the law firm and, although it's hard work, he says he couldn't be happier.

"Let me get you a coffee. Or a brandy – isn't that what you need when you're in shock? Or a coffee and a brandy?"

I laugh. "I'm not in shock, it's just a twisted ankle."

"It's not your ankle I'm talking about," David shoots me a look.

I go red.

"Come on!" he says. "You and Sam. You were so into each other, I was sure you were going to be together forever. I couldn't believe it when I bumped into him that New Year's Eve and I could tell he was gutted you'd found somebody else."

"What?"

"The year after you were here, when you and Julie came down before. I'm sure it was New Year's Eve, it must have been, because I seem to remember he was dressed as a Chuckle Brother, and Luke was the other one. Barry. Well, I guess it was Barry. It's hard to say, they look so alike... what's the other one's name, anyway?"

Despite the mental image of Sam and Luke as the Chuckle Brothers, I'm not smiling. "So you saw Sam, and he knew I was with somebody else?"

"Yes, and you were, weren't you? We'd had a Christmas card from you, and your new *amore*, was it Greg?"

"Geoff," I say flatly. "So you told him I was with Geoff?"

"What? No! He already knew you were with somebody. I'm sure he did. Unless I'm getting confused, it was during my Drinking Years. But I seem to remember it clearly enough, Sam saying you'd met somebody back home."

Well, this is weird. How the hell would Sam have known about Geoff?

"Yes, that's right," David continued, "because he'd been in that accident, hadn't he?"

"What accident?" I almost shriek.

"Sam, he said he'd been injured in a car accident.

89

Sounded nasty. Some drink-driving grockle had run him off the road."

"And… he was OK?"

"Well, unless that was a ghost you bumped into today…" David says drily.

I can't believe it. Sam had a car accident, and I didn't know. And he had known about Geoff, but how could that be? I try and work it out but I'd been so heartbroken about Sam, I hadn't really kept in touch with Bea or David very well. I probably had sent them a Christmas card, yes, and I remember now, how Geoff insisted I sign his name on the cards I sent. And that he checked who I was sending them to, and he hadn't really wanted me to send that one to Bea and David, but had relented when I explained David was gay, and Bea my ex-employer.

Would Julie have told him, or – more likely – somebody who knew him? This seems the most likely possibility, but I don't think Julie was any better at keeping in touch than I was. She'd barrelled off to university up in Scotland, and barely even contacted me while she was away. I didn't mind; that was just Julie, but I doubted she'd have made a better job at making contact with people she'd known for a handful of months.

"I think I will have that brandy, please," I say to David.

When I get back up to the flat, it's baking hot. The windows are closed, none of the curtains are drawn – not that they make a great deal of difference – so my first job is to hobble around, opening the windows and welcoming in the fresh air, the voices of people passing below, and, not far off, the constant, slow churn of car motors turning over as a queue of hot, red-faced visitors form a slow procession through town, stuck on the one-way system, on their way out, or looking for a parking space.

I lower myself gently onto my bed and I lie there, letting the events and the revelations of the last few hours wash over me. So many thoughts are dancing through my mind. I am still exhilarated from that close contact with Sam; I can still feel his arm round my waist, his warm skin and the soft, blond hairs brushing against me.

And he'd said I owe him a drink. Did he mean it? If only I had a way of getting in touch with him. Although I wouldn't admit this to many people, I can still remember his old mobile number, but that has long since been cut off. I know, because that autumn after the golden summer (the grey autumn) I had rung it again and again, but I always received the same long, high-pitched reminder that the phone was no longer in action. That was my only way of getting in touch with him, aside from writing – and I'd stopped short of that. I wanted to speak to him, to actually hear his voice and his reaction to me. If I sent a letter, I wouldn't know if he'd received it, and I wouldn't know how he'd received it.

Mum has a stack of letters Dad wrote to her when they were first together. They had only lived about forty miles away from each other, but could only see each other at weekends because of work and not having their own cars, so they had kept in touch by letter and by phone. I think it's romantic and lovely that she still has those letters. Dad's lost his from her, but I've seen them both reading through the ones he wrote, very occasionally, and smiling at each other as they remember their younger selves and those early days of their relationships. For a while I kept all Sam's texts, which is not the same at all, of course, but I would scroll back through them, and sometimes it would make me feel good – but usually it would make me feel awful, and then Geoff came along and I caught him looking at my texts, and I decided to delete the whole lot. I knew I had to move on, anyway.

So now I have new information, what am I going to do about it? I can ask Julie if she knows how Sam knew about Geoff. I could ask Luke too, I suppose. I definitely want to ask him about the car accident. But I feel like if I ask too much, I'll be showing my hand. It will be so obvious that I've never got over Sam.

Maybe Julie could arrange for us all to go out one night… but I know that's not quite right, either; too much like a double date.

All I can do is hope that I bump into Sam again, and I vow that if I do I will insist that I get him that beer – even if it's seven in the morning – and get to the bottom of all this.

I must have dozed off, despite the whirling thoughts. When I wake, I can tell that the light is different and it must be early evening. I hear a knocking sound and David's voice calling, "Hello-o?"

"Hello," I croak.

"Mind if I come in?" He pushes the door tentatively and I see he has a tray, with one of those dome things people use to keep food warm, a glass of wine, and a can of Coke Zero. "Room Service!"

"Wow," I say, pulling myself up. I wince at the pain in my ankle. "David! You didn't have to do this."

"Well, I couldn't have you limping around up here trying to sort something out on that crappy little cooker! Look," he pulls the dome away, "Thai green curry, with jasmine rice, all veggie of course." The aroma reaches my nostrils and I feel suddenly very hungry.

"And you don't need to worry about work, I've called Bea and I'm filling in for you tomorrow."

"David!" I say. "This is meant to be your week off!"

"It's fine! You know I love camping it up for the tourists."

I must admit, that's a bit of a relief. I hadn't really thought about work, but I don't suppose a limping waitress is a great idea. Hopefully, a day of rest will sort my ankle out. "You are too kind. Really, really, too kind."

"Well, you seem like you could do with a bit of looking after. Seeing as your mate's dumped you in favour of her new love."

"She hasn't… well, I suppose she has, a bit."

David raises his eyebrows at me. "Erm, she has totally… what happened to her summer of fun?"

"I don't know," I sigh, "And I really, really don't mind being alone a fair bit, if I'm honest. I'm used to it. And I don't mean that in a self-pitying way. I enjoy my own company. But you're right, we did come down here with the intention of enjoying the summer together."

"And now she's got together with Luke… who is looking *fine*, by the way." David gestures to the chair by the window. "Mind if I sit?"

"Go ahead," I say, taking a mouthful of the curry. "Oh wow, this is delicious. Luke is looking good, isn't he? He's such a nice bloke. Do you know about his mum?"

"Yes, I had heard something. You know what this place is like. You can't even get a terminal illness without everybody having to know about it and have an opinion on it!"

"It must be awful. For Luke, I mean. So maybe it's good that he's got Julie."

"But you're worried that she's on the rebound?"

He's good, this one.

"Yes, if I'm honest, I suppose I am. I am worried for her; she was meant to be marrying Gabe, for god's sake. And I'm worried for Gabe, too; he's a very nice bloke. You'd love him. But most of all, I think, I'm worried for Luke. He's already going through so much. I don't think Julie should have jumped into this so quickly but if I say anything it sounds like sour grapes." I dip a crispy spring roll into the sauce. I don't know if I've ever felt so hungry.

"I don't suppose there's much you can do," says David, "except watch and wait."

"Mmm," I agree through a mouthful of curry.

"But if you need some extra company, remember I'm always downstairs... or at Martin's," he admits. "But you're very welcome to come and hang out with us both, we won't make you feel like a gooseberry, I promise."

"Thank you, David, that is really, really lovely of you."

"It's no problem. Listen, I've got some cheesecake downstairs, and I'm going to bring my DVD player up here. You can borrow all my old boxsets. I've got *Friends, This Life, Spaced...*" He waves away my attempts at a protest. "Just rest up, and you'll be right as rain soon. Then you can come and wait on me someday."

"It's a deal," I smile, and I want to cry with relief, and the thought of David's kindness. It's been good to talk to somebody who gets it, and to know that my concerns about Julie and Luke aren't completely unreasonable. I decide to do as I'm told and make the most of this chance to rest.

13

Julie obviously got my note last night, as she didn't come crashing into my room to wake me for work. In fact, when I wake up it's because of a car horn somewhere in a nearby street and when I check my clock, I see it's nearly 10am. I can't believe it and I experience a moment's panic until I remember David's kindness, and my swollen ankle. I tentatively circle it, and I'm pleased that it already feels a lot better. However, I decide to give Pilates a miss. I'd told Casey I'd try to get to her Thursday class this afternoon, which she said is busier than the Monday night one – though full of grannies, according to her. I gently ease my way along to the bathroom, using the wall for support and stopping to put the kettle on. I retrieve my phone from my bag before heading back to bed with a cup of tea. Then I sit up and send David a text thanking him once more, and Casey a message to say I'm sorry but I'll have to miss her class.

I don't know why I feel I have to let her know, but there's something about her which makes me think she will appreciate a bit of extra support. She is quick to respond:

Oh no that's not good. Take it eezy, hopefully you'll b bak on Mon. KCx

I thank her and say yes, I hope to see her Monday, and I hope that her class goes well today.

Thanks luv, I was just thinking, do u fancy a drink tomorrow night, if ur foots better? KCx

I wasn't expecting that. I type back:

Can I let you know? I should check with my friend what her plans are, I haven't seen her all week!

Casey's response is short: **OK**

I'm immediately wrong-footed. Have I offended her? This is one of the reasons I hate text messages. It's very hard to know what somebody means if they just type 'OK'. Is she annoyed? Or is she just distracted by something? It's just that compared to her other friendly messages, this one sounds abrupt. I feel compelled to send her something a bit friendlier back, just to make sure things are alright.

Thanks for the offer – if not tomorrow then defo another night x

I even add a kiss, to show I'm being friendly. I'm well aware it's pathetic. This is not how I behave in other areas of my life. If somebody asks me face-to-face if I want to go out and then seems offended if I say no, or I'm not sure, I would generally just leave them to it. I don't like to be pressured into things, and I feel far less inclined to do something if I think that somebody is behaving like an arse.

However, I suppose that right now, from a selfish point

of view, I don't feel I have many options open to me socially in Cornwall. Julie has jumped feet-first into bed with Luke, and while I'd obviously love to go for that drink with Sam, I suspect that it's not really a realistic prospect. Casey seems quite nice. Maybe I should just say yes, and if Julie's at a loose end tomorrow night, it's tough.

In fact, I think, yes, I'm just going to do it.

Sod it... I'd love to go for a drink, yes please.

Another super-quick reply:

Fab! I'll come round to u about 8? Send me ur address. KCx

Now I'm sure she was sulking before. Oh well. Maybe she thought I was trying to give her the brush-off. It can't hurt to go for a drink or two with her, anyway. I can always blame my ankle if I want to leave early.

***

After a day's rest, my ankle is much better and I am up bright and early with Julie on Friday morning, ready for work. David had pretended to be disappointed when I said I was going to go back.

"You can't! There's a really hot couple in Room Three, and I think I've worked my charm on him. I'm pretty sure they're going to split up over me."

"Well, all the more reason for me to go in and make sure they patch things up. You can't just go turning straight men gay all over the place, you know. What will happen to the human race? And what about Martin?"

"He knew what he was getting into when we started going out. You can't be in a relationship with somebody as gorgeous as me and expect to be the only person who falls for me."

"You've got a point," I concede. "Still, I think I'd better get back to earning my living. Otherwise your sister might think I'm not worth employing anymore."

"Oh, OK. Be like that. Glad you're feeling better," David had hugged me. "Don't forget what I said about me and Martin being here for you if you need a bit of extra company."

"Thanks, David, I won't. I'd love to hang out with you guys, maybe we can go out next week?"

"Or you can come down here, for dinner, one night. See if you can drag Julie away from Luke, too."

"Ha! Actually, I'm sure he was only planning to be here for a couple of weeks this time so maybe he'll be back in London next week."

I ask Julie about this as we walk through the town to the Sail Loft.

"Oh, well he's decided to stay here… he says he can work from Cornwall at the moment, and he doesn't want to leave his mum."

"Oh," I say, "well I don't blame him. I wouldn't want to be away from my mum if she was ill."

"No. And he says he doesn't want to leave me, either!"

This was more like it. Not that I'm doubting Luke's devotion to his mum although, between spending time with his parents, and Julie, I'm not sure how he's getting any work done. Maybe he doesn't sleep. It's none of my business, though.

"I'm sorry," Julie looks at me.

"Why?"

"Because I've abandoned you."

"You haven't." She has.

"It's just… I feel like I've known him forever."

I remember those exact words coming from her mouth when she got together with Gabe. I wonder if the two of them have been in touch again. I can't believe she could just leave their relationship, up sticks, and never give it a second thought. They were meant to be getting married, for god's sake.

"I know," I smile thinly, and pull myself up the steps into the Sail Loft, using the banister.

"Are you going to be OK?" Julie asks.

"What, with my ankle, or being abandoned by my friend?"

"Both," she smiles at me and I can see she wants me to smile back. She's not quite sure what mood I'm in, but neither am I. I walk through to the kitchen to find Bea, leaving Julie to follow.

Work is busy and I don't get a moment to chat to Julie, which I am meanly pleased about. We do, however, have lunch together: fish and chips for Julie, and a sandwich for me, sitting on the harbour wall in the sunshine.

"I am sorry," she tells me again.

"Oh, you don't have to be," I cave in. "Not on my account. I'm OK, you know I'm happy in my own company."

"Yeah, but we came down here together. You wouldn't have come if I hadn't suggested it."

"That's true, but that doesn't mean we have to spend every waking minute together."

"I feel like Luke needs me, too," she says. "He's

heartbroken about his mum. She's going into a hospice, you know. They're just waiting for the place to be confirmed."

"That's really sad," I say.

"Yep."

We both sit quietly, staring into the dark green water of the harbour, which gently splashes against the hulls of the boats.

"I don't want to ask this," I say after a while, "and I promise I won't again, but are you really sure about you and Luke? It's not just a reaction to splitting up with Gabe?"

"No, it's not." I know Julie so well, I can tell she's making an effort to answer calmly and rationally. I know my question has annoyed her, but I can't help feeling that with Luke already in such a sad position, the last thing he needs is to be used as a pawn in Julie's relationship with Gabe. Not that I'm suggesting she'd do that knowingly, or cynically. She's far from a nasty, calculating person. But she has a tendency to act before thinking.

"I really like Luke," she continues, "I couldn't believe it when I saw him again, and how lovely he is now."

"He was always lovely," I say.

"You know what I mean," she shoots a semi-sharp look at me. "Yes, he was a lovely boy, but he's found his feet and grown into himself, and yes, I do mean physically. I know that sounds shallow; it's not meant to. But I didn't fancy him ten years ago, and I do now."

"OK," I say, "I'm sorry. And I know I said I wouldn't interfere again. Luke's going to need a lot of support, though."

"Do you think I don't know that?"

"No, sorry. Of course you do."

"Look, Alice, I know what you're thinking. I haven't thought this through, I'm too impetuous. Well maybe I am a bit, but life should be an adventure. Not some tedious treadmill of work, Pilates, running club…" she looks at me as if slightly unsure of how much she should say but she goes on. "Look at you. You're hung up on Sam, but you haven't spoken to him properly in ten years. He might be a totally different bloke. You might not feel the same at all about him now; you were only eighteen back then. I feel like Geoff has ruined you, stopped you taking a chance on anyone else and so Sam is your little escape clause. Your reason not to meet anybody new. But you're – we're – nearly thirty, and I know Geoff was a twat, but he's long gone. If you want to get together with Sam, go for it. Go and find him, and speak to him. But if you're just using him as an excuse, it's time to get over it, and move on."

I feel my face growing redder and redder as she speaks. Partially from anger, and also from embarrassment. She is right to some extent. I've become boring. I've let myself be that way. Geoff scared me, and I feel stronger and safer on my own. But I am also sure that I'm not imagining my feelings for Sam; he is not just an excuse. Still, if I'm not going to do anything about it then I really do need to move on.

"Right." Is all I can think of to say.

"I'm sorry, but it needed saying."

We finish our lunch in silence then walk back to the flat. I ask Julie if she wants to go for a swim but she says she's going to have a siesta instead. I inwardly shrug but outwardly offer a bright, unconvincing smile. "OK, see you later." I change into my bikini and stuff a towel and a book into my bag, grabbing a handful of change so I can get a coffee after my swim.

Stepping out into the sunshine is a relief. There is an atmosphere between Julie and me now, and I am not quite sure how to change it. I won't interfere again, but it's clear what I think and I can't take it back. She knows it, and a part of me wonders if she's annoyed because there's some truth in it, but I really have to say no more. I have to trust her that she's not going to mess Luke about now, when he most needs some stability in his life.

I decide to head to the more sheltered beach, on the west side of the town, where the waves are smaller and I can have a proper swim, without being swamped by a breaker or knocked out by a surfer. The early afternoon sun beats down, heat rising from the tarmac of the road. I move into the smaller streets, lined with fishermen's cottages, stable doors open at the top, the sounds of music, TV and conversation drifting out.

In contrast to the quiet streets, the beach is busy. The tide is a long way out but even so, the vast expanse of sand looks gridlocked. All the tables under the awning of the café are taken. I move past them, along to the rocks where I sat the other day. A large family group have already commandeered the sheltered side, with beach tents, blankets and windbreak making their camp for the day. I move on.

At the far end of the beach it is quieter and I find a spot where I can leave my bag. Without hesitating, I pull my dress off and head straight for the water. It closes its cold jaws around my ankles but I ignore it and plunge on in, soon acclimatising. I swim out, away from the children who are having a whale of a time with their dinghies and body boards. It's not long before I am out almost on my own; this is it. Heaven, for me at least. I swim back and forth, the salt tingling on my skin and stinging my eyes.

This is what it feels like to be alive. I am put in mind of Luke's mum again, who is never far from my thoughts. I can't remember if she was a swimmer but I wonder what it feels like to live here and know that you can't get to the beach; that you will never again step on the fine sand, or paddle in the shallows. The hospice is in a nice spot, and probably has some good views of the bay, but is it better or worse to see what is out of reach? I really don't know.

I think of Julie again. I do feel bad. Maybe I'm letting my personal situation make me bitter, cloud my judgement. Maybe I'm jealous. It's very possible. I must admit, I envy her ability to just go for it, see how things turn out. Maybe it's not the most sensible way to behave, but she's not over-cautious, or scared to give something a go. I hope that she'll still be in when I get back to the flat, and we can have a chat – or just have a drink together, and forget about all that. I'll see if she wants to come out with me and Casey, in fact.

I move onto my back, adopting my favourite position. The water is cold as it rushes into my ears, but it fills them with a welcome whooshing sound, so that once again it is the sea, the sky, the sun and me. I feel the goose pimples softly prickle my belly where it is exposed to the air. I lie as still as I can, just gently circling my hands from time to time, and I float, letting it all wash over me.

When I start to feel cold, I know it's time to return to shore. I look at my position and see I've drifted a little way, but a few strong strokes soon have me heading back in the right direction and I enjoy the feel of my limbs slicing through the water until it's too shallow and I walk the rest of the way, smiling at the kids I pass as I head back to dry(ish) land and return to my bag. I towel myself dry then wander to the café, in search of coffee. Instead of staying on the beach, I take my drink and my book, and I climb the steep steps at the other end of the sand, up onto the clifftop, where benches are spaced around a large lawn, interspersed with well-kept flowerbeds. An older couple sit on my favourite bench - the one facing away from town - but there is plenty of space for me and I sit along the length of the seat, legs stretched in front of me, sipping my coffee and reading, occasionally distracted by a bird or the sight of the miles of twinkling sea in front of me.

I haven't brought my phone with me; if I had, I'd text Julie and see if she wants to meet up. We'll be OK, I know that, but I'd like to make sure we're OK sooner rather than later.

When my coffee is finished, I pack away my book, toss my cup into a bin and head towards town, keen to get back to Julie. But by the time I return to the flat, she's gone. She's left a note saying she's staying at Luke's and will see me at work in the morning. I try to read the tone of the note but it is flat, perfunctory.

Alice,
Gone to Luke's, I'll be staying there tonight. See you tomorrow at Sail Loft.
J

There is no kiss, in the style of Casey, but Julie's not really like that. It's a perfectly functional, factual note but I can't help feeling that it bears the undertones of somebody who is not happy with me.

Still, there is nothing more I can do now. I check the time. It's half-four; later than I'd thought. I decide to have a bath, then I can phone Mum and Dad, and get a salad ready for tea, in a bid to be healthy.

At half-past seven, my phone goes. It's Casey. "I'm outside."

"Oh," I say, "right." Didn't she say eight o'clock? Maybe we got our wires crossed, or she forgot. "I'm still getting ready. I'll come and let you in, if you don't mind hanging on a few minutes."

"No, that's fine."

I dash down the stairs, and open the door to see Casey wearing a very short, very tight blue dress. She can certainly get away with it, with her Pilates-toned body, but I was planning to wear jeans and a top. Now I feel distinctly underdressed.

"You look nice," she says, kissing my cheek. I see she is holding a bottle of Prosecco. "I know I'm early," she says, not exactly apologetically, "but I thought we could drink this before we go. Is this whole place yours?"

She looks admiringly into the cool, dark hallway which David has painted Farrow & Ball Stone Blue ("Martin said it would look cold, but I think it's just cool... and kind of nautical."). The floorboards are bare, and the wooden staircase stripped and polished. It is a beautiful house.

"No," I say, "sadly not. Julie and I are at the top of the house."

"Julie's your friend from home?"

"Yeah, that's right. She's not in tonight, though, otherwise I'd have seen if she wanted to join us."

"I don't mind, it'll give us a chance to get to know each other better. Where's she gone?" Casey follows me into the hallway and up the stairs.

"Oh, she's out with her bloke," I say vaguely. I may not

be on the best terms with Julie but she's still my best mate, and I don't really want to talk about her with Casey.

When we get to the top, I say, "We'll have to hang out in my room, I'm afraid, there isn't really a lounge to speak of. Or at all."

"That's OK!" Casey says brightly. "You get some glasses, and I'll open this baby up." She sits on my bed, stretching her tanned, muscular legs in front of her. I momentarily consider getting changed but I think no, this is what I want to wear. And besides, whatever I wear, I will pale in comparison to Casey.

The wine froths out of the top of the bottle and she expertly catches it in her mouth, giggling. I laugh, too, and hold out both glasses to catch any excess. She fills them up and taps her drink against mine. "To new friends."

"To new friends," I agree.

We polish off the bottle within an hour, and in that time I feel the bubbles fizzing to my brain. I sit on the chair under the window and Casey remains on my bed. At first, talk is fairly polite – where and why she studied Pilates (in Penzance, and because she wanted to make a living out of something she really believed in); how Sophie was getting on at school and what it feels like to have a daughter who's approaching secondary school. From there, with the Prosecco oiling our thoughts and letting them slip more freely into the room, it's talk of secondary school, first boyfriends, first kisses. I tell her about mine, with a boy called Damien Parker, playing Spin the Bottle at a party in Year 8. "He just stuck his tongue straight in my mouth," I say, "I was absolutely shocked. I can still feel it now; sort of slimy and cold, like a dead slug." I continue as Casey splutters with laughter, "I don't think I kissed anybody else till I was sixteen! And then I was dreading it."

"I was a bit of a late-starter," Casey admits, "I was really shy at school, and a bit overweight. But I made up for it. I was sixteen when I first kissed a boy, and he was my first real boyfriend. We were together till I was eighteen then he broke my heart. I didn't really have many friends and I'd given them up for him, really. He went off with the girl who had been my best friend at school. Turned out they'd been seeing each other behind my back for a year."

"That's awful," I commiserate. "Are they still around here?"

"He is, and she's not far away, in Launceston I think. Her mum's still in town, and he's married for the second time, got two kids from the first wife and one from the second. They all go to Sophie's school."

"That's a bit weird, isn't it?"

"Not really, it's quite normal here. If you grow up here and don't leave, you see your exes all the time, and their wives, and their kids. I know somebody who's married to her ex's brother."

I laugh.

"There's not much choice, I suppose," Casey grins. "And after Jon left me, I played the field a bit... well a lot, I guess. Until Sophie came along."

"And are you still with Sophie's dad?"

Casey goes quiet. "No."

"Oh, sorry. I wasn't sure. I knew you were rushing off to meet him that time; I thought you might still be together."

"We were too young, really," Casey says. "But I don't regret having Sophie."

"Of course you don't," I say, and I try to imagine what it must be like being a young mum. Casey is only a couple of years older than me but she has a daughter who is nearly ten, and I have no idea when I might – or even if I will – have kids. I hope I do; I hope I can. But it has to be right.

"Come on!" she says, draining her glass. "Let's forget about all that stuff, and get going!"

We head down the stairs, and out into the warm Friday evening. There are families and couples out; men in short sleeves, women in dresses and heels. Casey receives admiring glances as she walks confidently along the cobbles. I hurry to keep up with her long-legged stride, and she apologises when she remembers my ankle.

"You should have told me to slow down!" she says. "Come on, let's get one in at the Rack."

The Rack (full name: The Rack o'Lamb, not very veggie-friendly) is a locals-only pub, or at least it was when Julie and I were here the first time round; as we discovered to our dismay when we went in on the first night, giggling and pooling our coins for a couple of cider & blacks. They weren't unfriendly, exactly, but a bit… well… stary. And we soon finished up our drinks, walking with relief into the more tourist-friendly harbour area where we spent our last pennies on a bottle of cider and a bag of chips, and sat on the harbour wall until it had long gone dark.

Tonight, though, I am with Casey, who is greeted warmly by the barman. "Alright, K? Not seen you for a while."

"Yeah, you know, been saving up for Sophie's school camp, and getting the business going."

"That's right, Celia said you were doin' somethin' new… yoga, is it?"

"Pilates," Casey corrects him, just as a long, low whistle comes from behind us. She turns, grinning. "Watch it, Pete."

It's hard to put an age on Pete; he's very, very tanned.

His skin looks like leather, and his teeth flash white in stark contrast to it. His hair is also white, and wiry, and he's wearing a Metallica t-shirt.

"Just admirin' your dress," he says, and his eyes move to me. "Who's this, then?"

"This is Alice, she's a friend of mine, so be nice!" Casey instructs.

"When am I anything but?"

We have a cider in the Rack, taking our drinks to a corner table. Casey clearly knows most of the people in the pub, which means they are friendly enough, but I feel out of place and I'm relieved when we've drunk up and she says it's time to move on.

She links her arm through mine and we wander along the meandering back streets. There must be some kind of plan, but I've always found that, like an errant sat nav, my sense of direction goes askew when I'm walking through the town, and I used to be constantly surprised at where I'd find myself, when I'd been sure I was heading to the beach but ended up at the art gallery, or back near David's house when I thought I was nearing the opposite side of the town. Now I know my way around confidently but it doesn't mean it makes sense.

"Where to now?" I ask. I'm happy to let Casey take the lead.

"Why don't we go to the Ecuabar?"

This is the poshest of the three clubs; sitting above one of the flash restaurants, on the harbour road, it boasts 'the best view… and the best cocktails… in town'.

Casey must see my look. "Don't worry," she says. "We won't have to buy more than one. It's always full of the yacht brigade, down from Padstow and Rock. I bet you I can get us our drinks paid for."

"OK," I say. "Let's give it a go!" I feel swept along by Casey's confidence, and full of a sudden energy and excitement. It feels good to be out, and going somewhere new.

The Ecuabar is loud, full of smartly-dressed, loud men and women in posh frocks or expensive linen trousers and tops. Some kind of Spanish guitar music is being released into the room from the vast speakers, and the glass bar is lit from beneath so that different coloured shards of light shoot into the air. I don't know how the bar staff manage to work without being blinded but they are all smart efficiency, in their black shirts and smart haircuts. "What's it to be, ladies?" asks a good-looking barman, polishing a cocktail shaker.

"Can you do us something special?" Casey asks him. "We've had prosecco, and cider. We want something to compliment them, please."

"A challenge... great," the barman grins. "Take a seat, and I'll sort something for you."

He scans the myriad bottles and pulls a few out in turn, mixing and shaking, then placing two ice-cold glasses in front of us, pouring in his creation, and finishing with a few sprigs of mint and a wedge of lime.

"Here you go, ladies. Elderflower gin, apple juice, spiced rum, and a dash of tequila. What do you think?"

We both take a sip. It's delicious. I tell him so.

"Fantastic," he pulls out a smile like a magician pulling a rabbit from a hat, and disappears to his next customer. The bar is heaving but Casey says we should keep our seats. As we are nearing the bottom of our glasses, the smart barman comes back, topping them up with what is left of our drink. "Same again?" he asks smoothly.

I am about to say no, when a voice comes from behind me, "I'll get these."

Casey raises her eyebrows at me. *See?*

I turn to see a forty-ish man, in a shirt and chinos, offering his card. "And I'll have the same again please, Nick."

"No problem, Charlie."

"I was going to introduce myself," the man smiles, "but Nick's just done that for me. I'm Charlie," he offers his hand, first to me, then to Casey. "That over there is my brother, Nathan."

I'm about to say my name when Casey pipes up, "I'm Tallulah, and this is Daphne." I almost spit my drink out.

"Tallulah?" Charlie raises his eyebrows and smiles. "Fancy joining us? After you, *Daphne…*"

We walk with him to his table, where he places himself next to Casey and introduces me to Nathan who, he says, is married, "So don't get any ideas."

Nathan, while a nice man, is not likely to put any ideas into my head. He drones on and on about the intricacies of sailing, and how he's been doing it since he was a boy.

"I nearly made it to the Olympic team," he says earnestly.

"Wow, you must be really good at it," I say, only half-listening to him; aware Charlie is getting quite 'friendly' with Casey. He has his arm draped around her shoulder, and he's moving in to whisper something in her ear. I want to know she's OK with it. I find out soon enough.

"Ow, you bitch!" Charlie exclaims.

"You shouldn't be such a slimy bastard, then," Casey says. She downs the rest of her drink and takes my hand. "Come on, Daphne, we're out of here."

"What happened?" I ask her as she storms out, dragging

me behind her.

"He put his hand on my thigh. Almost up my skirt. I squeezed his bollocks really hard and asked him how he liked it."

"You didn't!"

"I bloody did," she says.

As we head into the night, I become aware of how drunk I am but not, it seems, as drunk as Casey. She pulls me into a side street, and doubles over. "I think I'm going to be sick."

I hold her hair back for her, and she retches, spitting out what she can bring up. Suddenly she doesn't seem quite as glamorous. We walk back out into what light remains of the day, and I sit her down on a bench by the harbour, checking that there is no sign of Charlie before nipping into the chippy to buy a can of Coke. "Here, have this," I hand it to Casey.

"Thanks," she says, "I'm not really meant to have full fat Coke."

"It'll make you feel better," I say firmly. I sit next to her.

"That bloke was such a prick. Why do I always attract men like that?"

Sitting at bars waiting to have drinks bought for you doesn't really help, I think, but I don't say anything. Instead, I let her continue. "It's like, since I had Sophie, blokes think I'm a slag. Which is just stupid, because I'm not, I'm really not. OK, I'm not with her dad, and I've had a few flings round town, but nothing major. Sophie's my life, my world, I don't want her to get mixed up with any old bloke I fancy seeing."

"I know," I soothe.

"I've been on my own with her since she was two, nearly three, and it's been just me and her since then. I'm allowed to go out and have some fun though, aren't I? Just sometimes. I don't mean like every weekend."

"Of course you are. Is Sophie's dad looking after her tonight?"

"Yeah, she's staying at his place."

"Shall I walk you home? Make sure you get there OK?"

"OK," she sniffs.

This time it's me supporting her. My ankle's much better and it's easier walking at this slow place. Casey is attracting more glances but I fear that this time it's for a different reason. She is crying openly, and I can only half make out what she's talking about; I assume she's talking about Sophie's dad. "I wish we'd never split up... she really loves him... I might do, I think, I could do..."

"Is he single?" I ask.

She nods. "I think so. I don't think he's really been with anyone else since we split up. When he's not with Soph, he's either working or studying, from what I can make out. I don't know. He's kept it quiet if he has been with anyone, but that would be just like him. He's a very private person. He's lovely."

"Well, it sounds like you still have feelings for him. Have you tried talking to him?"

"No. Well, yeah. Sort of. I don't know. He says there are good reasons it didn't work out between us. And I've got to give him credit for always being there for Soph. I can't believe I let him get away."

"Come on," I say, "try not to worry about it tonight. We've had fun, haven't we?"

"Yes," she sniffs again. "I guess you won't want to do it again, though; I've made a total tit of myself, haven't I?"

"Of course we can go out again! And no, you haven't made a total tit of yourself. Just a bit of a tit."

I'm pleased to see her smile at this. "Thanks, Alice. I don't really have many friends, you know. It's been good having a night out."

"No problem."

We walk quietly, in step with each other, concentrating on making it up the steep hill, until we reach a block of flats. "This is me," she says.

"Want me to come in?"

"No, it's fine. Thank you, Alice."

"Are you sure? I can make you a coffee, help you sober up a bit before you go to bed."

"No, thanks, I think that Coke helped. And being sick. I knew it would make me feel better."

"OK. Well, thanks for a lovely evening." I grin and she laughs. "Really, it was a lovely evening. It's been a laugh. And hopefully Charlie'll think better of trying it on so readily in the future."

"I can't believe I did that!" Casey laughs.

I give her a hug then I turn and walk back down the hill. Although it's a total pain having to walk up here, there's a view of the bay which you don't get from town. It's dark now, of course, but the moon is rising and the sky is clear, so that a strip of sea is illuminated, and the odd star popping out above matches the twinkling of the lights on the boats below.

It's not late, and I'm relieved. I have to get up and work in the morning. I stop at a restaurant for a large takeaway latte, and I carry it home carefully, heading back to the flat. My ankle is aching a bit, and I feel dehydrated. I smirk to myself about Charlie's come-uppance. An evening out with Casey is definitely an experience. Maybe one I don't want to repeat too often.

14

I stay up late to try and rid my body of its alcoholic embalming fluid, reasoning it's better to be tired than hungover at work in the morning. I drink my latte then I clean the tiny kitchen, and the bathroom. I decide to have a bath and read my book but I'm flagging and afraid I'll fall asleep in the water. Ever since I was a kid I've had a fear of falling asleep and drowning in the bath. Is that a real thing? Or a scare story my parents told me to make me be careful? I'm not sure but to be on the safe side I decide to go to bed. I still have David's DVD player so I decide to watch some of *This Life* while I have the chance. I suppose in some ways the show is dated but the characters, mostly in their twenties, and their messy love lives and fledgling careers, are all too familiar to me.

I must have fallen asleep about a minute into the show because when I wake at 3.37am, my mouth thick with sleep and unbrushed teeth, the screen is glowing a deep, blackish blue and I don't remember anything that happened in the programme. Now I am wide awake, and I watch the thin curtain at my small dormer window blowing gently back and forth in the dim light. I sit up and take a sip of tea, immediately regretting this decision. It is cold and unappetising.

There is enough time for me to get a bit more sleep before I have to get up but there's something unsettling me. I can't place what it is but I slowly recall that Julie is annoyed with me. Once I let that thought in, others come to join it. Unsurprisingly, many of them revolve around Sam. I can't understand how he knew about Geoff. I don't even like to think of that name; all its associations are negative. I was a young student, and heartbroken; he made full advantage of this. He was a little older so I believed he was wiser. He had a good job, with a good wage, so I believed he was reliable and would look after me. He was adamant about his feelings for me. Even when he was telling me what to wear, who I could be friends with, what music to listen to. It was for my own good. It was because he loved me.

A cold unease creeps in when Geoff is on my mind. It is impossible to sleep. So, instead, I open my eyes. I have a shower. I put the kettle on and place some veggie sausage rolls in the oven to bake while I stealthily pack my work clothes in a bag then get dressed in a hoodie and joggers, with a body-warmer over the top. I get my tartan flask - I miss Julie – and fill it with hot coffee. I grab an apple and a banana, wrap the sausage rolls in foil, and I'm good to go.

I tiptoe down the stairs so that I don't wake David, then ease out of the front door, pulling it shut so gently – as the house is in the middle of a terrace, I run the risk of waking not only David but all of our neighbours.

The town is quiet. The light of the day is gradually swirling into the dark sky. I think the only other times I would have been out in town at this hour would be coming back from nights out. I feel like I've turned a corner somehow; like this is symbolic of getting older. I know that sounds daft. As my footsteps echo along the streets, I imagine the fishermen in decades and centuries past, walking down to their vessels in the early morning – in all weather, all seasons. History hangs heavy in these streets; there is no option for much to change; no room for new houses, no space for pavements to be built. The town is stubbornly itself, even though it is now largely inhabited by holiday-makers.

I walk along the harbour road, continuing along this line of thought; those men and women who used to live here, their struggles to make ends meet, the dangers they faced every day. What would they make of their homes turned into luxury holiday cottages?

There's a town museum, walls hung with black-and-white photos, showing the fishermen and their families; the tiny school classes; the weekly market. The people in those pictures look out almost confrontationally, daringly meeting the eyes of anyone looking in on them; their own with that eerie, translucent quality typical of old photos. Like they know you; your thoughts and your wishes, and like you don't know what life is about, or how hard it can be. You've spent your money, earned in a nice little office, on a week in one of their homes. Where it used to be cold and damp and dank, with a fire to heat the room where a family would huddle in the winter, to bake the bread and heat the water. When a bath was a weekly necessity, and the family would be placed in order to bathe in the same, increasingly murky, water, one by one.

Why is it I feel such an affinity with this place? My family do not come from here. We are a landlocked bunch, from the middle of the Midlands. I have never lived by the sea, never sailed. I'm a vegetarian, I do not eat fish. I've had a comfortable upbringing and never really had to struggle like the people of this town once did – and like some up in the far reaches, on the estates built uphill, still do today.

Why am I any different from any other tourist, bewitched and bedazzled by the beautiful sea and the white swathes of sand where it meets the land? I am not, I tell myself. I'm on holiday. This is not real life. And yet, I believe I belong here.

Now, as I walk past the harbour, the small fleet of boats making their way out through the incoming tide, the bars and restaurants are closed. The lone arcade is shuttered. Remnants of the previous day's ice creams and fish-and-chip suppers still litter the pavement, awaiting their saviour, the street cleaner. These are the trimmings and trappings of a town so beautiful that everybody wants a piece of it. I don't want a piece of it, I want a place in it.

I walk around the little path which curls to the headland, zipping my body-warmer and pulling my hood up against the cold – the air has yet to warm today and there is a cold wind coming in across the waves. I walk determinedly around, across the car park and the small piece of headland which separates it from the beach. As I top the brow, my breath is literally taken away, by a strong gust of sea wind, reminding me who is the boss here, and then the view. The beach: vast, inviting, entirely empty. With the sun barely making a dent in the sky, it is too early yet for even the surfers. It won't be long, I know, till a few brave souls make their way here, catching a wave before work, and before all the novices swarm in, saturating the sea like a cloud of jellyfish.

But for now, the beach is mine.

I take my shoes off at the top of the path and I run, faster and faster, onto the sand, which is cool beneath my toes, becoming colder still as I come closer to the shoreline, where the water seeps readily through the grains. I am out of breath – I am no runner – but I am filled with an intense joy.

And then I'm knackered.

I walk the rest of the way to the rocks, clutching my side against a stitch.

I set out my breakfast and pull myself up, keeping an eye out for any early-rising gulls. The sky is becoming a rich assortment of colours, with a bold pink suggesting 'shepherd's warning'. There's been talk of a storm coming. I think I would like a storm. There's a lot that needs clearing up.

As I take my time, sipping my coffee, eating first the sausage rolls and then the fruit, I have the absolute luxury of watching the sun rise across this beautiful town. I did this with Sam, the day before I had to leave. We had been out all night and set up a small tent on the far reaches of the beach.

We'd both fallen asleep, zipped into the tent, and wrapped in each other's arms. There was barely room to move but it hadn't mattered; in fact, I had loved it. Sometime in the early morning, I had become aware of a hazy light leaking into the tent, and I'd unzipped the door, shaking Sam gently. We had lain there, together, watching as the day came to life. I had been so sure that the practicalities of life would not get in our way. Convinced we were meant to be together. I am older now, and harder in my outlook, but maybe Julie is right. Perhaps I do need to be more like her.

Sod it, I think, downing the last dregs of coffee, I am going to bloody well do something. Sam said I owe him a beer. Well, he's going to have that beer. And I am going to

119

find out whether I really and truly am in love with him — or whether it's time to forget it all and move on.

Work flies by. Despite my lack of sleep, I am full of energy. Chatting with the guests, laughing at their jokes, nothing is too much trouble this morning. Bea smiles at me, a question in her eyes. I just smile back.

Julie is frosty with me but I bluff right over that. We've both annoyed each other and I know I need to talk to her but it's going to have to wait. I have bigger fish to fry. I take orders to her, say thank you, give feedback from guests, even return a plate of bacon twice as it is not crispy enough and then it is too crispy. She rolls her eyes and I can't help rolling mine too. Then we smile. She sends back the exact same plate of food, having wiped some of the bean sauce and rearranged the fried potatoes, and the gentleman is quite satisfied this time.

I can feel a thawing between us and, after Julie has dished up my scrambled eggs and grilled tomatoes, she sits down next to me, a cup of coffee in each hand. She slides one over to me. "Peace offering," she suggests.

"Looks like coffee to me."

"Peace coffee, then."

"Lovely. Thanks, mate."

"No problem, mate."

We sip in silence, then at the same time say, "Sorry."

Then, "Jinx."

Then, "I Jinxed first."

We have to play Rock, Paper Scissors to determine the winner. I lose; my paper to Julie's scissors. I sit in silence.

"Ha!" she says. "Now you have to listen to me. You can't speak until I say your full name."

I pretend to zip my mouth shut.

"That's better. OK, here goes. I'm sorry, Alice, for being a crap friend." I open my mouth, to respond but, "No! You're not allowed to speak. I have been a crap friend to you. I got you to quit your job, and I dragged you down here, and then I abandoned you on nights out and now I've abandoned you for Luke." She takes another sip of her coffee. I look at her. "Ahh," she sighs, grinning. "I quite like this. But really, Alice, I know I've not been great, and I know exactly why you're worried about me being with Luke. Maybe I shouldn't have just jumped into it, head-on, but I have, and he needs me. And he makes me feel good. You may now speak."

I sit in silence.

"OK, you knob... Alice Emily Griffiths."

"A Jinx is a Jinx, as you well know. OK. Let me answer. Look, I don't mind being on my own a lot of the time. You know that. I don't feel exactly abandoned, but I would quite like to see you a bit more, with or without Luke. You know I think he's great, too. I'm happy to hang out with you both. And you haven't 'dragged me' down here. I am so happy that I'm here. I love it. I don't want to leave. So you don't need to worry about that. It's not like I'm longing to be back selling paper clips and printer cartridges."

"OK..."

"And yes, I can't deny I'm worried about you and Luke, a bit. And I also know it's none of my business. But I don't want either of you to be hurt – and most of all, believe it or not, it's you that I'm worried about. You and Gabe were so happy. You were going to marry him, have kids, rent an art studio, open a café. You had plans. I just don't want you to regret giving all that up."

Julie looks thoughtful. "He called last night, you know."

"Who, Gabe? What did he want?"

"I don't know. I didn't answer. He's left a message, I'll listen to it after work." Julie checks the clock. "Uh-oh, you've got about three minutes now. Best gobble that lot up and transform yourself into Reception Woman. The other thing I haven't said is that I'm sorry for what I said about Sam, and Geoff. I worry about you, too. I admire your restraint and your self-reliance, but I hope that you don't miss out on chances of happiness because you're too scared of losing control. You can have both, you know. Not every bloke is a Geoff."

"I know," I say through a hurried mouthful of scrambled egg and toast. "And I can see that it looks quite mad that I am still hung up on the boy I was with when I was eighteen but... well, I'll tell you later..."

"What?" she asks, "You can't just say that."

"No, sorry, got to go," I laugh meanly and push my plate towards her. "Thanks for breakfast."

"You're going to tell me," she says.

"We'll see," I practically skip out of the kitchen, so relieved that Julie and I are on good terms again.

On our way back to the flat, I ask her what she's doing for the rest of the day.

"I don't know," she says, and I can tell she doesn't really want to answer. "Do you want to do something?"

"I'd love to if you haven't already got anything planned."

"Well, Luke said he'd like to do something this afternoon," she says apologetically, "but I can always cancel him..."

"No, no, that's fine." I really don't want her to feel bad and I need to ask her a favour, which involves Luke.

"… I think he might need some company, though. It's today that they're moving May into the hospice."

"Really, it's fine, I promise," I hasten to reply. Now I feel bad. "Actually, Julie, I wondered if you – and Luke – could do something for me."

"Oh yeah?" she turns her green eyes on me, narrowing them slightly.

"Yeah. I, well, I forgot to tell you I saw Sam the other day." Julie says nothing so I stumble on, "I kind of... bumped into him... anyway, we had a bit of a chat and I said I'd get him a beer sometime, but I don't know how to get in touch with him. I don't know where he lives now and I don't have his phone number."

"I wondered how long it would take you to tell me," Julie laughs.

"What?"

"About Sam! I know you saw him, you idiot. He told Luke."

"He did?"

"Yes!"

"Have you seen him?"

"No, not yet. I can't believe it's taken you this long to mention it, though!"

"Well, you were out…" I say, half-embarrassed, feeling like I've been punishing her for being with her boyfriend.

"Yes I was, wasn't I? And then we fell out. Sorry," she says sheepishly. "So what was it like? Was it love at second sight?"

I tell her what happened; how I came skidding out of the undergrowth and practically fell at his feet.

"Ha! So he saw you coming down from your little cottage. The place where you first…"

My cheeks grow hot. "Oh my god, you're right. I can't

believe I hadn't thought of that before. He must have known where I'd been, that I was…"

"… revisiting your past?" supplies Julie.

I laugh. "Oh, don't I look like a twat? I was going to ask you to see if Luke will pass on his number. But I don't think I can face him now! I'm acting like a fifteen-year-old."

"Don't be daft. I'm sure he was flattered. He didn't mention any of that to Luke, I don't think. Luke didn't mention it, anyway. He just said that Sam was really happy he'd seen you."

"Did he?"

"Yes, he did. And so he should be! Listen, Luke's coming round about half-two. Why don't you ask him for Sam's number then?"

"I can't!"

"Yes, you can. Now you really are acting like a fifteen-year-old. You said you'd buy Sam a beer. You can just text him: 'what about that beer', or something like that."

Can I? I suppose I can. "OK. Thanks, Julie."

"No worries. Now, let's stop at the deli, get some olives and cheese, and we can have a nice salad for lunch, out in David's garden."

Julie makes lunch while I sit and rest my ankle, soaking up the rays in David's suntrap. The carefully tended flowers and plants emit a subtle sweetness. I sit on the wooden bench, my legs stretched along it, and I close my eyes for a moment or two. So Sam's mentioned me to Luke, and if he didn't want to see me, surely Luke would have said something to Julie. To try and put me off. In an hour or so, I could have Sam's number, I could be texting him, we could be arranging a date.

Not a date, I quickly tell myself; a meeting. A catch-up. Two old friends filling each other in on what they've been doing for the last ten years.

Who am I kidding?

"Here we go." The tray Julie puts on the table holds two beautiful salads, a bottle of water, and two glasses. I probably wouldn't have gone to all the trouble she has to make lunch, but this looks delicious. There are fresh green leaves: rocket, spinach, and some kind of red lettuce; olives and sliced apple and cucumber; salted tomatoes and a sprinkle of cheese, walnuts and chilli. I'm very grateful that she's such a great chef, and also that she's a bit more weight-conscious than me as I'd probably have just rustled up a cheese and tomato sandwich and some crisps.

She pours us both a glass of water and raises hers to mine. "Cheers."

"Cheers," I agree. "I'm glad we're friends again."

"We were never not friends, you idiot."

"I know."

"This garden's lush, isn't it?" she says, sighing.

"Yeah, I think the only thing that's missing is a sea view." The walls around the yard are painted white. It feels very calm and sets off the multi-coloured flowers that David has so carefully cultivated. There is a wooden door, painted midnight-blue, which leads out onto a set of steep steps down to the town.

Above, the house peers down at us, under the bright blue sky. A few sparrows twitter from the gutter, keeping an eye out for crumbs, and a gull I'm pretty sure is the same one as last time I was out here lands on the back wall, strutting along it and pretending not to be looking at our plates.

"Are you enjoying it as much as the first time?" Julie asks.

"What, being here?"

"Yes."

"I think so. I don't know. It's totally different, isn't it? I suppose I knew all along that it would be. We're ten years older. We've experienced working, and paying rent, and arranging mortgages. Last time, we were just beginning to enjoy our freedom. Coming down here was such an adventure. It's a different kind of adventure now."

She nods. "I listened to Gabe's message when I was making lunch."

"What did he say?"

"That he's sorry, that he had been taking me for granted, that he's missing me. That he wants to come down."

"Oh."

"Yes, oh."

"What are you going to do?"

"I don't know."

"Shit."

"Precisely."

We discuss Julie's options and can't really come up with a good idea. Gabe has no idea about Luke, of course, although Luke knows about him.

"I wonder what he wants," she says.

"I think that's obvious. He wants to get back together with you."

"I know," she sighs. "It is obvious."

"And how do you feel about that?"

"I don't know. I don't want to think about it. I'm happy here, I'm having fun with Luke, and I really feel like I'm good for him, without wanting to sound big-headed."

"I'm sure," I say. "He's having an awful time and you've come along and given him the chance for some happiness. Maybe it's not possible to take his mind off his mum, but you're something else to think about. But how do you feel about him?"

"He's so lovely!" she says. "And he makes me feel great. And he's pretty hot, and a successful businessman."

These aren't necessarily the right answers, I think, at least from Luke's point of view.

"And what did you feel like when you heard Gabe say those things – that he's sorry? Could you imagine being back together with him?"

"Oh god, I don't know," Julie says. "I just want to enjoy this summer. I feel like coming down here is a holiday – even though I'm working – but a holiday from life, do you know what I mean?"

"Yes, I do. I do, exactly. But the problem is, life is still going on. And Gabe is still in your home, still going to work, so for him he's still living life as normal – the only difference is you are not there. And Luke is here, dealing with his mum's illness, and clearly falling for you. And I'm not judging, I promise. I just don't think that it's possible to have a holiday from life."

Julie's face seems to close in on itself, her long-lashed eyelids downcast, then she looks at me. "I know. You're right. But I don't know what to do."

Then the doorbell goes, and we look at each other.

"That'll be Luke," I say.

"I'd better answer it."

Julie rubs her forehead and gets up.

I hear her move through the house, and greet Luke brightly. "We're sitting outside," she says, "in David's

127

garden. It's lush, come and see."

"Hi Alice," Luke's large frame seems to fill the doorway, then the yard. I smile at him and he leans over to kiss me on the cheek. "How's the ankle?"

"Oh, much, much better, thank you. How are you? How's your mum?"

"She's OK. Well, obviously she's not OK. She's dying." He speaks matter-of-factly. "But she likes the hospice, and the people there are just amazing. They see it every day, of course, but they manage to make you feel special, cared for, and they try to make sure it feels as much like home as possible. There's a lady who has her dogs come in to see her every day and I've heard they brought somebody's horse in to say bye to them! It's lovely, for a place where there's so much sadness. Mum will be happy there, she says." He looks away, and I don't say anything.

Julie touches his arm, "Do you want a cup of tea?"

"If you're making one." Luke sits heavily on the chair next to the bench.

"I am." She smiles. "Alice had something to ask you, didn't you, Alice?"

I glare at her and Luke looks at me, "Oh yeah?"

As Julie makes herself scarce I say, "Yeah, well the thing is, I saw Sam – well, you know that – the other day."

"He did mention something about it."

"OK," I smile, wishing Luke would be more forthcoming, and make this easier for me. "Well, I said I'd get him a beer, to say thank you for looking after me…"

"Of course." Luke is smiling at me.

"The thing is, I don't have his number. Do you think it would be OK if you gave it to me? I mean, don't worry if you don't feel comfortable, I know you can't just go round giving out your friends' numbers to just anyone."

128

"Alice," Luke says, "it's fine. Sam actually asked me to give it to you."

"He did?"

"Yes! He said you could decide then whether you wanted to get in touch or not. I know he'd like to see you again."

"Oh, right." Now I don't know what to say.

"So do you want his number then?" Luke has his phone out, and is scrolling through his contacts.

"Oh, yes, yes of course." I scrabble in my bag and pull out my phone.

"Sent it to you," Luke says, and a contact card pings onto my screen.

Sam Branvall.

A shiver of excitement runs through me to see that name on my screen. There is also a message from Casey, by the looks of it.

"Thanks, Luke."

"No worries."

"There was something else I wanted to ask," I say, feeling suddenly brave now that I know Sam does want me to get in touch.

"Oh yeah?"

"Yeah, well, it's a bit weird, really. But David – you know, who owns this place."

"I know David, yes."

"Well... he said that the year we met, you know, after the summer and I was at uni and had... lost touch with Sam, he saw him, and Sam knew about the guy I was seeing."

"Yep, I remember. After the car crash."

"Yes!" I exclaim. "What happened? I had no idea he'd had an accident."

"You didn't know?"

"No, not till David told me. How could I? I only had Sam's number, which went dead, and his address here, of course. I tried phoning again and again but I thought he'd changed his number."

"OK," Luke says thoughtfully, "well I think probably you ought to speak to Sam about all that."

At that moment, Julie comes outside, with a pot of tea, a jug of milk and three mugs, on an Alfred Wallis tray. "Sorted?" She looks at me.

"Yep," I smile, tapping my phone.

"Great. You texted him yet?"

"No! I've only just got his number."

"Well, what are you waiting for? Get on with it, girl."

I suppose I probably should. Julie pulls her chair next to Luke's and he puts his arm round her. They are both grinning at me.

"Oh stop it, would you? I'm going inside to do it."

I walk into David's kitchen, where I tap in about twelve variations of the same message. In the end I settle on:

I owe you a beer. Are you free tonight? Alice

I think it sounds quite cool; not too cheesy, not too suggestive, but fairly confident. I press 'send' and experience anther little shiver of excitement, then head back out to the garden, shoving my phone deep into my pocket. I will sit and drink my cup of tea and I WILL NOT check for a response until afterwards. I remember I have a message from Casey but I think that can wait, too. If I pull my phone out now to read it, Julie and Luke will just think I'm desperate to hear back from Sam. Which, of course, I am.

15

The next thirty minutes are some of the longest I've ever experienced. I mean, obviously they're not as they're exactly the same length as all of the other minutes I've lived through. However, they feel longer. OK?

We talk about Luke's mum, which does take my mind off the Sam situation. The doctors have not said how long she has left but Luke is sure that it can't be long. He says she is no longer really herself, anyway. But the hospice staff actively encourage visits from him and his dad and sister, and May's friends, to sit with her, read to her, play music. Luke says that it's a really peaceful place. I can't imagine a hospice being anything other than unbearably sad but he says it's not like that.

"Do you want to come and see her?" he asks Julie, taking her by surprise. I see her look up, slightly shocked and quickly trying to recompose her features.

"Me? Would you really like me to? Would she mind? And your dad? Doesn't she want to settle in first?"

"They'd be very happy for you to come. I told Mum that we'd got together, in one of her more lucid moments. She was happy. And you know they both remember you from way back – you too, Alice."

"If you want me to come, of course I will," says Julie, but I can see she's not one hundred per cent comfortable with the idea. This seems to go over Luke's head, however.

"Thank you," he smiles at her, lifting her hand and kissing it.

I decide to leave them to it. "I'm just going to the bathroom," I say.

"OK," Julie says, shouting after me, "Let us know what he says!"

Damn her. My hand is admittedly already on my jeans pocket, itching to see if Sam has responded. In the shade of the house, as I head up the steep staircase, I see I have three messages.

One: *Sam Branvall*. Oh my god. My heart starts beating and I have to stop halfway up the staircase to steady myself.

Hi Alice, thanks for your message. A beer sounds good. Beach Bar at 8? Sam

Aaarggghhhhh!! He has actually said yes. And he wants to meet tonight. This is real!

I check the next message, in case it's him again with a change of mind. Another text from Casey, I haven't had a chance to check her first yet. I see what she has to say.

Hi, fancy coming to mine instead, for wine and a girlie film tonight? He's busy ☹ KCx

Who is 'he'? Has Casey got a man she hasn't told me about? I scroll back to the first message from her.

Hi, gr8 nite last nite. Fancy doing it again tonite? I'll see if S's dad can come round KCx

Ah, so she's been let down by Sophie's dad. Poor Casey. I wish I'd replied sooner. But I suppose I didn't know I was seeing Sam until just now. And if I'd agreed to go out with her, I'd have either had to dump her or tell Sam I'm busy. And after my morning's resolution, I am not willing to wait another moment, selfish though that may sound. Ten years is long enough.

I'm really sorry, but I can't make it tonight. Maybe we can have a drink after Pilates on Monday? Hope you enjoy the rest of your weekend x

OK

There it is again. The 'OK'. I am now sure that is her being pissed off via text message. I can't say I care for it much. I hadn't actually arranged anything with her – and we only went out last night! I'm not going to apologise. I feel sorry for her because it must be hard being a single mum, but it's not like I owe her anything. Anyway, I have to concentrate on this evening, with Sam. I can't believe it. After all this time, we're going out together. I keep telling myself it's nothing; two old friends catching up after a long time apart, but somehow I can't quite convince myself of that.

"We're going out for a bit," Julie calls up to me. "I've left the lunch stuff in David's kitchen, do you mind bringing it up in a bit?

"OK!" I shout back.

I hear their footsteps, the front door open and close, then the house is mine. What shall I do? I check my watch.

It's 2.57pm. I have five hours and three minutes until I am meeting Sam. But who's counting? (I am). First thing's first. I trek back down the stairs to collect the stuff from the kitchen. I know David is meant to be out at Martin's all weekend but I don't like leaving his place a mess anyway.

As I come back up the stairs, I formulate a plan. I need to decide what to wear. I need to have a bath, wash my hair, and, if at all possible, have a siesta. I have been up since ridiculous o'clock this morning and I don't want to be yawning all over Sam.

I set the bath taps going; clouds of steam rising in the bathroom. Opening the porthole, I peep out at the town. There is a light mist coming in off the sea, and the sky's greying. I hope it isn't going to rain all afternoon and evening. Although it could be nice, if we manage to grab one or two of the beanbags in the Beach Bar, and get a place to sit and watch the mist drifting in over the waves, the rain pocking the sand. I allow my imagination to run away with itself; if there is just one giant beanbag, and Sam and I are forced to share it. Our bodies close together, his arm slipping around me, his mouth brushing my bare shoulder...

Enough! I tell myself. I have until the bath is full to decide what to wear. I pull out my beach dresses. No, they're not right. I need Sam to see me as I am, and I'm not really a dress kind of person. I never was. I find my knee-length denim shorts, bought from FatFace on Fore Street, and a long spaghetti-strapped top, cut on the bias, in chunky, multi-coloured stripes. I'll take my shoulder bag and a hoodie in case it gets cold. Perfect. If he is the Sam I remember, he won't expect me to dress up anyway. And besides, I remind myself, this is not a date.

I check the bath, adding more bubbles, which puff up

into cloud mountains. Slipping off my clothes, I slide between the cool bubbles, into the hot water below. It's just the right side of too-hot, it feels like it will scald the dead skin cells from me, and I will emerge red and raw and new, ready to face the world. Leaning back, the bubbles fizz in my ears and all over my hair. I feel excited and relaxed at the same time. Sam's words run through my head, but there is much to be gleaned from his text: *A beer sounds good. A beer sounds good.* What could it mean? Oh yeah; that a beer sounds good.

I remember the night I met Sam, that first golden summer. I'd actually seen him earlier that day at the beach, but I wasn't going to tell him that. He was with Luke, and some of their other mates, playing a pretty informal game of volleyball. He was wearing his long swimming shorts, and nothing else. I remember his tan, and those shoulder blades gliding up and down his beautiful back as he jumped and reached and fell into the sand, laughing. I could see how well he got on with his friends, and how good-natured he was; and also that he was absolutely gorgeous. Sitting at the café table with me, Julie had seen me looking. "Oh yeah," she'd said, "he's nice."

"I saw him first," I'd half-joked, but there was a part of me which meant it because I had been so drawn to him and, unlike Julie, I didn't go round snogging half the boys we met. That sounds bitchy and it's not meant to. It's just that, as we have already established, Julie is a bit more gung-ho about things than me. We'd been in Cornwall about three weeks, been to lots of parties, pubs and clubs, and Julie must have got off with at least four different boys in that time. I was more reserved, even then. But something clicked when I saw Sam. Which perhaps makes me a bit mental more than anything, but I knew that I wanted to get to know him better.

Julie, being Julie, went up to the boys once their game had finished and asked Luke their names and where they'd be that night. I saw him looking after her as she walked back to me. She sat back down and said, "They'll be down the beach tonight, they're all skint."

"OK," I was grateful for her forwardness and determined to try and become a bit better at that side of things.

When we'd got to the beach that evening, there was nobody there save for a large family group packing up after a barbecue. I'd sat heavily on the sand, disappointed, but Julie had said it was early, and she was right. As the family moved off, a few of the lads from earlier began to appear but it was a while before Luke and Sam got there. "Hi," Luke had said, waving, and they'd come over. He sat next to Julie, and Sam had sat on the other side of them to me. Julie and Luke had begun chatting and we'd passed a bottle of cider back and forth along the row. I didn't know what to do. I could hardly lean forward and make subtle, relaxed conversation with Sam across Julie and Luke, could I? Then I surprised myself. "I'm going in," I said. I had my bikini on under my clothes and I just decided to hell with it. I kicked my things off and Julie, laughing, said she'd join me. That was enough for Luke; he was pulling off his clothes, too. It didn't take long for Sam to do the same. They weren't in their swimming things so they emptied their shorts pockets and we ran, holding hands in a line, down into the sea, laughing and shouting as the cold water reached up our limbs and I fell, bringing Julie down with me. The boys helped us up; Luke had Julie and so Sam came to me. I could see his smile through the salt water tears which were stinging my eyes.

We mucked about a bit more; splashing each other, and then I decided to show off, swimming out to a buoy and back. "Careful," Sam had called, but I'd just smiled. I was a strong swimmer. I knew I shouldn't really be swimming after drinking but we hadn't had that much. As Julie and Luke headed back up the beach, Sam waited for me. I got to the buoy, turned, and focused on getting back, trying to look elegant and graceful as I moved through the waves.

He waited for me, watching me, and I could see he was concerned. I liked that. And I was fine; I made it back to him, but he told me off. "You shouldn't take chances with the sea. We've been drinking. It's dangerous."

I felt silly; I'd thought it would impress him. "Sorry," I said, and thought he'd never be interested in me. He'd see me for the idiot I was. But as I started trudging through the shallower water towards the beach, I heard a huge splash behind me and felt myself soaked once more. I turned, to see Sam grinning. "Hey!" I said, starting to smile too. I kicked at the water, sending droplets flying into his face. Soon we were in a full-on water fight and my embarrassment was forgotten. I could see Julie up the beach, laughing at us. I ran from Sam, and he ran after me, pulling me down into the warm shallows. At this moment, we were panting, face to face, and if we'd have been braver and more confident, it would have been the perfect time for our first kiss. But we looked away, shyly. "Shall we go and dry off?" I asked him. He nodded. But he didn't have a towel, so I let him share mine and, while our friends began building a fire, we sat huddled together under it, our damp legs sticking to each other, and our bodies growing warm and dry together. As darkness moved in, and stars began to prickle the sky, Sam offered me his jumper, and we moved closer to the fire. More kids came and joined the group, and we sat and sang songs while someone played a guitar. I didn't want that night to end. We walked back to the flat in the early morning; Luke walking with Julie while Sam and I lagged behind. I felt his hand reach for me, his warm, soft fingers interlacing with mine.

We stopped at the top of a steep flight of steps, under a streetlamp. Before I could say anything, he lifted my chin, looked into my eyes, and he kissed me.

16

When I get out of the bath, leaving little clouds of bubbles in my wake, I wrap a big fluffy towel – which is actually Julie's but she's not here to complain - around me and I pad into my bedroom. I switch the TV on, wrap a smaller towel around my hair, and lie back on my bed. The local weather forecaster is predicting another humid evening. I smile. I love summer; not having to get wrapped up in sweaters, coats, gloves, scarves, and boots. I love the fact that even when it rains, it's warm, not miserable and cold-inducing. When the weather map on TV is a mixture of yellows and oranges, I'm a happy girl.

There follows some sort of daytime made-for-TV film, which I leave on, though I'm not concentrating on it. I feel my eyelids become heavy and I turn to make myself more comfortable on the bed. Sleep comes and goes, and I'm aware of a small pool of saliva dribbling from my mouth to the pillow. I know I am seeing Sam this evening, but I also know I am tired and I want to sleep. I push thoughts of Sam away, for now, and let myself float into a deep afternoon slumber, punctuated by sounds from the street below and odd dreams. Mum and Dad stuck in a car which is in turn stuck in some mud, but they're laughing. They won't stop laughing. I'm getting annoyed with them. I wake up. Some of my hair is plastered to my face, and my skin is damp with sweat. My mouth tastes strange and I have that feeling of needing something sweet, which I always get when I sleep in the daytime.

I wander to the kitchen and get the orange juice out of the fridge, filling a glass and gulping it down. The clock on the microwave says 6.37.

6.37!

How did that happen?

I'm meant to be meeting Sam at eight. I need to eat – and I feel like I really need a shower after that sleep – and I need to get dressed, factoring in the fact that I will probably change my mind about what to wear, try on lots of different things, and end up coming back to my original choice.

Ten minutes to walk to the Beach Bar. Should I be late, or early? Or on time?

I check my phone to make sure he hasn't cancelled. There is just a text from Julie:

L and I going to hospice. Any word from Sam?

So she's going to see Luke's mum. I hope she knows what she's doing. Luke will be pleased, but it feels like a commitment to me, if she's going to visit his dying mum with him – which is of course why Luke will be pleased. No time for me to worry about somebody else's mess, though. It's already 6.41. Where did those four minutes go?

Yes! I'm going to meet him, at eight. Arghhhhhh.

I get in the shower, pulling my shower cap on as I really don't have time to wash my hair again, although it's dried

140

at some interesting angles thanks to my unplanned sleep. I feel much better, more awake, now, and I get another fresh, fluffy towel – Julie is going to kill me, she only went to the laundrette yesterday – and wrap it round myself. 6.53. No time to eat a proper meal. I push two slices of bread into the toaster and go into my room, selecting matching underwear, because it feels like I should, and pulling on my top and shorts. I look in the mirror. OK. OK. I'm going to be strict, I am NOT going to try on other outfits. I don't have time for that.

Twenty-five minutes later my White Stuff dress, my Sea Salt linen trousers, and about eight different tops are lying on my bed. I am back in my denim shorts and stripy top, as predicted, and I have toast crumbs round my mouth. I am trying to brush my hair into some sort of sensible style, and wondering what to do about make-up. I don't often wear it but I feel like I should make a bit of effort tonight. I apply a bit of eyeliner, and use my extra-length mascara, noting that my eyelashes look exactly as long as they did before. I look in the mirror. I check the time. It's 7.28. I will have to do.

In the kitchen, I try to practice some deep-breathing, as I push a couple of ice cubes from the tray into a glass and pour a liberal helping of gin, with a dash of tonic and a squeeze of lime.

"Chin, chin," I say to myself, and I drink slowly and steadily, leaving the flat at 7.42. I may be a few minutes early but I will take my time.

As I walk down through the town, I feel like everyone must know. It is written all over my face. I am so nervous and so excited. *It's just a beer, it's just a beer,* I keep telling myself, but who am I kidding?

When I get to the wall above the beach, I scan the

141

length of the sands, to see if Sam is walking across, but there is no sign of him. Great. I get to watch him arrive. I can get to the bar, order a drink, and sit looking sophisticated when he comes in.

I walk down the slipway and this time leave my sandals on to cross the sand, which feels weird. The music from the Beach Bar is mellow and trancey; maybe Chicane. I feel myself drawn towards it and wonder if I was in this spot exactly ten years ago. It's a distinct possibility. I imagine eighteen-year-old me heading excitedly across the beach. Did I used to feel as nervous as I do now? My stomach is twisting like somebody trying to wring out a dishcloth.

"Alice!" I hear a voice as soon as I step onto the decking. Sam is already at the bar, a half-drunk beer in front of him and an empty stool next to him. No going back now.

"Hi," I say, trying to sound perfectly calm and collected. He stands up and gives me a slightly awkward hug. He smells nice and his navy shirt is soft, open to reveal just a tempting glimpse of that tanned chest with its dark curls.

"What are you having?" he asks, smiling at me and gesturing to the stool next to him.

"Can I have a gin and tonic, please?" I ask, fumbling in my bag for my purse.

"I'll get this," he says and smiles.

"But I owe you a beer!" I say, and I can't help smiling back at him, I'm so happy to be here.

"Well, you can get the next round."

So there's going to be a next round, I think excitedly. I know, I know, I'm so pathetic. I am truly channelling eighteen-year-old Alice Griffiths tonight.

Sam calls to Andrew, who brings over another bottle of

beer and pours a generous gin and tonic. I'm pleased to see him add a squeeze and a wedge of lime.

"Cheers," Sam says, and we push our drinks together then both take a big swig.

"Thanks for helping me out the other day," I say.

"That's no problem," Sam smiles, "it was my pleasure." I remember his arm around me and I think it was actually my pleasure.

"How's the ankle?" he asks, gesturing towards my leg.

"Oh, it's fine now," I say. "Do you remember David? We're staying at his place again this year," of course he probably already knows this, "well, he did my shift for me the next day, bless him."

"He's a good bloke. I see him around a bit, with his... boyfriend? Partner? I never know what to say."

"I think he's happy with boyfriend – although I think he'd be happier if it was husband."

"Oh yeah?"

"Yeah, I probably shouldn't say that, should I? He's over there every weekend, though, which is cool because it means we get the house to ourselves. Although actually, as Julie is pretty much with Luke full-time, the house is mine..." I trail off. Does this sound like I'm suggesting something? Sam doesn't seem to notice.

"He's having a hard time, Luke," he half-frowns.

"I know. It's so awful, about his mum, I can't imagine."

Sam's mum lives in Spain; she moved there with Sam's little sister Janie when Sam was sixteen and he stayed on in Cornwall with his auntie, Lou. His dad left years ago, not that long after Janie was born, but I think is still in Cornwall somewhere, or at least he was when I last knew Sam. I used to get the feeling that Luke's family provided a second home to Sam, and he always used to tease May in a nice way; it was obvious he really liked her. He must be very sad about her illness too.

"I haven't seen much of him these last couple of weeks, him and Julie are full-on, aren't they?"

"Yes," I say carefully, "in fact she's gone with him to the hospice this afternoon."

"Really?" Sam sounds a little surprised but doesn't say any more.

"Yes. Have you... been to see May?"

"Not in the hospice, no, but I've been round their house, I was helping Jim with some shelves he wanted to put up, and I had to help move a bed downstairs; Luke was up in London trying to sort some work stuff out before he came back here."

"That's great... that you were helping, I mean." I don't know where to go with this conversation. It's so sad. Possibly not the best topic to start an evening off, but that's just selfish, I know. I look at Sam sneakily while he's drinking. He looks just the same. Well, he doesn't; if anything, he looks better than ever. Julie says Luke has grown into himself and I can only say the same of Sam. Except he has dark shadows under his eyes, like he's tired. But his tan manages to conceal them unless you look closely. His dark-blond hair is still thick and wavy, and he has a fine stubble around his chin, which I'd like to rub the back of my hand against. Probably a bit of a weird thing to do, though.

He looks back at me. "It's good to see you," he says.

"You too."

"I can't believe it's been ten years."

"I know, it feels like nothing's changed. Well, I've got a bit older, and wider..."

"Don't be daft! You look as great as you ever did." His

voice is soft and I am not quite sure I heard him right, but he's looking at me earnestly.

God, I want to kiss him. Right here, right now. I can't. I take a big gulp of my drink. "Shall I get us another, and we can maybe grab some comfier seats?" I point towards one of the low tables by the open front of the bar, which is just being vacated by a group of lads.

"Sure," he says.

"Same again?"

"Same again." He smiles, and walks to the table. I sit at the bar, my heart pounding furiously. I catch Andrew's attention.

"I'll bring 'em over," he says. "We'll sort out a tab if you're staying."

"Great," I say, thinking that I hope we're staying. If we've got a tab maybe there's more chance of us hanging on longer.

Sam is sitting on a long, low, dark red settee, with faded seaside-designed cushions, which I am sure I remember from ten years back. He looks at me as I walk towards him and I feel self-conscious. I flop down next to him, and sink into the cushions. We both look out, towards the sea, where there are still plenty of surfers and even the odd swimmer.

There is so much I want to ask Sam. When Andrew has brought our drinks over, I decide to jump straight in.

"Sam," I say.

"Yes?"

"David, you know, my landlord..."

"Yes," he says.

"Well he said something that I've been wondering about. He said that you'd mentioned someone to him... a guy I knew, called Geoff."

I see a slight cloud cross Sam's expression. "Yes," he says flatly.

"And he also said you'd had an accident."

"Yep, that's right."

"So… I don't know what to say, or how to ask this, really. But what happened to you? To us, I suppose. And how did you know about Geoff?"

Sam looks long and hard at me. "I thought you must have known about the accident."

"Luke said the same thing, but I didn't. How could I? I only kept in touch with you, and with Bea a bit, but she never mentioned anything."

"Oh. Maybe she wouldn't have known. We don't exactly mix in the same circles," he smiles.

"So what happened?" I press.

"I don't remember the accident itself," he says, "all I know is, I woke up in fucking agony, in hospital, my crappy old Golf was written off, and I couldn't remember much for weeks. I couldn't make sense of anything. I knew Luke, I knew Auntie Lou, but I didn't know much else. It started to come back to me, bit by bit. And the guy who crashed into me was charged with dangerous driving, the stupid fucker," Sam growls. "Only good thing to come out of it was my compensation, though that took long enough to come."

"God, it sounds awful." I can't believe all this was going on whilst I was just back home, going to uni, completely oblivious.

"It was, but it's a long time ago."

"I had no idea, no idea. I thought…" I feel childish and selfish for even beginning to think about how I felt back then.

"You thought I'd just decided not to bother with you?"

Sam laughs humourlessly.

"Yes, I'm sorry, I know that sounds really childish."

"It doesn't. I was gutted about you. It didn't take long for me to start remembering that side of things, but there was nothing I could do. My phone was totally wrecked. I knew where you lived, but it was miles away. I knew where you were studying, though. So I came up, when I was better, or better enough to get the train. I came up and I came to your uni. I found out when your course lectures were, and I waited outside one day but your bloke warned me off," he said bitterly.

"Geoff?" I exclaim but now I am not surprised. I know it makes perfect sense.

"Yep. Geoff," he says. "What a tool. Sorry, you're not still with him, are you?"

"No!" I say. "And I had no idea, no idea about any of this." I could kick myself. Why hadn't I tried harder to find out if Sam was OK? It was pride, I suppose. Those unanswered texts and calls. I just thought he didn't want to know.

"Good. He seemed like a tosser."

"He was." And I find myself telling Sam the whole story; how I'd thought he was no longer interested. How Geoff had taken me out, charmed me, started to control me. I can see Sam's face growing darker all the time.

"He did what?" he says angrily when I tell him about Geoff cutting up a top I had because it was too 'low-cut' and 'trampy'. I tell him everything I can bear to; how my parents didn't like Geoff, and how he took me away at Christmas so I couldn't spend it with them. The expensive presents. The shouting, the bullying, the black eye. The restraining order. The court case. Geoff killing himself.

By the time I reach the end of the sorry, sorry story, I

147

am crying and Sam has his arm round me. Which is what I'd been longing for, but not like this.

"Oh my god," he says softly, "you've really been through it."

"So have you," I sniffle, trying to pull myself together.

"I think yours beats mine, though, hands down."

"Let's agree it's a draw, and move on, shall we?" But I can't help thinking of what might have been. If Sam hadn't had his accident we could have carried on, tried that long-distance relationship which we had promised each other. I would never have got together with Geoff.

Or if I'd seen Sam when he came to find me; it would have been before things got out of hand with Geoff. There would have been no question of carrying on seeing Geoff when I found out what had happened to Sam, that he still wanted to be with me.

For Geoff, I feel like his fate was sealed. If it hadn't been me, it would have been someone else. It took me a long time and many of hours of counselling to believe that, but I got there eventually. I've learned to be happy on my own, and in control of my own life.

"So what did you do, when Geoff sent you away?" I ask, trying to picture a nineteen-year-old Sam returning, dejected, to Cornwall.

"Oh, nothing, really. I still had physio to get through, and I was behind on my studies so I delayed for another year. I suppose I just spent time with the boys and pretended none of it had ever happened."

Andrew, who has been keeping a discreet distance, signals to Sam, asking if we want more drinks. Sam looks at me and I nod. "Please, mate," Sam calls.

"Well, that's not entirely true," he says. "There was…"

"… a girl?" I ask the question I've been dreading, even though I know I couldn't expect Sam to have been saving himself for me all this time. He nods.

"And you're still with her?"

"No!" he laughs, "God, no. I mean, sorry, that makes me sound like a total twat. She was… let's say, high maintenance, shall we?"

Inwardly, I'm thinking, *Yes!* But I try not to show it.

"Were you together long?"

"About three years. Which was two years too long. Three years too long, if I'm being really honest."

"Quite a while, then?"

"Yeah, well it was… complicated…"

Andrew brings our drinks over, with some bowls of olives and bread. "These were going spare," he says, "so I'd rather you have 'em than they get chucked away."

"Thank you!" I say. I'm really hungry, I realise.

"Yeah, cheers mate," says Sam. His arm is no longer around me, but we've settled in close together. It feels so right, which I know sounds horribly cheesy, but it's the only word I can think of.

We tuck into the snacks, and our drinks. I suddenly don't want to talk any more about the past.

"So you're working now?" I say.

"Yeah, doing Facilities at a place in Falmouth. Been studying too, though. I never quite finished my course back then, what with the accident, and Kate and everything."

Kate, I think to myself, squirrelling that tiny piece of knowledge away.

"That's great," I say, "do you still want to get into conservation?"

"Yeah, I've been volunteering for years anyway, with

149

the RSPB and a bit of work with the Wildlife Trust. But I want to work for them, properly. Need some qualifications, though."

"So you don't want to leave Cornwall anymore?"

"No," he laughs, "not for any longer than I have to."

"I don't blame you," I say, "I can't bear the thought of having to leave again at the end of the summer."

"Do you have to?"

I'm in the middle of trying to spear a particularly awkward olive with a cocktail stick. I look up at him. "I suppose so. I can't see a way of earning a living here. And I've got my own flat at home now. And a job, well I did have."

Jason has told me that there's always a job for me if I want to come back. I suppose in my heart of hearts, that's what I see myself doing. These golden summers are all very well but I know they can't last forever.

"That's a shame," Sam says. And he leans forward and kisses me. Just like that.

His mouth is salty, from the olives, and tastes mildly of beer. I kiss him back, and I don't want to stop. But we are in a bar. And we are nearly thirty years old. We can't sit snogging like teenagers.

He looks at me, raising his eyebrows. "Sorry, I couldn't resist any longer."

I smile, not quite sure what to say. We finish our drinks and settle up with Andrew, an unspoken agreement between us.

Walking out onto the beach, the sun is setting just round the bay, casting shadows over the land and throwing splashes of colour across the sky and the sea. We hold hands as we walk, suddenly shy with each other, but we both know where we are going. We trudge along, pushing

150

hard, determined footprints into the sand, all the way to the end of the beach, and up the steep stone steps which meet the coastal path.

Sam helps me up the last few steps and at the top we turn back towards the beach, and the town, where we can see the sun squeeze the last few drops of life from the day, before vanishing behind the rooftops. Sam stands behind me, his arms around me and his mouth finding my neck. He kisses me and goose pimples break out all over my body. I turn and my mouth finds his, sliding easily open to allow his tongue in. Now the sun has gone, it's slightly cooler but the heat of the day still hangs in the air and tiny insects hover around and above us, while the birds sing their evening songs to each other.

Sam's hands are in my hair, then one is sliding down my back, pulling my body close in towards his. He feels at once familiar and incredibly exciting. He stops for a moment, and smiles at me, his eyes on mine, then he's pulling me back, further away from the edge of the cliffs, to a warm, mossy clearing, back from the path and surrounded by gorse. We sit down, kissing eagerly again, then his hand is inside my top, finding its way inside my bra, gently stroking then teasing my nipple. I place my hand on his warm skin, unbuttoning his shirt and seeing how his teenage body has developed into that of a man. I shiver.

"Are you OK?" he asks, pulling back.

"I'm fine," I croak, and I kiss him again.

He eases his hand out of my top. "Sorry," he says, "I was getting a bit carried away with myself."

"Really, it's fine," I assure him.

He kisses me. "Plenty of time for all that," he says, and he pulls me towards him, turning me around so that I am leaning on him, and looking out to sea. "I've missed you," he whispers in my ear. And although I'm disappointed that we've stopped just as things are getting exciting, I feel a rush of warmth. He never rushed me back then, and maybe now, given everything I've told him about Geoff, he's being even more thoughtful, and cautious. I let myself relax, and I listen to him breathing. I just can't believe I'm here, in my favourite place, with the man I've dreamed about all these years. He's right, I hope; there is plenty more time.

17

I wake up happier than I have felt for a long, long time. My waking thought is, of course, Sam, and I lie in bed, the sun peeking in through the window, letting the memories of the previous evening wash over me − new waves of happiness coming again and again.

After we'd sat for a while, we walked − along the edge of town, along all three beaches, and then into the Mainbrace for a nightcap. We left the deep stuff behind and we just chatted, and laughed. I'd almost forgotten just how funny he is. We punctuated the laughter with more kissing, ending the night outside David's front door, in a full-on romantic clinch on the doorstep, the moonlight shining on the narrow street.

After I'd got into bed, I'd picked up my phone to send him a message saying what a great night it had been, but he had beaten me to it…

That was the best night. So happy you came back xxxx

I read that message now, smile and hold the phone to my chest, then laugh at myself for being such a saddo. In the other room I can hear murmuring. I guess Luke and Julie have stayed here for a change.

I creep to the bathroom. I don't want to talk with Julie about the previous night while Luke is here but you can guarantee I'll have the full inquisition as soon as she sees me.

I go to text Sam, but think I'd better wait. I don't know why; he's not the type for 'playing it cool' but I don't want to wake him. It is, after all, only 8.00am on a Sunday morning. As I tiptoe back to my room, I hear the church bells start up. I sigh contentedly and lie back on my bed, looking at Sam's message again. As I do so, two, then three messages ping in.

Casey.

Morning ☺ Did u hav a gud nite?

Fancy meeting up today?

Lunch at the beach? Have S with me KCx

She's keen, I think, but I don't mind. She is obviously a bit lonely, and I think it's nice to have a 'local' friend – it makes me feel like I belong a bit; a pretence I'm happy to continue for as long as I can, until I have to traipse back to the World of Stationery, so far from the sea.

Sure, let me know where you'll be, I'll come and meet you. I'll bring cakes! X

I'm feeling like celebrating, though I'm not going to tell her why. She might even know Sam; it's that kind of small town.

Gr8. Text ya l8r. KCx

For now, I am going to laze in bed, reading, and pretending not to think about Sam. I close my eyes and listen to the church bells, unable to stop the smile which is stretching across my face.

In time, I realise I must have dozed off. I hear the door go downstairs, and then Julie's footsteps carefully tracking their way back up to the flat.

Here she comes, I think, and prepare myself to tell all. But she doesn't knock on my door; instead, she goes into her room, closing her own door quietly behind her. Weird. Maybe she's tired. I check the time; it's nearly 11am. I need to get showered, packed for the beach, and pick up those cakes I promised. I wonder if Sophie considers herself too old for playing in the sand? I am hoping not.

By the time I'm out of the shower, it seems that Julie has gone out. She probably shouted through to me and I didn't hear her. Once I'm dried off, I send her a message telling her where I'll be, and inviting her to join us – although I am not sure if Casey will approve of me bringing another friend along.

As I press 'send', a message pops up from Casey:

We're here! Surf beach. Near that rock we met u at. KCx

Great, I reply. **See you soon x**

I'm looking forward to an afternoon at the beach. I stop at the bakery and pick up three jam doughnuts and three chocolate brownies – as well as an olive loaf, a slab of cheese, and some apples. Next stop, a seaside tat shop, as Julie calls them – where I get a couple of buckets and spades.

My bags bang against my legs, the plastic spades gently grazing my skin, as I walk up the cobbled hill, but I have a sudden need to see a particular view, as it is a perfectly clear day, with a dazzlingly blue sky and an equally dazzling turquoise sea. I am hot and sweaty by the time I get there but it's worth it. I reach the crest and turn my gaze slowly from left to right, surveying the town in all its unbelievable beauty, with the miles and miles of glowing, dancing water reaching far into the distance. I just love it. I love it. And my eyes focus on something moving, quickly and confidently, across the bay. A pod of dolphins, swooping and diving, egging each other on. I don't know when I last felt this happy.

Eventually, I move along, aware that Casey and Sophie are waiting for me. I take careful steps down the steep hill, looking up every now and then to catch a glimpse once more of the sea, and trying to see if the dolphins are still there, but they are now nowhere to be seen.

I trek along the tiny streets and round the corner to that welcoming blast of fresh sea air. Up there, on the cliffs, is where I sat with Sam last night, I remind myself. I hug that thought close and congratulate myself on not having bombarded him with texts yet. Although I should message him soon, I think, just to check everything's OK.

The beach is busy but I know where I'm heading and it's easy to identify Casey, in a small orange bikini which fits comfortably over her well-toned body, and a large straw hat, complete with flowers on the brim, plus a pair of oversized sunglasses. She is every bit the glamorous film star. You would never guess that body had carried and delivered a child; of the two of us it is definitely me that looks more like I've gone through a pregnancy.

Sophie looks up and waves. I smile to see she is already hard at work, digging away at the sand near the rock.

"We are going to make the best fort!" I say, smiling.

Casey looks up. "Hi, Daphne!"

Sophie looks quizzical. "I thought this was Alice..?"

"It's a long story," I say.

"You two are weird," Sophie says, grinning.

Casey smiles back at her, and reclines on her towel. I pull out my newly acquired buckets and spades. "Can I join in?" I ask Sophie.

"Of course! Daphne," she looks at me as she says this, to see what kind of reaction she'll get. Her brown eyes shine mischievously.

"Thanks very much, Cynthia."

Sophie giggles. "Cynthia!" she says to herself, turning back to her digging.

"So what's the plan?" I ask.

"I'm trying to build an Iron Age hill fort, like Maiden Castle, we went there on a school trip this term."

"Did you?" I smile, "I went there when I was a bit older than you. My mum and dad took me and my friend Julie on holiday."

"Wow! I'd love to go on holiday, we never go anywhere."

"That's cos all your school trips and after school clubs cost so much!" Casey says, and I think she is only half-joking.

"Do you know what? You live in the best place ever," I say to Sophie. "Do you know how much people pay to come on holiday to the place where you live?"

"No, how much?"

157

"Well, er, a lot. A lot of money."

I wonder about Sophie's dad; how much input he has into her life, financially. Whether he could be the person to take her on holiday? Casey is trying to set up her business although, to be fair, that can't take up all her time. She only does a couple of classes a week. *None of my business*, I remind myself.

"OK… anyway… Maiden Castle, eh? I'd say that's going to be pretty tricky with sand. What if we just try to build a huge hill first off, and we'll put a moat around it."

"Dad always does moats, too," Sophie says.

"Well, he sounds like a very sensible person," I say, wondering if this is OK with Casey.

"He's not, he's really silly," Sophie giggles.

"Even better!" I say, and set to work digging.

While Casey lies back and tops up her tan, I dig and build, making regular trips to the shoreline with Sophie to bring back buckets of water in an attempt to make the sand easier to mould and hold in place. I don't mind because I really enjoy this kind of stuff but I wonder what Sophie and Casey would be doing if I wasn't there. Would the girl be left to her own devices, or would Casey help her? Was I being treated like some kind of unpaid au pair?

After a while, Casey sits up, pulling her sunglasses down so she can see our construction. "Wow, that looks great," she flashes Sophie a smile. "You two have been working hard, shall I go and get some drinks?"

"Yes please, Mum," Sophie says. "Can I have Orangina?"

"Of course," Casey says. "Alice, do you fancy a beer?"

"I think I'll have an Orangina as well, please. I'm trying not to drink during the day." I don't drink during the week, at home, and I have been feeling like I've had a bit too much since I've been here. After all, I'm not on holiday. I'm here all summer. I can't carry on as if I'm on a fortnight away.

"Suit yourself," Casey shrugs mildly. "Don't mind if I have one, do you?"

"No, of course not." I hope I didn't sound judgmental. It's only a beer, after all. I just don't really fancy one at the moment.

While Casey has gone, I check my phone. There's a message from Sam. My heart leaps when I see his words:

What are you doing tonight? xxx

I think for a moment. I would really like to spend the evening with Julie – or at least *an* evening – but I have no idea where she is and I haven't heard back from her since I sent her the message earlier. I presume she is with Luke. And if I'm honest, I don't want to pass up the chance of seeing Sam.

No plans at the moment xx

That's what I wanted to hear (read)! Can I take you to dinner? We have more to catch up on xxx

I can't believe how nervous and thrilled I feel. This is what is known as a dream come true. I'm back in the place I love, and tonight I will be seeing the man I love. I don't see the point in pretending otherwise, although I'm not intending to tell him that. I don't want to sound mad.

That sounds lovely. I should be ready any time after seven xxx

Another message comes back super-quick.

OK... I might be a little later... I'll try to be with you between half seven and eight, that OK? xxx

Perfect xxx

I look at Sophie and smile. She returns a wide, innocent smile, the bridge of her nose wrinkling a little, changing the pattern of freckles on her face. She's a lovely girl.

"Mum!" she exclaims, and leaps to her feet, running to Casey as if she hasn't seen her for weeks. Casey is carrying a small polystyrene tray with two takeaway coffee cups and three bottles of Orangina.

"I thought I should follow your good example," she says to me.

I feel bad. "Oh, you shouldn't have, it's only a beer... it's just I've had quite a lot of nights on the booze lately," I say. "And it's so hot today, a beer would just dehydrate me."

As Sophie shakes her Orangina then opens it and gulps half the bottle in one go, Casey leans in conspiratorially. "I drink every night. Every night," she reiterates.

"Do you?" I ask, wondering what is the right thing to say. "What do you drink?"

"Oh, sometimes just a glass of wine."

"Well, that's OK," I say, not really sure it is, but wanting to reassure her, "I'm sure they say a glass of red wine every day's good for your heart."

"Ha!" she laughs, "It's normally white wine, or rosé... and really, it's more like half a bottle a night, at least."

"OK..." I say, grasping for the correct response. "Is it bothering you?"

"I don't know."

"Why don't you just try and cut out a couple of nights a week?" I've read somewhere that giving your body two alcohol-free days a week gives it a chance to redress the balance. I can imagine how tempting it is when you are a single parent, and your kid's gone to bed – to just pick up a bottle, have a glass, maybe two… After all, you're kind of stuck, I guess. Not that I tend to go out anywhere much in the evenings, back home, but I suppose I know I could, if I wanted to.

"Yes, yes, you're right, I might do that."

I'm not convinced. Still, she's opted for a non-alcoholic option now, which is a start.

"Mum, can I have something to eat?" Sophie asks.

"I'll see what I've got in my bag," Casey says. "I don't really bother with lunch," she says to me. "Sometimes I forget on weekends that Sophie needs to eat."

"So do you!" I say. I can't bear to miss any of my meals. The thought of Sophie having to go without isn't great. "But you're in luck! I got these earlier…"

I bring out the cakes, bread and cheese. The apples roll out of my hand onto the sand.

Casey wrinkles her nose. I see a real similarity between her and Sophie as she does so. Sophie, however, jumps up. "Oh wow, Alice… I mean Daphne! They look so nice. Can I have one, please, Mum? Mum doesn't like me having cakes," she tells me.

"Is it OK?" I ask Casey, wondering if I have stepped on her toes by bringing all these fattening things. But Sophie is a growing girl and from what I've seen of her, she never stops moving. Casey's the one who's just lounging about. "And what about you?"

"Oh no, I'm fine, really," she says.

"Come on, you should have something. You can afford to have one little cake. Or a bit of bread and cheese..?" I'm starting to get an idea of how she manages to stay so slim, even if she does drink every night. "It's hot and you're out in the sun, you should have something to keep you going so you don't get heatstroke." I am not really convinced by my argument, but it's the best I can come up with.

"Well, OK, maybe I'll have a bit of the bread. And one of the apples." Casey smiles at me and again I see the similarity between her and Sophie. Behind all that make-up and underneath that perfectly tanned skin, I suspect she is really not very confident. I suppose her life took a different direction when she became a mum, and then Sophie's dad left, and she's been on her own – with Sophie – ever since. It must be hard. But she shouldn't forget Sophie needs lunch, I think. And again I have to tell myself off. It's easy to judge from the outside.

Meanwhile, Sophie is patiently, politely, waiting. "Tuck in," I say, "Help yourself! That is, as long as it's OK with your mum." I myself have just taken a huge bite out of a very jammy doughnut.

"That's great. Thank you, Daphne!"

I laugh. "No problem, Cynthia."

I watch Casey with the bread. She takes a very reserved bite. Then another. She must be starving, I think. I take another bite of my doughnut, the jam oozing over my fingers and sugar sticking to my lips. I must look disgusting in Casey's eyes, I think. Sophie is gobbling her brownie as if she hasn't eaten for weeks, but I feel I should be more restrained, given the speed at which Casey is eating. "More bread?" I ask her but get that pretty nose-wrinkle in return. "Sophie?" I offer it to the girl.

162

"Yes please!" she replies enthusiastically. I'm glad she hasn't caught her mum's resistance to food.

"Sophie's dad's coming down in a while," Casey says. "I thought I might ask him to have Sophie tonight then you and I can go out."

"Oh," I say, "I don't know if I can tonight, I'm... otherwise engaged." I am too excited about Sam to keep it quiet any longer and I am about to tell Casey about him when Sophie jumps up, knocking her drink over on the towel.

"Dad!" she calls. I must admit I'm intrigued to meet Casey's ex. I hastily pick up Sophie's bottle, trying to save as much of the drink as I can, as she goes flying across the sand. I turn around to see her leap into a man's arms and my stomach drops like a cable car cut loose.

18

Sam looks as shocked as I feel. For a moment, we stare at each other but Sophie, seemingly oblivious, pulls Sam's hand, guiding him over to the Iron Age fort, which is crumbling but still standing. A bit like me.

Sam casts an apologetic glance over his shoulder, and I quickly glance at Casey, who is giving me a weird look.

I have to think fast. What do I say? What do I do? I decide on: nothing. I have no idea what the hell is going on and I don't think I should make a scene on the beach, for Sophie's and Casey's sake. I'm not feeling too worried about upsetting Sam.

"Me and Daphne made it," Sophie is telling her dad.

"Daphne?" Sam queries.

"Yes, this is Daphne. Though sometimes she's called Alice!" Sophie giggles. "And she calls me Cynthia!"

"Does she?" Sam smiles at me, but I don't feel like returning the favour.

"I'm going to have to get going pretty sharpish," I say to Casey.

"Oh yeah, you've got a date, haven't you?"

"I didn't say it was a date," I half-snap and she looks taken aback. "Sorry," I say. "I am meant to be going out but I don't feel all that great, actually. I might just have an early night."

I don't look at Sam again. I gather my things together and tell Casey I'll be in touch. Sophie gives me a hug. "What about your cakes?" she asks.

"Your dad can have them," I smile at her, turn, and stalk off up the beach.

By the time I've journeyed through the warren of tiny streets, my anger has turned to tears, and my mind is wrapping itself in knots. I want to know what's going on. I want to ask Sam. But I also don't want to speak to him, ever again. I get to David's, tiptoe quietly up the stairs. I don't want to talk to anybody right now.

Julie is not in. Her door is shut but it's completely quiet. I'm pleased. It means I can go into my room, put some music on, and sob loudly for as long as I want.

Every now and then, my phone vibrates on my bedside table. I ignore it.

For the first time since I've been here, I miss home. I want to be at my parents'. It's Sunday; they've probably had a nice lunch and gone for a walk to blow away the cobwebs. Tears stab my eyes as I think of them and I wish I could just be there, now, and forget all this. My room is a mess; there's a pile of dirty clothes in one corner, and what little space there is feels stifling and humid in the afternoon heat. There is seagull poo on my window, and the bird I assume is the perpetrator is busily shrieking on the roof just above. Outside, the street is a stream of tourists, sticky with ice cream or wobbly with beer, patting round tummies, full after a lazy, protracted Sunday lunch. They have no worries, I think angrily. Here they are; the couples, the families, wandering smugly along, hand-in-hand, not a care in the world.

Somewhere out there is Julie, with Luke; and then there is Sam, with Casey and Sophie.

I know I'm being silly; I know I'm being childish. I don't care.

Eventually, after I've worn myself out from crying, I take my phone. I slide my finger across the screen and type in the pin code. I can see I've missed five calls, and I have seven new text messages. Well, it's nice to be popular.

I check the messages first.

Sam: **Alice, I'm sorry, I wanted to tell you all about it tonight. Last night didn't seem the right time. Xx**

Casey: **Hey, let me know if you change your mind bout tonite KCxx**

Sam: **I really hope you're OK. I'm sorry xxx**

Mum: **Hi darling, I tried to call just now. I bet you're at the beach, Dad and I were wondering about coming down for a few days. What do you think? We miss you. Love, Mum xxx**

Sam: **Alice, please can you answer your phone? I just want to talk. I'm back home now xxx**

Julie: **Are you still at home? Xx**

Sam: **I promise I won't text or ring again. I guess you're angry. Please can you give me a call when you're ready to talk? She wants me to have Sophie**

**tonight but I've told her I'm going for dinner. I
hope this is still correct. I didn't say who I was
going with xxx**

I check my call register: two missed calls from Mum, two
from Sam, and one from Julie. I wonder where she is. I'm
not ready to call any of them back right now: Mum will
know something is wrong just from hearing my voice, and
want to know what it is. Julie will be somewhere with
Luke, and I am not in the mood for their loved-up
happiness. I have no idea what I want to say to Sam.

I think about Mum and Dad coming down here. I
would love to see them. Normally, I see them a couple of
times a week; just popping round for a cup of tea, or a
meal, or meeting Mum for coffee at lunchtime. It suddenly
feels a long time since I've seen them, and aside from Julie
they are the two real constants in my world. I miss them.
The thought makes me sob again.

I quickly text back to Mum: **Hi Mum, you guessed it!
It's another beautiful day. I would love it if you
and Dad can come to visit. I think you'd really
like it here. Can I ring you tomorrow and we can
sort out when – and I can look into a place for you
to stay. There might be room at the Sail Loft for
you! I love you, and miss you too. Alice xxxx**

I think Mum will be happy to read that message and that
makes me feel a bit better.

I go into the kitchen and make a cup of tea. Julie's door is
open, which is weird. Has she come back and gone out
again without me noticing? I check her room; the window

is open so maybe the breeze just blew the door. I make a cup of tea, carry it into the bathroom, and give my face a wash. Then I decide that actually I want a shower. I turn the water on hot, and I pull off my clothes. I think I'll just get my pyjamas on after this, watch some TV, maybe call out for a takeaway later.

The water is almost scalding and makes me gasp, but it feels good, washing away the sand from the failed beach outing and soothing the achy, miserable feeling.

I step out of the shower, leaving wet footprints across the soft green carpet as I walk into my room. I hear the door go downstairs. Is it Julie? No, it sounds like David. I feel relieved. It's not that I don't want to see Julie, but the chances are that she is with Luke, and I really don't want to see him. It wasn't his place to say about Sam, and Casey, and Sophie, and his loyalties lie with his friend, of course, but I still feel aggrieved that he could have let me go headlong into this without a clue.

I know, of course, it's nobody's fault. Not even Sam's. He had a life after me; he thought I'd moved on. Geoff scared him away. He was perfectly entitled to go ahead and meet somebody – get married, have a family, whatever. I am angry because I was shocked; embarrassed, even, by not knowing anything about it. And I don't know why he didn't tell me last night; after all, I told him about Geoff. And if I am very honest, I feel really weird that Casey and Sam have been together. That he's the father of her child, for god's sake! It's just so much to take in.

I send a short text to Sam:

I can't see you tonight. I will call you soon.

Then one to Casey:

Sorry, I'm shattered and I've got a headache. I'm going to have an early night x

I pull on my pyjamas but I hear David calling upstairs. "Anyone up there?"

"Hello?" I call back, in what I hope is a cheerful voice.

"Alice! Is Julie up there?"

"No, I don't think so…"

He is already bounding up the stairs. He rounds the corner, swinging round the banister and clearing all three of the last steps with one leap. "Alice!" He says, grabbing me by the shoulders, "Alice! I'm so glad you're here. I needed to talk to you. I'm getting married!" He swings me round, which is not easy to do in the tiny space, then pulls back. "You're in your pyjamas!"

"Oh? Yeah, I am, I… just got back from the beach, had a shower, and thought I might as well just put these on. You're getting married?" I change the subject back to him. "Oh my god, that's amazing!"

"I know!" he laughs. "Martin asked me last night. It was so romantic. We were at the Cross-Section, dining al fresco, and he got down on one knee. I thought he'd dropped a crab claw or something, but he pulled this out of his pocket…" David shows me his left hand, where a plain silver band shines from his ring finger.

"Wow!" I say, and I genuinely can't help smiling. "That is just the best news. I'm so happy for you, David."

His eyes are shining with tears. "I'm so happy, too. I can't calm down. Will you come and have a drink with me? In your pyjamas?"

"Of course I will!" I laugh.

"Great… tell you what… I'll put my pyjamas on too, then we'll be equal. I won't drink much, I promise. But I think one to calm my nerves would be OK, do you?"

"I do," I say.

"I do! I'll be saying that soon!" David exclaims and gallops back down the stairs. "See you in five!"

I pull myself together. I'm pleased to have the distraction. It's far better than sitting on my own, eating a takeaway in bed. I get my phone and text Julie back:

Yes, I'm in. David, too. I'll be down at his, having a drink xx

I leave my phone where it is. There are no new messages from Sam, as he promised there wouldn't be. I'm disappointed even though I know that's unreasonable of me.

I brush my hair, pull a hoodie around myself, and go down to David's. He's sitting in his lounge, the patio doors open, an unopened bottle of champagne on the table in front of him. He is humming to himself.

"I am so happy for you!" I say. "Have you told Bea yet?"

"No, I've been trying to ring her but she's not answering! Here, you open this and I'll try her again."

I take the bottle from him and peel away the foil as he picks up his house phone and dials Bea's number. *Pop!* The cork hurtles into the air, rebounding off the ceiling, just as he says, "Where have you been, big sis?" He listens for a moment. "That was a gunshot. Yeah, it's that waitress-cum-receptionist of yours, causing trouble. You know what she's like."

He winks at me before continuing. "I've got some big

news, Bea, wait till you hear this... I'm getting married!"

I hear shrieks from the other end of the telephone line. David is grinning. He waits until the whooping has stopped and listens. "Yes, to Martin, you daft cow! Who else? He asked me last night!"

I hear more exclamations from the phone. I can't help smiling. I pour two glasses of champagne while David listens to his sister.

"I'll tell you all about it tomorrow. What if I come over in the morning? I could walk down with the girls. You know I won't be able to sleep tonight anyway..." he listens, "... that would be really lovely, thank you, Bea. Thanks so much." David is becoming teary, and I feel myself welling up. "I love you, too."

He puts the phone down and looks at me. "Look at me," he laughs, "I'm a total wreck! Come on, let's get some of that down us!"

I hand him a glass and then I raise mine high. "To you and Martin."

"To me and Martin! God, I miss him already!"

We take our drinks and the bottle into the garden and sit there, in our pyjamas, talking and chatting. I think I've cheered up until David says, "So what's up with you?"

"What... oh, nothing. Nothing, really."

"Come on!" he says. "I can tell there's something bothering you. Do you want to talk about it?"

"No," I say, unconvincingly, "this is your happy day."

"Yes, it is, and unless you tell me you're having an affair with Martin, I don't think you're going to put a dampener on it. Come on now, spill!"

So I end up telling him about Sam. About our night out, then about him and Casey.

"Casey?" David asks, looking puzzled. "I don't think I know her. Is she from round here?"

"Yes, she is, I'm guessing you must have gone to school together. She's a similar age to you, too. She's the one who's running the Pilates classes."

"You mean Katie? Katie Collins?"

"No, Casey..." as I say it, my mind starts to whirr. Casey... KC... Katie Collins... Sam mentioned he'd had a girlfriend called Kate... "Oh," I say. "Well I suppose that's something that makes sense, even if nothing else does."

"I did go to school with Katie, she was the year below me, but I remember her being really quiet and cute. Sort of cuddly, if you know what I mean, in a nice way. I remember some of the other girls didn't like her. They were bitches, though, in her year. She had a transformation after she'd left school, though, became a bit... popular with the boys, shall we say?"

This fits in with what Casey... Katie, I correct myself... told me about herself.

"So your Sam went out with her, did he?"

"Yes, but not just that. They've got a daughter. Sophie."

"Have they?" David looks surprised. "Well, I knew Katie had a little girl, but I didn't know she was Sam's. I guess this all happened in my hazy years, though, I don't know if you can trust me to remember anything much from that time! So what's bothering you most: the daughter or the ex?"

"I really don't know," I sigh. "All of it. Maybe most of all it's the fact he didn't tell me."

"Yes, I can see that," says David. "Can I try and offer a different point of view, though? You and Sam are only just getting to know each other again. It sounds like you told him a lot of things about your scary dead ex last night. And Sam did tell you he'd been with somebody else. Maybe introducing the subject of his daughter at the same time just seemed too much."

"Hmm, maybe," I'm not convinced but I think of Sam's text from the beach. *We have more to catch up on.* Then the later one. *Last night didn't seem the right time.* "He did say he'd been planning to tell me tonight."

"Well, maybe he was, and maybe he wasn't, but is it worth giving him the benefit of the doubt? After all, it sounds like he got together with Katie after you'd rejected him. I know, I know, you didn't reject him. But he thought you did. And OK, he's got a kid, but these things happen. We're all a bit older. We've all got our history to lug around with us. God knows I've got mine. And he's not with Katie any more, is he?"

"No," I reluctantly admit.

"So… let's try and look at this logically. You and he fell in love one summer. You went home. He had an accident. You thought he didn't love you, and got together with freaky psycho man. Sorry, I know I shouldn't speak ill of the dead but, well… And Sam came to find you but got scared off. So he came back and got together with Katie. And they had a daughter who, you say, is a great kid."

"OK so far…"

"And Sam still sees the girl? His daughter, I mean?"

"Mm-hmm."

"So he's a good dad? He's still the good man you think – or thought?"

"I suppose." I know it all makes sense. I know it's not so unreasonable. But it's bloody messy and I don't know if I want messy. And to top it all off, it's Casey, and Sophie. Not some random strangers. "Thank you, David, it's really helped talking to you about it. I think I need to give it a couple of days to let it settle and then I can think again."

"I'd steer clear of Pilates tomorrow night, though," David grins.

"Yes, I guess I'd better. I've got a headache just thinking about it all."

"Well don't, then," David smiles. "Let's think about me instead!"

I smile back. We talk about him and Martin; their plans for a local wedding, in the winter. "Oh, Bea said she wants to have a celebratory meal this week," David says. "Do you and Julie want to come?"

"I'd love to," I say, "if you're sure that's OK with Bea?"

"I'm sure it will be fine."

"Oh, I wanted to ask her about my parents coming to stay, too, if she's got room for them."

"Why don't we ring her now?" David says. "No time like the present."

Before I know it, David has rung Bea again, and made me ring my parents, and plans are in place for them to come down on Tuesday, to stay at the Sail Loft for four nights thanks to a late cancellation, and for them to be coming to celebrate David's and Martin's engagement, too. I am really excited to think I'll see my parents so soon, and I think some of the bubbles have gone to my head.

"I'll go and ring Julie," I say, "see if she can come out on Wednesday as well. I won't tell her your news, though, you can do that. Hang on, I'll grab my phone…"

I trip up the stairs, suddenly happy again – putting all thoughts of Sam aside, I am happy for David, and really touched that he and Bea are including me and my family in their world down here. I unlock my phone to see that

Julie has got there first; there are three missed calls and a voicemail from her.

"Alice, it's me," she sounds like she's crying. "Alice, I don't know what to do. You need to help me."

19

I manage to get Julie to calm down long enough to tell me where she is, but she won't say why she's so upset. I can't tell if something has happened to her, or she's been drinking, or both. I rush back downstairs. "Julie's in a bad way," I say, "She's down at the harbour, I need to go and find her."

"I'll come with you," David looks concerned and is up on his feet in a flash, grabbing his keys and a jacket. I shrug my own coat over my pyjamas. There's no time to worry about being seen out in my nightwear.

We walk quickly down through the town. My ankle is aching still, but feels much stronger. My heart is thudding. It's not like Julie to behave like this – she has never been a drama queen - and I don't know what to expect when we find her.

We scurry past the people milling leisurely around the tables outside the Mainbrace; there's live music tonight so it's very busy. It's a beautiful evening; the tide is in and the boats in the harbour are bobbing gently on the rippling water. I look along the harbour wall. I think I know where Julie will be, and I'm right – she is sitting in our favourite spot, and she has her head in her hands.

"There she is!" I say to David. "I'll go ahead, if you don't mind."

"No, that's fine – I'll hang around here for a few minutes; you can give me a signal if you need me urgently."

I rush along the uneven stone surface; worn away over the years by the comings and goings of fishermen and, more recently, tourists.

"Julie!" I cry, out of breath, as I get near to her. She looks up. Her eyes are rimmed with red and she looks pale. "Are you OK?" I ask.

She shakes her head and I sit next to her, putting my arms around her. She cries deeply into my shoulder, and I don't say anything for a while, I just let her cry, while I try to work out what's going on.

"Has somebody hurt you?" I ask eventually. "Are you OK?"

She shakes her head. "No… nothing like that. More like I've hurt them."

"Who?" I ask, "You've hurt who?"

"Gabe… and Luke…"

OK. Now I know a bit more about what I'm dealing with, I don't feel quite so worried. I thought something had happened to her, the way she was carrying on. In fact, I feel a bit annoyed at her. But I don't suppose now is the time for that.

"What's happened?" I ask her.

"Gabe was here," she says.

"Here..?" I ask, wondering what he was doing at the harbour.

"Last night. He came down to Cornwall. I didn't know he was coming."

"Blimey. Did he find you? Was Luke with you?" I'm building a picture in my head: Gabe and Luke facing off. Julie stuck between them. Luke is a lot bigger than Gabe, who has quite a slight build, and is not that much taller than Julie. I don't fancy his chances in a fight. But I don't think either he or Luke is the fighting type.

"No, Luke wasn't there. I... I didn't go in to see his mum. We got to the hospice but I chickened out. It was so weird. I don't know her; I mean, I know we used to hang out at theirs, but it was a long time ago. He was so happy that I was going to see her with him, and then I told him I couldn't do it. It just felt wrong, somehow. Disingenuous. He kept saying how happy she'd be to see him with somebody before she died and when he was saying that, I kept thinking of Gabe. Of his mum, and dad. And I miss them. And I miss him. Gabe, I mean. Shit, I'm such a stupid bitch."

"No you're not," I say, but my heart is aching for Luke, whose own heart must be breaking twice over right now. "And when did Gabe come into all this?"

"Well," she sobs, "I left Luke, saying I thought it would be better for him if I didn't come in. He had to go and see his Mum, she was expecting him. I went home, thinking you'd be there. But instead, there was Gabe, on the doorstep. I couldn't believe it."

I think of the murmuring voices I'd heard this morning. I thought it was Julie and Luke but it must have been her and Gabe. "Did he stay the night?"

"Yes," she sniffs, and I want to shake her. I am finding it very hard to feel sorry for her, but it's no use me getting annoyed. I think she knows what a mess she's made of things.

"Come on," I sigh. "David's over there. We'll go home together. Maybe you should just have a good sleep and see how you feel in the morning."

I sound like my mum, saying that. I can't wait to see her

on Tuesday. Right now, I feel like coming down to Cornwall was the worst thing Julie and I could have done. Luke would certainly be much better off, for one thing. And I'd never have got mixed up with Sam, and Casey, and lovely little Sophie. Life may have been boring but I'm not sure boring is so bad.

David and I walk on either side of Julie, our arms around her. She's been stupid but she's still my best friend. David had raised his eyebrows at me when Julie and I got to him outside the Mainbrace. "Tell you later," I mouthed to him.

The half-drunk bottle of champagne is on the table when we get in. "Have you been celebrating something?" Julie asks.

"Yes," David can't keep the smile from his face, despite the slightly miserable situation, "Martin and I are getting married!"

"Oh that's great," Julie promptly bursts into tears. "I've ruined your celebrations as well!"

"Shush, no you haven't, don't be silly," David puts his arms around her. "Come on, let's get you upstairs, I'll bring you a hot chocolate, and you can have a good sleep."

While David sorts Julie out, I go into my room. I check my phone, wondering if Sam's been in touch, even though he said he wouldn't. He and I should have been out having dinner now.

There is one message, from Casey. My heart sinks. I open it up. It's a long one.

Sophie wants to no y u left so quick. I told her to ask her dad. He sed u and him were havin dinner

2nite. She sed r u his GF and he said maybe. Wot's goin on? U knew I wanted to get back wiv him. Why didn't u tell me u & Sam had history? Can't belive u kept that from me.

Well, I think, seeing as I had no idea that you and Sam even knew each other, never mind had a kid together, why would I have told you anything about it?

Ask Sam

I send just those two words. I've had enough for today. I can hear David talking softly to Julie in the next room. He is a lovely man, I think; Martin is very lucky.

In time, I hear David sneaking out. I go to my door. "She's asleep," he whispers. "Poor girl."

"Hmm," I say. I'm not feeling that much sympathy for my friend, if I'm honest.

I go back downstairs with David and he refills both our glasses. "To complete and utter fuck-ups," he says, and I can't help but laugh.

20

Monday is a quiet day. Julie and I walk to work in silence in the morning, but close together, shoulders and arms brushing on each step. She knows I am always here for her, and she knows enough that she has made a mess of things. She really doesn't need me to keep reminding her.

Over a hurried cup of tea this morning, Julie filled me in on everything that had happened. Gabe had stayed the night but had to go back up to the Midlands as he has a job interview today; something I found hard to believe. He's been happy doing a few odd jobs – barman, hospital porter, delivery driver - these last few years, not wanting to commit himself to anything and preferring to keep plugging away at his art. And he is a really, really talented artist. However, apart from the occasional sale, it isn't paying the bills and I can see how it's difficult for Julie. It seems that Gabe has now realised this himself. The job is with a graphic design consultancy and Julie says he's really excited about it. Apparently he told her he'd been thinking about how he'd acted, and why she'd left him, and had come up with a plan, to show her he appreciated her. He wanted a well-paid job so he could contribute more financially and she wouldn't feel like she had to work all hours to keep them afloat. And he realised he had taken her for granted and let her do too much around the house.

"Apparently it was his mum who made him see it!" Julie had laughed drily; she and Gabe's mum had not always got on brilliantly well. "I never knew that she could see how hard I was working, or that he was... well, taking the piss, really. I used to think it must have been because she spoiled him when he was growing up, but he says that wasn't it. He said it was his own fault, and nobody else's."

"Well, good on him," I said fondly. I suppose if he's going to work in graphics, he might be able to use his artistic talents, even if it's not entirely in the free-spirited way he'd like to.

"I know," she said. "I can't believe he's come up with all this, by himself. It's what I always wanted him to do. I did spell out to him on more than one occasion how fed up I was getting..."

"I'm sure you did!" I grinned.

She nudged me but grinned as well, "... but it never made any difference. He'd say all the right things and maybe make an effort for a day or two but then we were right back to square one."

"So what now?" I asked.

"What now," Julie repeated. "I... I think I have to go back to Gabe. I love him, Alice. I still love him. Maybe I always knew that but him coming down here, with all his ideas, and his plans for us... it's made me realise how much I've missed him."

"But Luke..?" I ask.

"I know," Julie put her head in her hands. "Luke is so lovely. I can't believe I've done this to him, and what a time to do it, too, with his mum. I am such a stupid, stupid cow. I do love him, too, but is it possible to love two people at the same time?"

"Shit, look at the time!" I said as Julie moved slightly

and I saw the clock on the microwave. We had seven minutes before our shifts started. We gulped down our drinks and scurried off down the stairs. I could just hear the sounds of David getting up as we tiptoed past his bedroom. I smiled to myself that at least one of us was happy this morning. And I thought selfishly that at least all this mess with Julie had taken my mind off my own situation, with Sam.

It's busy at the Sail Loft and I don't have time to think; going from waitressing to gobbling my breakfast down with barely a moment to spare.

Bea is in a great mood this morning, I guess because she's so happy about David and Martin. Julie is dreading telling her that she's going to leave. She's decided to work a week's notice then head back home, to Gabe. She wants to have time to tell Luke that she's leaving. Gabe has no idea about Luke, and I don't know if she intends to be honest with Luke about going back to Gabe. I have to leave her to it.

While I'm on the phone, taking a new booking, I see Julie come out of the kitchen and knock on Bea's office door. She glances at me briefly, crossing her fingers, before walking in. She is in there for a while and when she comes out her face is pale and it looks like she's been crying. Julie is really not much for crying normally so I'm not used to seeing her like this. However, I am on the phone again so I can't go to her. I gesture for her to wait, and she does.

"Oh my god, was it that bad?" I ask.

"What? No, oh no, Bea was lovely. She said it was kind of lucky because her friend's son has just come back to town so she can ask him to fill in."

"You look like you've been sobbing, though."

"I know, I have, I've just been telling Bea about it. And she was so kind. I wasn't expecting her to be and the nicer she was, the more upset I became. She said that even if it wasn't for Jonathan, she'd probably have been able to get somebody, but not anyone like me!" Julie blows her nose. "She said I have to go back to Gabe if that's what's right for us. I guess seeing David and Martin so in love must be getting to her."

I smile to think of this. I really thought Bea might go mad. I had no idea she was such a romantic! A divorcee with no children, she had bought the Sail Loft when she and her husband split up, and turned it from a slightly twee, chintzy B&B into a really lovely hotel, pretty much all on her own. As far as I know, she's not had any relationship to speak of since then and the hotel has become her life. I really admire her but I wonder if it's a bit lonely being her, sometimes. Julie says it's why Bea and I get on so well; we've both shut ourselves away from relationships.

Looking at the state Julie's in, I'd say Bea and I have made the right choice. Maybe I've had a lucky escape with Sam. Still, as I think of him, I check my phone in case he's been in touch. There are no missed calls, no messages.

After work, I go back to the flat. I decide to get out of town for the rest of the day; take the train across to the other side of Cornwall, walk to a little sheltered beach I know where I can swim, and think, and get away from everything. It does seem slightly ironic that I am now trying to get away from the place where I'd come to get away from everything.

Julie is going to see Luke, and tell him she's going home in a week. She says she is going to be as honest as possible.

I feel so sorry for him. But it's better than leading him on. I agree to be back here in the evening so hopefully we can have a glass of wine and talk things through; I think she will need it. I won't be rushing back to get to Pilates, though.

I sit on the train, looking out of the window. We go round part of the coast, then weave in around some small villages, arriving on the other side of the ever-narrowing peninsula. I know this place well, but not from the golden summer. This is a place we used to come to; Mum, Dad and I, when I was little. Sometimes we'd be with Dad's brother and his wife and kids, so I'd have cousins to play with. I remember the walk to the beach; along the edges of fields, with tall crops swishing next to us, in the breeze; crickets chirping and butterflies flittering up, away from our brown legs and sandalled feet. I remember Dandelion & Burdock to drink, or Shandy Bass. A swim in the sea followed by a Mars Bar. Pasties or sandwiches for lunch and chips from a café not far from the station. The beach was recommended to my dad by the owner of the cottage where we used to stay. It is a 'locals' beach' and nowhere near as busy as those in back in town. I follow the same route we took so many years ago. The wheat and the sea breeze whisper, conspiring next to me as I stride along, and the clouds dash across the sky, their shadows sweeping the landscape and then the sea – which looks a dark blue today; more agitated than it has been for a while - trying their best to keep up.

As I get closer to the beach, my mood lifts, my footsteps quicken, and I feel lighter somehow. I have my ever-reliable bag slung over my shoulder, in it a bottle of water, a towel, a book, a change of clothes, a few coins, and a hoodie. The path down to the beach is rocky and steep so

I pick my way carefully down, landing on the sand after a short jump at the very end. The beach is deserted. I laugh for pure joy. The place is mine!

I set my bag down and I pull off my dress, then I run, crunching over the shale, the sharpness scratching the dry skin of my feet. Straight into the water, ignoring the cold; plunging deep into the depths, the salt stinging my nostrils and eyes. This is just what I needed.

I think of Julie, and Luke, and the conversation they could be having right now. I think of Sam, and wonder where he is. At work, probably. Is he thinking of me? I think of Mum and Dad, packing for their trip. That thought makes me happy.

I swim out a little way; wary of the choppy water and unfamiliar currents, I keep a close eye on my position and pick out a rock or two as markers so I can tell if I am being carried too far off course. It seems fairly tame, though; as long as I stay within the relative safety of this bay I think I'll be fine. I swim from one lot of rocks to the other, then back again. I can see my bag, clothes and shoes where I tossed them. There is still nobody else on the beach. As I scull along for a while on my back, I feel myself relax. My muscles seem to loosen and I gaze at the sky, watching the clouds pass overhead. I remember once more why I am here. It feels like all my thoughts have been of Sam lately but I didn't come back to Cornwall for him. I came because I love it here. I've just been swept away by seeing him again; by rediscovered memories. But there have been ten years that have passed since those memories were made, and much has happened in that time.

Thank god Mum and Dad are coming tomorrow; I can work in the mornings then spend the afternoons and evenings with them. Maybe we will come back here, and revisit some of the places where we holidayed. When they go back, Julie will be leaving, too. I could go as well but why should I? In just six or seven weeks, I will be heading back to the Midlands anyway and I am determined that I will not waste a minute more thinking of Sam. I have a chance to spend some real time in Cornwall and I may not get this opportunity again. I won't have it ruined because of a relationship which never was.

I swim back and forth a bit more to keep warm but when the sun disappears behind a large cloud, my skin prickles with goose pimples and I know it's time to get out. I swim strongly back to the shore and I head back to my things, wrapping my towel tightly around me. When the cloud moves off on its way, I soon warm up and dry off in the sunshine. I lie back on my towel, sand in my hair and sticking to my skin, and I let myself just relax, trying to remember some of the relaxation exercises I learned in my Pilates class back home. It makes me think of Casey and I feel sorry for her, but I didn't like the accusing tone of her message. I think it's safe to say that friendship has bitten the dust.

After a while, I think it's time to head back. Reluctantly, I say goodbye to the beach where still nobody else has set foot since I've been here. I imagine a house somewhere like this; where in the winter it would be bleak, and wild, and probably a bit scary. But it's real, somehow. It's not sitting in an office, selling stationery. It's not travelling on a bus back and forth to town, the same fellow passengers every day, all focusing on their screens, scrolling endlessly through social media updates made by people as bored as they are. I'd like to live here, and write here; get a dog, maybe two. I would pop into town once or twice a week;

have a chat with the shopkeepers who I'd get to know (I'm not totally anti-social), maybe go to a reading group or something, and then escape back here to a place which is mine and mine alone; where nobody else can tell me what to do or when to do it.

The wind is picking up as I walk back towards the small town and the railway station. I pull on my hoodie and wrap it close around me, my bare legs feeling the brunt of the weather. Soon enough, the blue sky is shrouded with grey, while long fingers of low-lying mist begin to stretch across the land. I sit on a bench on the station platform, drinking a coffee from the nearby café, where we used to buy our chips but which now sells artisan breads at extortionate prices. The mist advances and I am glad when the little train pulls slowly in and I hop on board, heading back for the north coast. The mist's attempt to swamp the land is thwarted as we rattle across the county. By the time I am climbing back out of the train, it is sunny once more, the sky clear.

David and Julie are both out when I get home so I head gratefully up the stairs and collapse onto my bed. The events of the last day or so, coupled with the long time I spent swimming this afternoon, have worn me out. I fall into a deep and satisfied sleep and I stay that way until the alarm goes off the next morning.

21

On Tuesday morning there is no sign of Julie but I don't have time to do more than send her a text asking if she's OK. I'm relieved when I get a message back from her:

Yes, see you at work, explain later.

Explain what? I wonder, but I have no time to think too hard about it as I jump in the shower, get dressed, and scurry off to the Sail Loft.

"Good morning!" Bea is smiling at me as I walk in, "I'm looking forward to meeting your parents today. Are you all free for a meal tomorrow night? I thought we could do it here; Jonathan – who'll be stepping into Julie's shoes next week - says that he'll do the catering, get used to the kitchen. Julie says she's coming."

So Julie's here already. "That sounds great, as long as you don't mind us barging in on your family celebration!"

"You won't be barging in at all; we'd love to have you. There'll be me, David and Martin, of course, and Martin's brother, plus a few of their friends. Then you, your parents, and Julie."

It sounds lovely and, best of all, we'll be safely tucked away at the Sail Loft; no chance of bumping into Sam, or Casey. I do wonder what I'd do if I bumped into Sophie;

189

the town's certainly small enough for that to be a possibility. I don't know if she'll have any idea about what is going on, or if she thinks me and her mum have fallen out – which I suppose, in a way, we have. I guess I'll just have to play it by ear.

Before the guests start trailing down into the dining room, I quickly push through the door into the kitchen. Julie is working away, whistling to herself.

"Julie!" I hiss. "How did it go?"

She turns, quickly. She looks OK. "Oh, it was fine. Much better than expected, in fact!"

"How's Luke?"

"He's OK. Well, he's not, but that's more to do with his mum than me. He said he knew he'd pushed me too quickly and that he shouldn't have done. He said he'd been thinking maybe he isn't in the right frame of mind to be starting a new relationship, anyway."

"Wow," I say, thinking that Julie's landed on her feet once more. "And he was OK about Gabe?"

"Well," she looks embarrassed. "I didn't quite tell him about Gabe…"

"Julie!" I say.

"I know, I meant to, I really did. But I started explaining about how I wasn't sure that we were right together, and then he launched into his side of the story, and then we got talking about his mum, and somehow… somehow it felt like I didn't really need to tell him that Gabe and I are getting back together. I will tell him, though, when I'm back home."

"And where did you stay last night?" I can tell from Julie's manner that she's not telling me something. She goes red. "Oh, Julie. You didn't…"

"I did… it, well, we just got really close again, and it felt

190

so intense, and romantic and…"

"Bloody hell, Julie." I feel really annoyed at her. Why can't people just be honest?

There is no time to continue our conversation. The first guests are seating themselves at their table; they are a fifty-something couple, staying for the week, who behave like newly-weds, but they say they're rediscovering each other since their children have now left home. It's more information that I need, to be honest, but I kind of like the way they are so into each other.

The dining room soon fills up and the only words Julie and I exchange are about food orders. We keep a distance from each other; she, I think, because she knows I'm annoyed at her and I think she is probably a bit ashamed. Me because I can't be held responsible for what I say so it's best if I don't say anything.

I'm on reception and busying myself identifying any empty rooms we can advertise at a slightly reduced price when the front door opens. "There she is!" I hear a very familiar man's voice say.

"Dad!" I exclaim, then, "Mum!" My parents are walking in, pulling suitcases on wheels. "We got an earlier train, we wanted to see you at work!"

"It's so good to see you," I say, confused that I feel like crying. I give them both an enthusiastic hug then Bea comes out to say hello.

"It's great to meet you," she says. "Do you know, of all the people I've had working here over the years, your daughter – and Julie – really stand out to me. I'm very grateful you've let me borrow her again."

"Not down to us, I'm afraid," Dad smiles at me proudly, "this girl knows her own mind!"

"Dad," I feel my cheeks growing red. It's funny how having your parents in your place of work makes you feel — like you can't be the professional, well-honed person you have become but instead you're their little girl again.

"I'll show you to your room," Bea says. "Can't distract the staff! If you settle in and have a cup of coffee, you can come and relax in our lounge if you want to; it's got a terrace with a great sea view. Alice can come and find you when her shift's over, if that's OK."

"Of course, can't interrupt the worker," Dad says.

Mum gives me an apologetic look. "We'll see you in a bit!"

The rest of the morning passes quickly. Julie has not emerged from the kitchen, although Charlie, who works with her, left some time ago. I feel like I should clear the air before she and Mum and Dad get together. I know my parents are sitting out on the terrace because I can hear Dad's Black Country accent drifting in through the open doors. I sneak to the kitchen and find Julie leaning against one of the counters, staring off into space. My entrance startles her.

"Hi," she says.

"Hi."

"You must think I'm an absolute idiot," she says.

"Julie," I sigh, "I don't think you're an idiot. Well, actually, maybe I do. A bit. Last night was meant to be your chance to clear everything up."

"I know," I can see she's trying to hid her annoyance and I must admit, I know I sound quite sanctimonious. I also know I am extra annoyed at her because I'm feeling sore from Sam's dishonesty and I am probably taking that out on her.

192

"You weren't there, though," she says. "It was such a great evening and I'd thought it was going to be awful. We talked about loads of stuff, and I was so relieved by all those things Luke said. When I was about to leave, he kissed me, and then one thing led to another, and it was… wonderful. I wish I could be with him; but then that would mean no Gabe. I wish I could have them both."

"Well you definitely can't do that," I snap, then apologise. "I'm sorry. You're right; I wasn't there. But don't you think you're being unfair to Gabe as well, now? He's at that job interview today, trying to make a future for you both. How would he feel if he knew where you were last night? Don't you think you should be honest with him… with them both?"

"Who are you to talk about being honest?" Julie snaps at me. "Gabe told me he'd gone to see you the night before we came down here. You never mentioned that, did you? I wonder why not."

"What… no, yes, he did. And no I didn't mention it to you. I was trying to protect you."

"Protect me?" she snorts. "Are you sure you weren't just trying to get one up on me?"

"What are you talking about?"

"Oh, you and Gabe always got on well, didn't you? Always mucking about together and laughing at my expense."

"I…" I am genuinely shocked. I had no idea Julie felt like that. Yes, I do get on well with Gabe and maybe there were times we had made fun of Julie, but never out of spite. And I'm pretty sure that anything like that was equal; we'd all take the piss out of each other as good friends do. I don't know what to say.

"Sorry," she sighs, "that was a stupid thing to say. I wish

193

you'd told me he'd been to see you, though. It felt weird that you and he had a secret."

"It really, really wasn't like that, Julie. I felt sorry for him, but I knew you'd made up your mind about coming down here and I thought telling you that he'd been to see me would just make you feel bad. Listen, Mum and Dad are here. Do you want to come and say hello?"

"I can't, at the moment. I just need to clear my head a bit. Will you say hi for me, and tell them I'll see them later?"

"Sure," I say, relieved, as there's no way I could hide the tension between me and Julie at the moment. And I wouldn't mind a break from her, to be honest. She needs to sort herself out. I can't believe she is being so self-centred.

I take a deep breath and head outside, to receive more hugs and exclamations from my parents.

"I'm sure she's grown!" says Dad.

"I'm nearly twenty-nine, Dad," I say, "so I bloody hope not!"

"You do look brown, though, Alice," says Mum. "You look really well."

"Thank you!" I say. "It's so good to see you. Do you fancy coming to the flat for a few minutes while I get changed, or is it easier to meet you in town somewhere?"

"Oh, we definitely want to see your flat, and meet David!" says Mum. "Will Martin be there?"

"No, not today. In fact, David will be out at work. But you'll meet him tomorrow; we've been invited to a meal to celebrate their engagement. Right here."

"Great," says Dad, "is Julie coming?"

"Yes, she'll be here," I say. "Come on, let's go."

I shepherd Mum and Dad off the terrace and we head away together into a day of Cornish sunshine. I show them around the town; we walk the length of the three beaches, and up onto the coastal path. I try not to think about the last time I was up here.

"What was that bird?" Dad asks.

"I don't know, I didn't see it."

"It was a beauty, it had a little yellow head and body, with brown on its wings."

"Oh, that sounds like a yellowhammer," I say airily.

I only know that because of Sam. Dad is impressed, though. "I can see it suits you, being here. You always used to love those holidays down here, when you were a kid. Do you remember?"

"I do," I say, and tell them about my trip yesterday afternoon.

After our walk, we head into town and stop at the Mainbrace as Dad wants a pint. Mum and I both drink bitter shandy. We sit at a table outside and Dad is impressed again when occasionally somebody says hello to me. A couple of the guys I met when I went out with Casey; and Marvin, who supplies the kippers to the Sail Loft. "Proper local, aren't you?"

"Hardly!" I say, but I feel proud all of a sudden. After all, I haven't really lived here long, but I do feel, if not a local, not a total tourist, either.

We stay at the Mainbrace for a couple of drinks and then head to a tapas bar. The afternoon seeps into the evening and before I know it we're drinking red wine at an outside table, surrounded by other chattering families, the night sky dark above our heads. I have barely given Sam a thought, I realise, as we walk back to David's house.

I say bye to Mum and Dad on the doorstep, checking

they know their way back to the Sail Loft.

"We can always ask a passing pirate," Dad says, in a poor imitation of the South West accent. I smile, and kiss him. Some time with my parents was just what I needed.

I unlock the heavy door and tiptoe into the house. Downstairs is in darkness but I can see a crack of light squeezing through the bathroom door, and I can hear the muffled sound of David's radio amidst some splashing. I creep past and go up to the flat, to find Julie's door closed. I knock softly on it but there is no reply. I use the bathroom, undress, and fall into bed. Then I think of Sam and I scramble out of bed, digging my phone out of my bag to check for messages. There is nothing.

22

On Wednesday, Julie and I are barely talking to each other but I need to make that right before the evening meal, if possible. If I get Mum and Dad involved, that could help. They love Julie and she loves them; as she and I have been best friends since primary school, we know each other's parents really well and are more like family to each other than friends. Which is why I know we'll get through this rocky period, and why I can be so honest with her. And why she can also be honest with me. I need to give some thought towards why she felt like that about me and Gabe – or was she just lashing out?

I also have to be honest with myself about how much of the anger I'm feeling is coming from my own situation rather than a reaction to Julie's behaviour.

It's funny seeing Mum and Dad at breakfast. Dad makes lots of jokes about me getting my comeuppance after treating their house like a hotel, and him as a taxi driver, Mum as a waitress, etc. Mum and I look at each other and roll our eyes.

I suggest that as they missed her yesterday, they might like to go in and see Julie after she's finished service. "Great idea, we've missed our second daughter, too," Dad says.

I decide not to warn Julie but to let them take her by surprise. She will have to be nice to them, and pretend everything is OK, unless she wants to tell them what she's been up to, and I don't suppose she wants to do that.

I hear them go in, Dad being his usual over-the-top self. My dad is great; for all the eye-rolling that Mum and I do, we wouldn't have him any other way. He is cheerful, and silly, and tries to make sure that life is fun. He's always been like that. The only times I've seen him down are when his mum died, and when I was going through all that stuff with Geoff. I hated seeing Dad sad. It felt wrong.

I can hear Julie returning my parents' exclamations and it makes me smile despite myself. And then, before I know it, they are ushering Julie out of the kitchen, and telling me we are all going for lunch. I look at Julie and she looks at me. And we start laughing.

"What's so funny?" Dad asks. "You girls, I don't know! Always giggling."

And just like that, the tension has gone. Trust my parents to sort everything out.

We head off to David's house, all talking and laughing together. As we hurriedly change, Julie and I shout apologies to each other.

"I shouldn't be so judgemental," I say to her. "I'm sorry."

"No, I shouldn't behave like such an idiot. I'm stupid, and I know it puts you in an awkward situation, with Gabe, and with Luke."

"Well I don't suppose I'll be seeing much more of Luke," I say. "Are you going to tell Gabe about him?"

"I think I might have to," Julie is downcast for a second, then looks at me. "What do you think?"

"I think it's going to be a very hard thing to do," I say,

198

"but I think you might have to. Otherwise you've got that hanging over you for the rest of your lives together."

"Shit, I know you're right. Why are you always right?"

I laugh. "I really wish I was." I realise that with everything that's been going on in her life, I haven't even told her about Sam, and Sophie and Casey. I'll save that for later.

We have lunch in the sun on the terrace of the Harbour Hotel, with a glass of prosecco. It puts us all in great spirits and in the afternoon Dad heads back to the Sail Loft for a snooze while Mum, Julie and I go to look for an engagement present for Martin and David. We end up all buying new clothes, for the party that evening, and being unable to decide on anything suitable for a present. I don't really know Martin's taste, although I feel like I know David's fairly well. It's nearly shop-closing time when Julie hits on an idea. We are on Fore Street, just moments from the harbour.

"Let's get them a tourist day!"

"A what?" I ask.

"A day to spend as tourists. I mean, they both live here, they probably don't do any of the things like boat trips or ghost walks. Let's ask David and Martin tonight to let us know a day when they're free and then book them a whole day's worth of activities! Starting with a dolphin-spotting trip in the morning; lunch at the Harbour Hotel, maybe surfing lessons, or paddle boarding, in the afternoon, fish and chips on the harbour wall, and the ghost walk in the evening."

"That is a great idea, Julie!" Mum says. "Maybe Phil and I should try out a few of those things tomorrow, too, then we can book them if we can get a date sorted tonight.

I might give the paddle boarding a miss, though."

Julie suggests we stop for a little drink to toast her genius, and we bustle into the Mainbrace for a gin and tonic before going our separate ways to get ready for the evening.

I have a shower and put on my new Seasalt dress. It's light blue and makes my tan look even darker. I peer at the peeling skin and freckles on my shoulders, then pin my hair up. I can't help but wish that Sam was coming with me tonight. I drift into a daydream, that it's our engagement party, but I quickly make myself snap out of it. I'm being pathetic.

Walking with Julie to the Sail Loft, I tell her about what happened.

"Oh my god, I'm so sorry I never even asked, I just assumed that you two were on the go-slow," she said. "And I've been totally wrapped up in myself, to be honest. Come to think of it, Sam tried to call Luke the other night – more than once – but Luke let it go to voicemail."

I wonder what Sam ended up doing on Sunday evening, instead of going out with me. Did he look after Sophie while Casey went for a night out with somebody else? I don't imagine so as she's told me herself she doesn't really have any friends. I feel suddenly sorry for her again. That thing she told me about drinking; it can't be good to drink that much, that often, all alone. I hope that things improve for her soon. Then it hits me that maybe Sam stayed with her and Sophie, maybe Casey and he got drunk together, for old time's sake… I turn the thought away. It's not a healthy way to be thinking.

As we reach the Sail Loft, I see some of the guests I served at breakfast this morning; a large, cheerful lady and her equally large, bearded husband, heading merrily down the steps.

"Come to join the party, girls?" she asks, and he pretend wolf-whistles at us.

His wife nudges him. "Like they'd be interested in you, you old goat!"

They laugh and head off in the direction of town, hand-in-hand.

Inside, there is laughter coming from the dining room. Julie and I go in, to be met by an exuberant Bea; more lively and colourful than I have ever seen her, in a dashing red dress, and a matching lipstick. "There you are, you two!" she exclaims. "Go and get yourselves a glass of bubbly!"

I see Mum and Dad chatting to Martin and David. They all smile at us and we greet Martin and David with kisses of congratulations.

"Have you seen Jonathan?" David nudges me. "Go and have a look in the kitchen!"

"Why?" I ask, smiling.

"He is gorgeous! Isn't he, Martin?"

"Who? Mr Chef? Oh, yeah. Go on, girls, go and sneak a look!"

"No!" I say.

Julie laughs. "Well, I will. I mean, it's my kitchen, isn't it? I'd better make sure he's treating it right."

Reluctantly, I follow her. A tall, slim man with short dark hair and chef's whites has his back to us, busily preparing a salad. Julie coughs and he turns around. David and Martin are right; he is gorgeous. But he's got to be younger than me, maybe no more than twenty-three.

"Can I help you?" he asks. His face is tanned and his eyes are a deep, dark brown.

"I just wanted to introduce myself," Julie says grandly; "I'm the breakfast chef."

"Oh, yes... Julie, right? Bea said you'd be here. You're leaving next week?"

"That's right."

"I'm sorry to hear it," Jonathan smiles at Julie and I see her melt.

"And I'm Alice," I say.

"Oh yeah... David told me about you. You're a waitress *and* a receptionist?" He grins.

"Yes." I see nothing funny in that.

"Well, I'm looking forward to working with you," he says. "I would shake hands, but..." He raises his gloved hands, which have tomato seeds stuck to them.

"That's fine, thank you." I smile now. "We'll see you in a bit."

I drag Julie out of the kitchen. "Two men's quite enough for you," I say.

She laughs. "Well at least you've got something to keep you occupied after I go!"

"Ha," I say, "have you seen how young he is?"

"You're hardly middle-aged yourself, Alice."

The meal is delicious. As well as being drop-dead gorgeous, Jonathan is clearly a very talented chef. There is crabmeat salad for starters, and an avocado version for me and the other two vegetarians (friends of Martin's); for main course we have roasted aubergines or lamb with cous cous, Moroccan style vegetables and deep fried potatoes (yes, that's chips to most people); dessert is a light chocolate mousse. Bea keeps the wine flowing and Martin and David keep us all entertained with far-fetched stories about people they have worked with, cases David has had to fight at work, and the most extravagant weddings they have gone to.

When it is time for coffee, Bea stands up and makes a toast: "I just can't say how proud and delighted I am that my little brother is getting married. If our parents were here today, they'd be just the same – once they'd got over the shock that their son was gay!" There is general laughter here. David has told me that he wishes he'd told his parents the truth but had been building up to it and then his mum had got ill, and he'd never found the right time, although he thinks his mum knew, really. His dad died within a year after his mum. "I couldn't hope for a better husband for David; a better brother-in-law for me, than Martin." Bea continues, raising her glass. "To David and Martin."

"To David and Martin," we all echo.

The sky, which had been clear just a short time earlier, has become moody; thick, grey clouds have moved in and taken over. Somewhere behind them, the sun is sliding down towards the horizon; every now and then it finds a chink in the grey armour and shoots a ray of gold through, making the sea twinkle briefly, but the clouds close ranks once more. I marvel at the difference this change makes to the view of the town; the rooftops seem to have changed colour, as the sunlight which was earlier making their orange lichen glow has disappeared. The clouds hang heavy and brooding overhead and I know it is just a matter of time until the rain comes. I feel quite heady – no doubt from the earlier gin and tonic, then the champagne, then the wine we've had with dinner. When it's polite to do so, I head outside to the terrace, to get some fresh air. My legs are definitely a bit wobbly. I stand quietly for a while, looking out to sea.

I'm surprised when I find that both Bea and David have come out to join me. Bea touches my arm, making me jump.

"Alice, have you got a moment? There's something we want to talk to you about."

My face must have fallen because they both laugh.

"Nothing bad," says David. "Let's sit down."

We all take a seat at one of the tables.

"Well, where to start, really?" David asks Bea.

"I think it's best if I go first," she says. "OK, you know I've been running this place for over twelve years? And how I always whinge that I never get a break?"

"Yes," I say hesitantly.

"Well - between the three of us - I'm going to go away, for a few months. I've actually… I've met a man. But he's American. He lives in America. And I'm going to go out and see him and hopefully… stay for a while."

"Wow, Bea!" I exclaim. "That's really exciting!"

"It is, isn't it?" she says. "But there's more to this. Now, I really don't want to give up the Sail Loft, because I've worked so flaming hard for it, and I don't know how it's going to work out with Bob. Yes, he's called Bob… don't laugh. So I wondered whether there is any chance you'd consider staying on, over the winter, maybe into next spring, and managing the place?"

"You want me to..? What? Really?"

"Yes, really!" Bea laughs. "But no pressure. Only if you'd like to."

"I'd love to!" I exclaim.

"I thought you'd say that," she says, "but look, take a few days. Have a chat with your parents, see what they think. Make sure it's what's right for you. And if you

204

decide you'd like to, we can talk terms then; pay and so on."

Wow. I have certainly not been expecting this. I look at David, who is smiling at me.

"The second thing is…" he says.

"What, there's more?"

"Yes! There's more! Now I don't know how you feel about this but Bea and I were saying it's too much for you to do everything here, so we thought it might be good to get a night manager. I can't promise it'll be Tom Hiddlestone, but somebody to take charge of things overnight so you can get away."

"OK…" I say.

"And Martin and I, now we're engaged, well, I'm going to move in to his place."

"Oh, that's lovely, David!"

"Yes, it is, isn't it? Well, anyway, what I'd like if you'd be happy to, is for you to take over my place… the whole of the house, while Bea is away. We can work out everything financially, between the three of us."

"What… I…" I am speechless. I feel like my jaw has hit the floor.

"Listen, it's a lot to take in," Bea says. "And we're all a bit drunk so let's leave it there for now. You have a good think, Alice, and let us know in a couple of days. Let's go back in and join the party."

I follow them obediently, and see Mum and Dad smiling at me. They clearly know exactly what's been said.

"Alright?" Mum asks, putting her arm around me.

"Yes," I say. "Yes, I am."

For the rest of the evening, my head is spinning. What an offer! What an opportunity. I can't wait to talk it through with Julie. I'm only sad that she won't be here. The only possible sticking point, I think, is living in the same town as Sam and Casey and Sophie. But I will just have to get on with it. They will just have to get on with it. This is much too good an opportunity to miss.

I walk home happily with Julie, our arms linked, and we talk about the evening. I want to tell her about Bea's offer but for some reason I keep it to myself for now. I think perhaps I need to make my own decision without anybody else giving me their opinion.

Julie is laughing, telling me about something Martin said, then she stops walking, and stops talking. We are on our street now, just a few doors away from David's house. I look up to see what's stopped her and there, in the streetlight, is Sam.

"Hi," he says gently. I don't say anything.

Julie moves forward, her footsteps sharp in the sudden silence. She knows he isn't here for me but it takes me a moment to understand this.

"Hi," she replies, in a similar tone. There's clearly some kind of understanding between them. In fact, I feel completely locked out of this situation.

"She's gone, hasn't she?" Julie says quietly.

Sam nods, and glances over at me. I suddenly understand.

"She died this afternoon," he says.

23

Shortly after Sam broke the news, and he spirited Julie away, the rain clouds broke as well.

I am in my room, looking out of the tiny window at the town, through a constant downpour. The rain pounds on the roof, gushes through the gutter and down the drainpipes. The gently sloping street has become a fast-flowing, shallow stream as the rainwater gathers, rushing down to meet the sea. No time to stop.

There has been thunder grumbling and rumbling, flexing its muscles threateningly; the occasional lightning flash splitting and lighting the sky. It is wild and angry out there now and I wonder how Luke and his dad are, and how Julie and Sam are getting on.

When the news was confirmed to Julie, she had sobbed, and turned to me. She looked so young. I moved towards her, and put my arms around her, and looked at Sam. He stood, his face illuminated in the dark, as if wondering what to say. "Will you come with me? To Luke?" he asked gently, and I knew he meant Julie.

She pulled away from me, giving me a short, strong look, and said, "Yes. Yes, of course."

How could she say anything else?

"Do you want me to grab a bag for you, Julie?" I asked, not really sure what else to say or do.

"No, it's fine, I'll go as I am," she said, and smiled at me. Sam smiled too, unsurely. "Bye," he said.

"Bye," I replied, and watched them go together down the street.

I entered the dark house and climbed the steps. I was tired, but wide awake. What a crazy night, and then that awful news. Even though we had known it was coming, it is still a horrible shock.

About ten minutes after Sam and Julie had gone, just as I was making a hot chocolate, the rain had started to gently tap at the windows and the roof, as if testing itself. With growing confidence, its strength increased and it has been hammering at the house and its neighbours ever since.

Now it's an hour or so since Julie and Sam disappeared. I've got my phone by my side in case she – or, let's face it, he – needs me, but I haven't heard anything. For once, I'm not so happy being on my own. I almost wish Casey would send me an antagonistic text, just so that I could have some kind of contact. David and Martin will probably stay at the Sail Loft, and Mum and Dad will be asleep by now. It's nice to know they're nearby, although I don't really think I could explain all about Luke, and Julie, and Gabe – or about me and Sam – to them.

Maybe they went through messy situations, though, before they got together. It's easy, as their child, to imagine that they have always been together, and happy, and settled. As though their relationship has always been straightforward, trouble-free, and nothing happened in their lives before they met. Maybe they have their own dramatic, or disastrous, stories to tell.

A great crack of thunder tells me it's close by now. I can't help wondering if this is something to do with Luke's mum. It's silly, I know; people die every day, and there isn't a storm every day, but the timing of this one seems ominous. I peer out of the window and see a figure hurrying up the street, coat pulled over their head, pulled close around them. Poor guy, caught out by what had looked like a promising sunny evening. I watch his progress then realise he's heading for the house and it dawns on me that this isn't just any figure.

I dash downstairs and open the door, just as he's about to knock on it. I look at him, and he looks at me, and just falls into my arms. My tears take me by surprise as I hold him and his wet clothes soak my pyjamas. His head on my shoulder, I stroke his thick, heavy hair. Of course, his heart is breaking too. Not as much as Luke's, I'm sure, but May had been a wonderful person to Sam, too.

"Come on," I say gently and take his hand, leading him upstairs.

I run the bath and I get the largest of Julie's lovely, fluffy towels. "Get those wet things off you," I say. "Don't worry, I won't look."

I pour what seems like half a bottle of bubble bath into the hot water and watch as the bubbles multiply. Sam comes into the bathroom, the towel wrapped around his waist. He looks so sad, I almost don't notice his beautiful, curly-haired chest, or toned, tanned arms.

"I'll leave you to it," I say, and I go into the kitchen and put the kettle on.

"Bloody hell!" I hear from the bathroom. "How hot is this?"

"Sorry!" I can't help grinning. I forget that not everybody likes their baths as hot as I do. "Put some cold in!"

I hear the tap going back on, and after a few minutes, the sound of what must be Sam's naked body slipping into the water.

"Do you want a drink?" I ask.

"Yes, please."

I make a cup of tea and I knock on the bathroom door. "Can I come in?"

"Of course," I hear, so I walk in and there, in my bath, is the man I have loved for ten years. Lying in a huge cloud of bubbles and looking so sad that all I want to do is put my arms around him again. Instead, I place the cup of tea on the chest of drawers and then look at him, and look away. I'm not sure what to do.

"Thank you, Alice," he says.

"For what?"

"You know," he says. "This…" He gestures with his hand and a puff of bubbles floats across to me. I examine it where it lands, on my right knee.

He laughs, and it is a relief.

"Join me," he says, and I meet his eyes. "Please."

It takes me a moment to realise what he means, and I keep looking at him. I'm not sure. But my hands find their way to the buttons on my pyjama top. He watches as I slowly undo them, and slide the top off my shoulders. I feel shy but strangely confident. The wildness of the weather is seeping into me. I step out of my pyjama bottoms and into the water. Sam puts his hand out to me as I slide into the bubbles. He is shaking. He pulls me to him, so that my back is resting on his chest. His arms are strong around me, and his head is on my shoulder once more. It rests there for a while but he is not crying this time. Slowly, he begins very, very gently kissing and nibbling my skin. It is sending shivers up and over me, again and again. I want to cry, and I want to laugh. I take one of his hands and gently kiss the back of it, then put his fingers into my mouth and suck them, one by one. I hear him moan gently behind me, and his other hand finds my left breast.

"I've been thinking about this, for ten years. Thinking about you," he murmurs. I turn my head and find his mouth, then I turn fully and kneel up in the water, kissing him with all the passion that has built up over these ten years, the energy of the storm and the emotion of the night taking over me. We stop for a second, looking into each other's eyes. Then we are out of the bath, wrapping towels around ourselves, but soon forgetting them as we make our way into my bedroom, our hands barely away from each other, and we fall onto the bed, the weight and warmth of him making me sigh with utter relief and joy.

In the dark of the night, with the rain still pouring down outside, rivulets trickling over the bumps of the roof and spilling out of the gutter, joining the torrents cascading along the road below, we hold each other. We don't talk about Luke, or his Mum. We don't talk about Julie. Or Sophie and Casey. We just lie there. I listen to Sam breathing, and can hear my own breath loud in my ears. Somewhere below my head, his heart is thumping, steady and strong. It makes my stomach tumble, thinking of it beating away in there, the centre of this man that I love.

The thunder and lightning are long gone; now the sound of the rain is soothing. Eventually, I fall asleep.

24

I'm awoken in the morning by a very gentle kiss from Sam.

"What time is it?" I ask, noting the dark grey, smudged sky through the open curtains. It's so quiet.

"It's about 4am," Sam whispers. "I'm sorry to wake you. I have to get back home, though, I've got studying to do – my exams are next week - and I'm meant to be looking after Sophie later. And I think I'll be heading to Luke's after that."

He looks apologetic as he says this.

"OK," I say, "and don't worry. Of course you have to look after your daughter."

Sam looks like he wants to say something but changes his mind. I see that familiar furrowed brow as the expression crosses his face, but it smooths out as he smiles at me. "Last night was great," he says.

"It was, wasn't it?" I can't help smiling. I don't know what to say; was it a one-off? I don't know where I stand. I don't want to think about that now, though; I'm happy to just remember last night.

"We should do it again," he says.

I raise my eyebrows.

"Get together, I mean, me and you. Well, and we should definitely do *that* again!"

He leans over me and kisses me full on my mouth. I probably have awful morning breath but he doesn't seem to care. I pull him in for a proper kiss, and I can feel his warmth and his soft skin, slightly bristled by morning stubble. *I love you*, I think. But there's no way I'm going to say it.

"I have to go," he says reluctantly, and he tiptoes out of the door, his shoes in his hand. I don't think he needs to be quiet; David and Martin were planning on staying at the Sail Loft last night and I doubt very much that Julie has come back. Sam casts a look back at me and his mouth turns up into another smile.

I pull the duvet around myself and sink into this delicious feeling. There's some time yet before I have to get up for work but I don't think I'll be able to sleep. Instead, I replay last night's events in my head. I'm caught between feeling sad about May, and ecstatic about Sam. And on top of all that, I'm filled with nervous excitement about Bea's offer. I don't know where it will lead, and I know I just need to enjoy it for what it is, while I can.

I spend over an hour drifting in and out of a very pleasant doze, but I know I need to wake up. I knock on Julie's door just in case she did come back but there is no answer. I push the handle down gently and I peer in. The curtains are open, the bed is fully made. She hasn't been back since yesterday.

I wonder what she and Luke are doing now. How Luke is. Will he have had any sleep at all? It's hard to imagine. While I wish for her own sake that Julie hadn't gone to him, I know why she did. How could she not? It's going to be an even worse wrench for him now, when she goes back home, but I suppose at least she was there for him in his hour of need. The first of many.

I feel guilty, feeling so happy at such an awful time, but I can't escape this feeling. I can't stop thinking about Sam, and me, and me and Sam. Remembering his breath on me; his hands.

Still, I must get ready for work. It's probably a good job he had to go back to study; I don't think I'd have been able to leave my bed if he was still in it.

I dress, humming to myself, and gulp down a cup of tea and a glass of orange juice. The two drinks slosh in my stomach as I hurry along to the Sail Loft. I am amazed to see all traces of last night's party gone. Jonathan is there and he looks up and smiles at me.

"Oh, hi," I say, "where's Julie?" I hope that didn't sound rude.

"She called Bea last night, while the party was still going. Her boyfriend's mum died, didn't you know?"

"Ex-boyfriend," I say. "Yes, I did. It's awful. So are you filling in?"

"Yes, for now. I might as well just get on with it, seeing as I'll be here next week anyway."

"I suppose so," I smile at him and I wander into the dining room, where all the tables are back in their usual places, perfectly made and resplendent in their thick white tablecloths.

Before long, the first guests appear. It's always the same people who come down first. You can put money on them being walkers, or bird-watchers. Usually aged 50+, and usually the man will say something about not wanting to miss the best part of the day, or the early bird catching the worm… that kind of thing.

Today is no exception. First in are Mr and Mrs Jones, who have stayed at the Sail Loft every year for five years now; I know this because they have told me, more than once. I greet them and ask what they'd like to drink, even though I know they both have decaf tea, every day.

They sit quietly chatting about their plans for the day and soon there is another table to wait on, then another, and another, and eventually my mum and dad appear.

"Morning, love!" Dad greets me.

"Shh!" Mum says, aware that it doesn't look very professional. Dad winks at me. I get them a pot of coffee.

"Some night last night, eh?" Dad says.

I go red. What does he know? Then I realise he's either talking about the storm, or the party.

"Oh, yeah. It was, wasn't it?"

"That Bea knows how to throw a party! Hey, and what about your new job? You are going to take it, aren't you?"

"Let Alice get on with her work, Phil," says Mum, smiling at me. "We can talk about it later, I thought maybe we could all go down to the south coast, revisit a few places, what do you think?"

"Sounds lovely, Mum," I say. I could do with some distractions today.

The morning passes quickly but I manage to text Julie while I'm working on reception.

How are you? Everything OK? Missing you this morning xx

It's some time before I hear back.

It's awful. Though Luke and his dad are being great. I'll tell more later. Are you around this afternoon? Xx

Out with Mum and Dad, they've only got another couple of days left here, but I guess we'll be back later.

Great, I'll try and get to the flat tonight, then. Have a good day. Say bye to Phil and Jane for me xx

Won't you be here in the morning?

I'm not sure. I'll explain later.

This is all very mysterious. Maybe she's decided to leave early. I guess there's no point being here longer than necessary, and being an extra complication for Luke. I feel so sad when I think of him. His heart broken twice over, though hopefully he'll realise that he and Julie weren't meant to be. And they've only been together a very short time. Maybe it won't even bother him; losing his mum is a much bigger deal.

I have a lovely day with Mum and Dad. We get the same train I caught the other day, my parents sitting across from me, chatting away good-naturedly. I love watching the way they interact. They really like each other. I know that sounds a bit odd – of course they do, they're married – but I'm not sure all couples who have been married so long still get so much pleasure from each other's company. For some I think it's more of a habit, being together. I don't want that to ever happen to me.

We walk past the cottage we used to stay in, then down to a tiny fishing village, which is almost painfully beautiful. The weather today is fresh and bright; the sun reminding us that even if those clouds blocked its presence yesterday, it is still here while they are long gone. It rises gradually into the rich blue of the sky until just after midday when it sits high above us, magnanimously throwing down heat and light, so much so that we beat a hasty retreat into a pub, for a bit of respite.

We eat thick homemade chips with mayonnaise, and drink bitter shandy, then we all wander down to the rocks, where we settle down to let our food digest and give ourselves a chance to relax in the sun. Unsurprisingly, Dad is soon snoring. Mum looks at me and smiles.

"So, are you going to go for it?"

"The Sail Loft?" I clarify.

"Yes, what else?" she asks. I think of Sam but I laugh.

"What do you think?" I ask her.

"I think you should throw caution to the wind and go for it."

"But my flat…"

"… you can carry on renting it out. Dad and I are always around to keep an eye on things, you know."

"What happens when Bea comes back and I have no job anymore?"

"Well, I don't know. You'll have to work it out. But you've got a few months to do that. I can't believe you've got any doubts about it, I can see how much you love it here! And you've got no real ties at home."

This is true. But it's a bit of a scary thought. And now Sam's back on the scene, for some reason it's scarier. I think last night when Bea made her proposition, I wanted to say yes because I wanted to show him I didn't need him; I could be here, in Cornwall, under my own steam, if I wanted to.

Now he's back, and he's so lovely. What if he doesn't

want me to stay, though? What if this is just a convenient little summer thing for him? And what if my presence makes things difficult for him with Sophie? I'm not too worried about Casey... Kate, I have to keep reminding myself... but it's not fair on his daughter if I mess up their relationship.

"I know," I sigh. "It's a dream come true, really."

"Then go for it!"

"Do you know what, Mum? I think you're right. I think I have to."

"That's my girl!" Mum puts her arm round me and I lean into her, looking out across the sea; its colour a thick, dark green here in this sheltered bay. A cormorant stretches its wings on a rock, then flies away. I watch its progress until it disappears behind the headland.

As Dad snores on, I find myself telling Mum all about everything – or nearly everything – which has happened since Julie and I came back down here. I give her a fairly diplomatic version of Julie's mess with Luke and Gabe, and Mum smiles to herself.

"What?" I ask her, feeling defensive on my friend's behalf.

"Oh, nothing," she says. "It just sounds like Julie. And no, love, I don't mean that in a bad way. It's just that ever since you two have been old enough to be into boys – and not just posters of popstars – she's thrown herself into it, hasn't she? I know you two thought you were so secretive and clever, but I knew what was going on. And no, I wasn't spying on you! There was Steven Wainthorpe, wasn't there, when you were about fifteen?"

"Fourteen," I say, remembering being a lookout for Julie and Steven while they snogged behind one of the temporary classrooms at school.

"I remember him because he marked the start of my worrying about you and boys. But my own worries never really came to fruition, well not until…"

"Geoff?"

"Yes, Geoff," Mum says grimly. "But Julie was different. Was she ever without a boyfriend from that point on?"

I think back. Was there ever really a time when Julie was single, after Steven? For more than a few days – or weeks, at the most? Even during those times, she'd be out on the pull pretty much every week, as she was in the golden summer, and again when we first came down here this year. And it's strange, because she's not one of those women who thinks she needs a man to validate her, or at least I didn't think she was. She is a strong and confident person. She is great at her job and came top of her class at catering college. She's outgoing and funny, and lots of other things I wish I was. But what she said about me and Gabe, well that took me by surprise. I know nobody is one hundred per cent confident but maybe Julie is more insecure than she'd let even me know. And Mum is right, she has never really been without a man. Which is why, I suppose, I shouldn't have been surprised that Julie got herself into another relationship so quickly. I only wish she'd taken a bit more time to consider Luke's feelings.

I look at Mum. She is pushing a stray wisp of hair away from her eyes, and tucking it back behind her sunglasses. I wonder what it was like for her when I was with Geoff; Dad never hid his feelings very well but Mum seemed to sit back and watch, never showing hers.

"You must have worried about me when I was with Geoff," I say.

"Yes," she looks sad. "I did. I could see what he was like,

although I didn't realise quite how extreme he was. If I had known, then I'd have intervened. But I never wanted to interfere. I think people have to make their own mistakes. But there's only so far you can go with that. When your nineteen-year-old daughter is being pushed about and bullied, then I think that's a time you can get involved. I wish I had."

"Well, you weren't to know, Mum. I think I was better at keeping secrets by then than when Julie and Steven Wainthorpe were going out!"

Mum smiles. "I think you'd come back from Cornwall so happy. You'd met that boy down here, and you'd clearly had so much fun with Julie. You were sad to be back but looking forward to starting university. It felt like a really good time. Then you got sadder, and you wouldn't tell me why, though I guessed it was to do with the boy down here. Then along came Geoff. He was older, and more adult – or so it seemed – and he worried me from the start. But for a while you seemed happy again. In a quieter way. Then the happiness went but the quiet remained."

"I've seen him again, Mum, the boy down here," I quickly clarify, for fear that she will think I'm mad, seeing Geoff's ghost or something.

"Oh yes?" she smiles. "And is he still a hunk?"

"A hunk?!" I exclaim. "This isn't *Neighbours*, Mum."

"But he is, isn't he?" Her eyes twinkle.

"Yeah, OK. He is."

"And is he single?"

"Yes, yes he is. But it's complicated."

"Well, that's life. Nothing much that isn't complicated I'm afraid, love. The older you get, the more you'll find that."

I find myself telling her another slightly sanitised story; this time about me, and about Sam. About the first time were together, that first golden summer, and how it's been this time. About his accident, my misunderstanding. Geoff. And I tell her about Casey/Kate. And Sophie.

"OK," Mum says slowly. "So you two splitting up should never have happened, not really?"

"No."

"And you both went into rebound relationships, and you both got more than you bargained for."

"I suppose we did," I agree.

"And Sam stayed with his girlfriend and daughter at first?"

"Yes, for a couple of years, I think."

"And he's still a good dad?"

I think back to what Kate has told me about Sophie's dad and I think yes, it sounds like he's been great. I nod my head.

"So he's basically a really nice bloke?" Mum's echoing what David had to say about Sam.

"Yes, but he didn't tell me about Sophie."

"OK," she concedes, "I can see why that might bother you. But how many times have you two been out?"

I think back. Other than our one night out, there was the time I fell at his feet on the coastal path; that hardly counts as a date.

"Just once, really," I say. I don't tell her about him coming back to mine, after he'd taken Julie to Luke.

"Right, and he's said he was going to tell you about everything? Didn't you say he'd sent a text saying he had more to discuss, or something? When he was taking you out to dinner?"

"Yes," I say.

"Well, I think, my love, that you might be giving him a little bit too much of a hard time. He could have told you about his daughter on the one date you had but is it possible that he just wanted to see if you two still had the same chemistry? It's probably a big thing for him, you know, getting involved with somebody when he's got a daughter to think about, too."

What's Mum doing? She's turning the tables. I feel myself bristle. But mostly because I know she is right.

"Maybe I have been a bit stupid," I say.

"Oh love, you haven't been stupid," Mum pulls me to her again. "It's difficult, being a parent, though. And I imagine even more difficult, trying to form a relationship when you've become a parent at a pretty young age. Sophie is... how old?"

"Nearly ten."

"Right, so how many people your age do you know with a ten-year-old?"

"None, except Sam... and Kate," I concede reluctantly.

"Precisely. So how did he know how you'd react if he just came out and told you he's a dad?"

"Dammit, Mum, stop making so much sense!" I laugh.

She laughs too. "Look, Alice, I've been so proud of the way you've dealt with things since Geoff... died... but you've made yourself diluted, somehow. You've been lovely, as always, but you've kept yourself under control. Regular job, paying off a mortgage, keeping fit... all great things to do but that's how you've spent your twenties and I wish you'd been a bit more wild! I know I'm not meant to say that, being your mum. But it's true. It's different now to how it was for me. I don't mean you should have been out there getting drunk every night, having loads of one-night-stands. But I wish I'd been able to be a bit more impetuous – don't tell your dad. I feel like Geoff scared you, made you a more timid version of yourself. Maybe it's time to just throw caution to the wind now, eh? Take this job. Call Sam, go out for that meal that never happened. Talk about it all. You don't have to throw yourself into a relationship but I don't think you should throw away your chance with him, either. To be honest, he sounds lovely."

"He is lovely," I say, just as Dad snores so loudly that he wakes himself up. Mum and I laugh, and Dad looks slightly bewildered. I sit between them both, as Dad slowly comes round, and I feel this knowingness between my mum and me. I am so glad I talked to her and I know what I have to do.

25

Now it's about the timing. I am impatient, eager to get on with things, to talk to Sam while I think I still have a chance. But of course there are other priorities. Luke's mum has just died and Sam is with him, and so is Julie. She's been back to the flat to get more clothes but she's done it while I'm at work and I think that her timing was by design.

Sam and I text regularly but they are short, sweet messages. I am not going to tell him what I have to say via SMS. Gabe phones me, more than once, but I don't know what to do so I ignore him, and feel my conscience gnawing away. I have no idea what Julie is up to now. She was meant to be returning home this weekend but after Mum and Dad left I sent her a message to see if she wanted a hand packing. She didn't reply. I know she must be in a bit of a state herself and I don't suppose she can very well up-and-leave Luke right now but she'd broken up with him and, as far as I know, Gabe is expecting her back home.

Sam has told me the funeral will be on Friday, just over a week after May's death. It seems a short time but I know Luke and his dad had made plans for the funeral with May herself, before she got really ill and went into the hospice. The wake will be held back at the family house. I wonder what it will feel like for friends and family to be there, eating and drinking, with May nowhere to be seen.

I am determined to be strong, and stoical, and bide my time. I go to work, I eat healthily, I run, and I swim. I haven't heard from Casey/Kate, and I certainly don't intend to get in touch with her. I still feel bad for her in a way but I also think she behaved like a bit of an idiot.

What I can't decide is whether I should go to the funeral or not, but I think probably not. I don't know if it would be weird as I didn't know May very well, and I think it's going to be a very, very full church. Maybe I will go to the church to pay my respects then make myself scarce.

Although I know what to say to Sam, I also know now is not the time. I must be patient, but it isn't easy.

I do, however, have to talk to Bea. Every day at work I can see she is trying not to ask me if I've made up my mind yet, but I don't want to keep her in suspense. She will have a lot to do before she goes away. So on Tuesday morning, after my breakfast – cooked by Jonathan and totally delicious (don't tell Julie) – I knock on her office door.

"Come in, Alice," she smiles at me.

I almost want to leave her guessing; I can see the anticipation written all over her face. It's very flattering, really. I look at her. She looks at me. I can't leave her hanging on any longer. I feel nervous all of a sudden.

"I'm going to do it," I say. "Take the job, I mean. If you still want me to."

Bea flings her arms around me. "Yes! Of course I still want you to. Why on earth would I not want you to? Thank you, Alice, you've made an old woman very happy."

"You're hardly old," I grin.

"I feel it sometimes," she says, "when I wake up and look in the mirror and I wonder who that is looking back at me. Then I realise it's me. Urgh."

"Well, clearly Bob doesn't feel the same way."

"No, he... he seems pretty keen," she says. "I don't know, I must be mad. I haven't been in a relationship for years and now I decide to throw it all in for somebody in the States. What am I thinking?"

"You're not throwing it all in," I reassure her. "You're taking a chance." I think of what Mum said to me, about throwing caution to the wind. "It's great, it's exciting!" I say, and Bea laughs.

"It is, isn't it?"

"Yes! And this is exciting for me. I thought I was going back to World of Stationery, and now I get to stay here, in this beautiful place, for a little longer at least. I will look after it for you, Bea, I promise."

"I know you will. And I didn't want to mention it before but we're all ready to go with the ad for a night manager so now you've said yes, I'll put it in the *Advertiser*, this week. You can help interview them!"

I look out of Bea's window; the bright white shutters frame a view across the rooftops of the town and across the dazzling sea. I feel excited and calm all at once. I am so sure now that I have made the right decision. The only slight niggle is that I haven't told Sam yet, but I haven't had a chance to. I hope that he won't mind. I hope that he'll be happy.

When I get back to the house, I dash up the steps two at a time. For the first time in days, Julie is there. She comes to the door of her room as I make it to the top step.

"Hi," she says, almost nervously.

"Hi," I say, and I look at her, move forwards, and hug her. I feel her relax, and lean into me, and then sob. "Come on," I say, and I move her gently back into her room, sitting on her bed with her while she cries into me, all thoughts of my exciting news forgotten.

When Julie is able to, she sits up a little, wipes her eyes, and looks at me.

"How is Luke?" I ask.

"He's... amazing." She gives a little laugh. "Him and his dad. They are both so... accepting. And positive. And determined."

"Well that's good, isn't it?" I ask. I think of what I've heard people say about funerals – how everything is focused on the organisation, and how friends and family are there all the time; how it's only after the event that it really sinks on. That life has to return to normal, only without that key person in it. Meaning it can't be normal, not really. Not for a long time.

"Yes, it is. It is."

"It's been hard, though, hasn't it?"

"Yes," she swallows back a sob. "Really hard. And I don't know what to do for the best. I really don't. What a mess. What a fucking mess."

I don't say anything. Julie continues, "It looks like I'm back with Luke now. I didn't really mean that to happen, but when Sam took me over there that night, I knew I couldn't go back to Gabe. I couldn't leave Luke like this. He was great. He was calm, he was focused, but so very, very sad. I know that's not surprising. But I couldn't leave him. Even after he'd finally fallen asleep, I lay awake. I thought about Gabe, and how great he is, and how much I miss him. But I sent him a message saying I'm staying in Cornwall."

"Bloody hell," I say, "how did he take it?"

"Not well. He tried to call me back straight away but it was about five in the morning. I couldn't speak to him; Luke was asleep next to me. I did call him back later that day and he was devastated. He got that job, by the way."

"Shit," I say. "He's tried to call me, you know, but I didn't know what to say to him."

"I know, I'm sorry. I didn't mean to put you in an awkward situation."

"Don't worry," I say, and I mean it. "Do you think you can be happy, though? With Luke?"

"Well, yes. I think so. I don't know. I mean, he's got to go back to London at some point but I don't see myself doing that. I think I've got to stay here; I can't go home, but I don't want to live in London. Do you think Bea will give me my job back?"

"I don't know," I say. "I think Jonathan's planning to stay, I don't think she can mess him about." I hope Julie doesn't expect me to get rid of Jonathan in favour of her, when I tell her my news. "Are you sure you want to stay here? You can't just make this decision because Luke's mum has died."

"It's not just that," she says. "You know I was confused already. And yes, Gabe says he's going to change... but how often do people really change? When he was here, I realised how much I missed him. But that night, when I lay awake with Luke sleeping next to me, I was looking at him and I just felt... overwhelmed... with feeling for him. And I know it might be sympathy, and it was an intense situation. But I thought to myself that I love Luke. And I do. I know I do."

"And Gabe..?"

"I don't know! I think I love him, too, but maybe we've

changed too much, or I have, over the last few years. Luke is a real adult; it's not just his business or his nice car and his own flat. Watching how he's been these last few days, I just can't explain it. He's dignified and sensible and serious. I think I really, truly have fallen in love with him."

"Well, if that's the case," I say, "then you are doing the right thing."

I know now that I just need to support her. How many times have I told myself that this summer, but then gone ahead and questioned her actions? I need to listen to myself now. I can see how hard this situation is for her. I feel very bad for Gabe but maybe she's right. Only time will tell.

"What are you doing right now?" I ask.

"I'm... I don't know. Luke's aunty Helena has just arrived, from Plymouth. I said I'd come back to his later but I think he wants to come here instead; I hope that's OK."

"Of course it is," I say, and I can't help wondering if that means Sam is free this evening too. "Come on, let's get some fresh air. Let's walk to Zennor and get an ice cream."

Julie smiles. "I can't think of anything I'd rather do."

As we walk that afternoon, I decide to take Julie's mind off things by telling her about the events of the last few days. I swear her to secrecy about the job, because I need to tell Sam about that myself; I don't want it coming second-hand, or third-hand, from Luke.

"So we're both staying down here?" Julie cries, delighted. "That is so great. I was going to ask David if he'd let me stay in the flat a bit longer. Do you think he will?"

"I don't know, I can ask him," I say. "But it might be a bit weird, if I'm in the main house downstairs!" I explain about David asking me to stay on in his place.

"That's fine," she says, "I'll be like your maid or something."

"Yes, I'll get a bell and you can bring me supper."

"Perfect, that's the new job sorted, then."

I go on to tell her about Sam returning after he'd dropped her at Luke's.

"No!" she exclaims.

"Yep."

"Bloody hell! This is crazy. Think back to a few months ago – April, say. Could you ever have imagined all of this stuff happening?"

I do think back. I remember April. I had a couple of days off at Easter and I did nothing with them. I went to my parents' a few times. I went shopping. I went to the cinema on my own. I was content living like that, I thought, but now I think I wasn't living at all.

"No," I laugh. "So I suppose I really need to thank you for dragging me out of my little spinster-like existence."

"Ha!" she laughs. "Now you know I'm always right."

"I wouldn't go that far."

As we walk, the sea sparkles and shimmers. Far off towards the horizon is a large, industrial-looking boat. Despite the storm and rain the other night, the ground is dry, and cracked in places. We pass a man and his dog; the man brown and leathery-skinned, like he spends his whole life walking this path. He smiles and nods at us but doesn't break his stride. The heat of the sun intensifies as we go and the path becomes harder work but it feels good. At Zennor we stop and rest, leaning our backs against an old stone wall while we eat our ice creams. The tables and benches are packed with families; children laughing or arguing with each other. One little boy crying because he doesn't like the flavour of ice cream he's chosen and he wants his sister's; their dad red-faced, managing to win the day by giving the boy his own ice cream. Julie and I laugh between ourselves at his face as he tries the blue bubble gum flavour he's been left with.

We sit for quite some time, taking it all in, letting everything wash over us. Just breathing and thinking, glad to be together. Happy to have each other. We refill our water bottles before we leave and begin the hot walk home; retracing our steps along the dry cracked path, sea on the other side of us now, sun on our necks. Back to the town and the flat, to our newly reformed lives.

26

The day of the funeral dawns sunny and clear. I've hardly slept all night - I've been tossing and turning and having weird dreams – so I feel like I'm awake to hear the actual crack of dawn, followed shortly by the screeching of gulls and then the steady whirr of the street cleaner.

Dawn is coming increasingly later in the day – there is still more summer to come but I always feel at this time of year like we've had the best of it. The anticipation during that long build-up to midsummer may be better than the summer itself as the days stretch out at either end and there's promise in the air.

Today, it feels like there is just a sweet sadness. If I listen hard enough, behind the noisy, attention-seeking gulls, there are the other birds' songs. I can pick out a robin, and a pair of blackbirds. I know that up on the headland the smaller birds are waking too, calling to each other, announcing the new day.

My thoughts move to Luke, and his dad, and Julie and Sam, both of whom have stayed over at Luke's the night before his mum is due to be buried.

I have seen Sam a couple of times but these have been short-lived occasions, and focused on arranging things for the funeral; I was up at Luke's yesterday baking cakes, as Julie had roped me in to helping her, and I was more than happy to. Sam had come rushing into the kitchen then stopped when he saw me and smiled.

"Hi," he said.

"Hi," I replied.

Julie had tutted and laughed to herself.

"What?" we both exclaimed indignantly, then we had all laughed.

I have so much I want to say to Sam but this week has not been the right time.

The funeral is at 2.30pm, so I am going to work as normal then I'll come back for a quick lunch and change and head to the church. Julie says it is likely to be packed out. I don't want to take anybody's place. I didn't know May very well, but I want Luke to know I am there for him.

The Sail Loft is full, and there are endless calls from people almost all wanting to find a place to stay for the bank holiday weekend. There is nothing at the Sail Loft but we have a list of other independent hotels which we can send out; there are eight in town which support each other and it works very well. I am wondering whether there is more we can do to work together but it's something for me to think about while Bea is away. I won't be able to make any decisions like that without her but I can present her with some ideas.

Anyway, the morning flies by. At the end of my shift, Jonathan calls me into the kitchen.

"Here," he says, "I know you've got a funeral to go to this afternoon and you can't have much time. Get this down you before you go, it'll save you some time."

On the gleaming chrome work surface are two plates, with pie and mash.

"One for me, and one for you," he smiles. "It's a new

creation of mine so you'll be doing me a favour, eating it. Sweet potato, spinach, and goats cheese – with a few pine nuts."

My stomach rumbles. "Wow, thank you!" I say, and he gestures towards the dining room. I walk in and he follows with the plates. There is a table for two set by the window.

"Funerals are horrible things," he says. "My gran's was last year. Mum was a mess."

"I'm sorry," I say.

"Yeah, it was a nightmare. I've got younger twin sisters, from Mum's second marriage, and they were crying their eyes out. I had to look after them and I didn't feel like I was able to say bye to Gran, really."

"That sounds pretty awful," I agree.

"I went travelling a couple of weeks later. I couldn't handle it," he admits sheepishly.

"I think that's OK," I say. "I'm sure your gran would want you to be enjoying your life, not sitting around and moping."

I look at him properly for the first time and he smiles almost shyly, his teeth white against his tan. He is really nice looking, with a sprinkle of freckles across his face, but he seems so much younger than me, even though the age gap can only really be four or five years. When I was his age, I'd been through the Geoff thing and was just starting to sort my head out. It made me grow up quickly, I suppose. And listening to Jonathan talk about his gran, and his little sisters, I feel like he is a different generation to me. He makes a mean pie, though.

"Ten out of ten for the pie," I tell him. "This is lovely."

"Really?" His smile widens. "I never quite know with veggie stuff. I mean, I like veggie food, but most people want meat, don't they? This takes a bit more work, getting the flavours right."

"Well, I'd definitely add this to the menu," I say. "Maybe we should put an emphasis on more vegetarian food – that might give us a different angle to some of the other places round here. Maybe in the quieter months, we could open the restaurant to non-residents, some evenings."

Ever since I decided to take the job, I've been having loads of ideas for the Sail Loft but I have to keep myself in check. This is not my hotel. I am simply caretaking for Bea. And I know it works very, very well as it is.

"Sounds great," Jonathan says through a mouthful of pie.

I smile. I am looking forward to working with him. He seems to be a really nice guy. I feel bad for Julie, not having a job here any longer, but she knows that the situation is of her own making. I can't exactly sack Jonathan to get Julie her job back, can I?

With a full stomach, I rush back to the flat and put on my funeral clothes. I managed to get a black dress in the charity shop, and some shoes. It's a hot day so I don't want a jacket but I fold a thin cardigan and put it into my bag. I haven't been to many funerals and I am suddenly nervous about the etiquette.

As I approach the church, I begin to feel a bit sick, thinking about Luke and how he must be feeling. I can see thirty or so people outside the church; talking in small groups. I shyly stand back. Aside from Luke and his dad, I can't see anybody I know here. Actually, scrub that. Just inside the doorway, there is Casey (Kate, I must call her by her proper name from now on) in a short black dress, with a fascinator in her hair – which seems somewhat inappropriate for a funeral, I think. There is Sophie, next to her, in a pretty light blue dress and red shoes. I want to say hello to her but I know I need to keep my distance. Presumably Sam and Julie are around too but I know they are both meant to be helping out inside the church; handing out little booklets of photos that Luke and his auntie have put together, from key moments in May's life.

I lean on the churchyard wall, out of the sunshine, and out of the way of the other mourners. I look around me, at the flowers, which sprout from tree trunks, cracks in old gravestones, and gaps in the wall. Then I am aware of somebody walking towards me. I look up.

"Hi, Alice," he says, and he is smiling at me.

"Luke, hi," I say, and I reach up to kiss him on the cheek. "How are you? Or is that the most stupid question ever?"

"No, it's not," he says, coming to lean against the wall next to me. "I'm meant to be greeting people by the door there, but I just can't do it. Dad and Marie are in church already. So is Mum. They brought her coffin in last night. We had a small service; Mum's sister and my cousins, me, Marie and Dad. Julie came, too." He smiles again. "I couldn't have got through this without her, you know. And I know it's been a total mess, with me and her, and her ex. But I feel like she was meant to come into my life when she did. That sounds horribly cheesy!"

I laugh and shake my head. "No, it doesn't. I'm glad for you, and for her."

"I don't expect anything, you know. None of us knows what life is going to throw at us so I'm grateful she is here, now, and I hope that we can make it work but my head is a total mess at the moment, about Mum. I know there is a long way to go with getting through losing her." He stops and I think he is going to cry, but he swallows and continues. "Don't be mad at Julie," he says. "She's been trying to do the right thing, all along."

"I know, I know she has," I put my hand on his arm.

"She needs you," he says.

"Well I need her, too!"

"I can't tell you how happy I am that you two have come back into my world," Luke puts his arm around me, and I hug him, suddenly fighting back tears myself. "And I shouldn't say this but I think Sam is pretty happy too."

As if he knows he is being talked about, I see Sam appear from the wide wooden door of the church, blinking as he steps into the sunlight, looking around, presumably for Luke.

"Duty calls," Luke says, and without another word, he strides across the churchyard. I want to shout after him but I don't know what to say. 'Good luck' doesn't seem right, somehow.

He cares so much about Julie, I think, to have come and spoken to me on her behalf – unnecessarily – at his own mum's funeral. I hope she knows how lucky she is. I think she does.

Sam turns and smiles at Luke, then his gaze falls on me. My stomach does a little twirl. He smiles, briefly, then Luke reaches him and Sam puts a reassuring hand on his friend's shoulder. The two of them walk into the church where Luke's mum lies in her coffin, surrounded by the people who love her most.

I stand at the back of the packed church, in the lobby area. I don't know if that's the correct term for this part of a church. I probably learned at school but if you don't use something, you often forget it and I'm afraid I don't use church at all any more. Now, as I stand in the beautiful, echoing building, I think maybe I should. I am not religious; I hate religion, in many ways, but churches are beautiful places, and peaceful by their very nature. The perfect setting for quiet contemplation and gathering thoughts.

There are people sitting in the pews, and lining the walls of the church, all here for May. So many people that I can't see Luke or his dad, or Sam or Julie. I can make out Kate's fascinator sticking up from one of the middle pews. I wonder what Sophie makes of this situation. Has she been to any funerals before?

There is an opening hymn, then a reading by a young woman, who could be Marie. I have never met Luke's sister but I can see the family resemblance in her dark hair and eyes.

Another hymn, some words from the priest, and then Luke walks falteringly up to the altar.

He reaches the lectern, turns, and looks out ahead of him, seeing, I suppose, a sea of faces. Hot bodies packed together quietly and sombrely, remembering his mum, and supporting him. I try to imagine how he feels. He is dressed in a black shirt and trousers, with a grey-blue tie. He loosens the collar of his shirt with his finger and coughs.

"My mum," he begins, and he gestures to the coffin which is set in the middle of the space between the pews and the altar. There are orange flowers on it – a mix of geraniums, crocosmia and roses, with wide green leaves pointing outwards. There is also a photo of May.

I catch my breath at Luke's words and he repeats them. "My mum," he continues this time, "would have been so happy to see you all here. Hopefully, she is somewhere that she can see all of this and she knows how many people care for her, and for Dad."

"And you, mate," a voice calls from one of the aisles. I smile, and Luke does too.

"She was a wonderful woman, Mum. She was a proper mum. She took me to school every day and brought me home, helped with my homework, had my friends round, all the time. She liked having people around and I know my friends loved her, almost as much as I did... do..." Luke stops for a moment, choked by his words. "She was more than a mum. She was clever, and talented. She was a great artist and you'll see some of her paintings back at our house today. I bet none of you knew she was great with IT, too. She was well into computers, secretly. It was her that got me started with it all. She was a secret geek." There is a light ripple of laughter at this and Luke grins. "But more than anything, Mum loved people. She loved her family. Aunty Helena and Mum were more than sisters; they were best friends. But Mum had so many other close friends, it's impossible to name them all, and I know that you're all here today. I know how much it meant to her that you kept coming to see her when she was ill and suffering. There was nothing to say sometimes, she told me, but you coming to see her said all she needed to know." I can hear open crying from more than one place in the church. I want to cry myself but I really don't feel it is my place to. I can't claim this grief as these people do. Luke takes a moment, carries on. "There are so many things I can say about Mum but you know them already. I was so lucky to have her, and I am lucky still because I know that whatever I do, I will have her in my mind, and my heart. And it is such an easy thing to say but I want to say it anyway – Mum was lucky that her friends stuck by her and she knew how many people cared about her, but sometimes we forget to let people know and then, then they die and it's too late. I don't know if Mum can see us all here or not but wouldn't it be nice to make sure that people know in life how much you care about them – if we make the effort for people *now*. Coming to a funeral is beautiful and respectful but making people feel loved in this life is the very best thing you can do for them. It's what Mum always did."

At this, Luke looks down, and I notice he has some notes in his hand but I am sure he hasn't looked at them once during his beautiful speech. I also realise that tears are streaming down my face and I am sure those of everyone else here.

Then a quiet clapping begins in one part of the church, and another pair of hands joins in, elsewhere, then another, until the entire church is clapping Luke, as he makes his way past his mum's coffin and back to his seat. The applause goes on for some time.

After this there is another hymn, and another reading, and then the priest says it is time to make our way to the graveside.

I walk out of the church; hang back, not wanting to escape but not wanting to get in the way. I will stay for this bit, I think, then go.

I follow on, and a nice older lady befriends me, telling me how she and May first met at an artists' group but discovered they had other friends in common, and began walking regularly. She tells me all this with a smile on her face. When she asks how I know May, I say that really it is Luke I know, but that May used to welcome us in when we were teenagers.

"Oh, yes, she was always welcoming," the lady says, still smiling. She excuses herself as we near the grave, and walks further towards the front of the people assembled nearby. Clearly a few people have dropped away from the church at this point but there are still many gathered around, to watch the coffin lowered into the ground.

The sun is relentless; there are no clouds, no places for it to hide. We are all sweating in our dark, smart clothes. There is a fantastic view of the sea from this graveyard – the best view in town, David says - and the water is glimmering away merrily, at odds with the solemn occasion. I listen to the birds in the trees which punctuate the graveyard. They sing heartily, providing a melodious soundtrack.

I can't bear the thought of seeing somebody I love so much buried in the ground. But neither can I bear the thought of them cremated. Either way is so final, I just can't stand it. But lucky me, I haven't had to, yet.

The priest speaks a few words and then the coffin is lowered respectfully into its grave. The mourners at the front have their arms round each other, or are clasping each other's hands tightly. Julie is there, next to Luke; his dad, sister and aunt on his other side, and Sam just behind him. The immediate family take it in turns to scatter earth on the grave, then step back and it is the turn of other mourners. I see Sam step forward, tears streaming down his face, and Julie takes her turn, too. She turns and Luke smiles at her. He is glad she's there.

We wait while everybody who wishes to has a moment in front of the grave, then Luke, his sister and his dad turn, and people begin the slow procession away, leaving May in her coffin, to be covered up for good.

I wait, about to peel away, but I feel a soft hand on my shoulder. It's Sam. His eyes are red but he's smiling at me.

"Alice," he says. "You're coming back to the house?"

"I, I don't know. I don't feel like I should. Should I?" I look at him.

"Of course," he says, "Luke will be really pleased if you come. He already said he wants people to come and make it a positive event. There are a few who he thinks can't help but put a negative spin on these things and he doesn't want that. And you've got to come and see May's paintings, too. They've been put up around the downstairs, with a proper display in the conservatory. They're beautiful."

I smile at Sam. "What about Kate, though?" I ask. I realise I'm a bit scared of her.

"Don't worry about her!" he says. "She'll just have to get on with it. I know Sophie would love to see you again."

"Really?"

"Yes, really!"

Sam takes my hand, and we walk together through the baking hot churchyard, where the shadows of the trees dapple the ground and the birds stay on, singing to Luke's mum, keeping her company.

27

Julie is also pleased to see me at the wake. "Alice!" she hugs me, her eyes red-rimmed. "I am so glad you're here. I feel outnumbered. And like Luke's family are suspicious of me."

From what I've seen, Luke's family are all extremely lovely, and welcoming towards Julie. I suspect she's just worrying because of the situation with Gabe.

"Look, none of them know anything more than that you're Luke's lovely new girlfriend," I reassure her, "which is totally true. You are his lovely new girlfriend. He really loves you, you know."

"I know," she says and the smile on her face tells me she is genuinely happy about that. "Poor Luke."

"You're not that bad."

"I mean, because of his mum."

"I know," I nudge her and she smiles at me. "Come on, let's get a drink, shall we?"

"Yes, we definitely should. You need to come and see May's artwork, too."

"Oh yeah, Sam said it's brilliant."

"Speaking of Sam, was I imaging things or did you two walk here hand-in-hand?"

"You weren't imagining things."

"Wow," she says softly, and we both smile at an old lady

who squeezes past us, a small dog looking at us with beady eyes, from the depths of her handbag.

Luke's dad is in charge of music and he keeps it upbeat. He and May used to go dancing a lot, and they both loved disco in the Seventies. It might sound a strange choice for a wake, but it works.

He is never alone, and I wonder if eventually he might prefer a bit of peace and quiet, but he is really the life and soul of the party in the house, filling people's glasses, reminiscing about May, celebrating her life.

The younger contingent have taken over the garden. I see Kate out there with Sophie and my stomach tightens slightly but this is not the place or time to be worrying about such things. I walk with Julie into the conservatory, where we admire May's bright, vivid oil paintings, then into the garden. Kate clocks me straight away and we give each other matching unconvincing smiles but then, "Daphne!" I hear Sophie's voice and she comes running up to me.

"Daphne?" Julie asks and I laugh. "It's a long story." I catch Kate's eye and the corner of her mouth curls slightly so I return a wide, genuine smile. Maybe this is the right time to just forget all the negative stuff.

"How are you, Cynthia?" I give Sophie a hug and she giggles. Sam turns, sees me and Sophie together, and smiles at us.

I feel I am far too happy for a funeral. But this is what Luke wants, I remind myself. He wants his family and his friends, and his mum's and dad's, around him, having a good day. Lifting and carrying him, his dad and sister, for a few hours at least. So this is what we do. We sit together in the sun, and drink wine, and eat until the enormous buffet is reduced to a couple of sad-looking sandwiches and piece of chocolate cake which was dropped and then trodden into the carpet.

"I will sort all this out," Julie reassures Luke's dad, Jim, who puts his hand on her shoulder and a kiss on her cheek. "Thank you," he says, and looks her in the eye. I can see he means for more than the food and the clearing up.

People start to head home in the early evening until there are just twenty or so of us left. Luke, Julie, Sam, Jim, Luke's sister Marie and their aunt Helena, her husband Joseph, and a handful of Luke's parents' friends. Kate and Sophie left at about five. Sophie hugged Sam, and me, and gave Luke the biggest hug of all, making him grin. "Careful," he said, "I'm old and decrepit, you know. You don't want one of my limbs falling off."

"You are not!" Sophie hugged him again and Kate kissed him. She said bye to Sam, and walked past me. I did say bye but I don't know if she heard me. I'm not too bothered, though; to be honest it was just a relief when she'd gone.

We sit on the grass, on blankets, or on the garden chairs which have been brought out. The old lady with the small dog in her bag is still here. She sits on a bench, the bag placed next to her and the dog devouring an egg sandwich.

There is music and wine, and plenty of laughter. As the sun goes down on this heady day, and the solar lights spring to life around the garden, I think that if May can see us now she will be proud, and happy.

Along with a few of the other guests, I help Julie clear everything up. "I'll get going soon," I say. "I guess you're staying here tonight."

"Yes, and we're going for breakfast to the Cross-Section tomorrow, with Helena and Joseph and Luke's cousins, and Jim and Marie, of course. If you fancy joining us. Christian's opening up specially."

"That's really nice of him," I say. "I'm going to be working, though. Otherwise I'd have loved to."

With the damp tea towels hung up and the various platters, bowls, plates and glasses stacked neatly on the side, I head into the garden.

"I'm going to get going," I say to Luke, and he stands and gives me the most enormous bear hug. It seems a long time since that first hug he gave me when we'd been reunited at the beach party.

"You take care now," I tell him.

"I will."

I say bye to his dad, and the other guests. I can't see Sam anywhere. As I head into the house, though, there he is. Standing in the hallway.

"Come on," he says, "I'm walking you home."

"You don't have to," I say.

"No, but I want to."

"Don't you want to stay with Luke?"

"He's fine," Sam reassures me. "I told him I'd go when you do. And we're going for breakfast in the morning, if you'd like to join us."

I smile. He offers me his arm. "Let's go."

We walk through the darkened town, and are nearly back at the house when a thought hits me. "Let's go to the beach."

"What, now? In our finery?" Sam laughs.

"Yes, in our finery!"

"Alright." He takes my hand, and we walk together

determinedly, not talking much, until we reach the beach by the station. We practically run down the steep steps to the sand, where at the far end there is laughter and the light of a fire. We head the other way, shoes off and quiet.

"I've got something to tell you," Sam says.

"I was about to say that!"

"Oh?"

"Yes, nothing bad, or at least I hope not. Why don't you go first?"

"OK, but let's sit." He pulls me onto the cool sand. I can hear the waves rolling in the darkness. "I couldn't tell you before. But I maybe should have. It's just it's not exactly my secret to keep. It's… well, I'll just tell you. Sophie isn't my daughter."

"She's… what?" Confusion hits me like I've been hit by a breaker.

"Well, that's not quite right, either. She is, to all intents and purposes. She is my daughter in that she has grown up with me and I am the only dad she's ever known. But when I got together with Kate, she was already pregnant. We didn't know, or at least I didn't. No, that's not fair; I am sure Kate didn't either. But then we did know. And it was either cut and run, or stay and do the decent thing. I couldn't just dump her because she was pregnant. She needed me more than ever, then. And I don't think I particularly meant people to think I was the father but they just assumed, and there seemed no harm in it. You were with… Geoff… I had long given up hope of us getting together. And then along came Soph." His voice softens and I can just see his face, lit by the light of the moon. He is smiling. "She wasn't my daughter, but she was. And she is. She always will be. The thing is, you mustn't tell anybody about this. Please. Sophie doesn't

247

know I'm not her biological dad, and I don't see any reason to tell her that now."

I wasn't expecting this. I take a moment to think about it. So Sam didn't tell me he was a dad, and now he's telling me that he isn't. But he is. I take a moment to try and digest it all. I wonder if it's right not to have told Sophie, but I don't suppose that's for me to worry about. And no wonder Kate resents me. She'd said, hadn't she, that she would like to get back together with Sophie's dad. I presume she meant Sam. I feel sorry for her. But overwhelmingly, I feel so much love for Sam who, at the age of nineteen, took on the worries and pressures of fatherhood unquestioningly. Who stayed in Sophie's life even after he and Kate had split up and who let people think Sophie was his.

"Say something," he says, and I realise I've been quiet.

"Sorry!" I laugh. "It's just a lot to take in. Are you the most amazing man ever?"

"No, not at all. And please don't think I am telling you this to make myself sound good. I just wanted to tell you, because I think we need to be honest with each other. But I have to beg you not to tell anybody else, not even Julie. Luke doesn't know, even. There's no need for anybody else to know. Sophie's the important one here."

"Yes," I agree, "she is."

"She's why I stayed, in Cornwall, I mean. And why I'm doing a regular job, to keep things ticking over. But she's starting secondary school next year and I've been studying so I hope I can make a change in my own life soon. Get back to doing what I love." He puts an arm around me, and I hear his breath as he rests his head on mine. "I still can't believe you're back here," he says. "I wish you didn't have to go again."

"Funny you should say that, it leads me neatly in to what I have to tell you..."

I explain to Sam about Bea's offer, and my new job, and staying on in David's house. The more I tell him, the more animated he becomes.

"But that's brilliant!" he says, kissing me. "You'll be doing something you love, living in an amazing house and... best of all... you'll be here! With me!"

I laugh, and I kiss him, on his mouth. He returns the kiss and we move together until we are lying on the sand, holding each other. Sam's body is warm and firm against mine. He presses against me and I want to undress him right here and now, run my hands across his smooth back, across the wiry hair of his chest. I feel his breath on my cheek, and his hand on my leg, but his fingers are cold and I shiver.

"Are you OK?" he asks gently.

"Yes," I tell him, "I've never been better."

Without another word, we get up, picking up our shoes and dusting the sand off our clothes. The moonlight spins a long silver sliver across the sea. Up above us many of the houses in the town are in darkness. I think of Luke and Julie, going to sleep in a house so definitely without May, and of Bea lying in bed, running through the lists of things she must do before she goes to the States. Somewhere on the other side of the estuary, David and Martin will be together and then back into the town, Sophie will be sleeping soundly, I hope; safe in the knowledge she has parents who love her. I think of Kate on her own and I can't help but hope things work out for her, too. She's a brave woman.

Here, on the beach, close together, Sam and I trudge, pressing firm footprints into the sand.

"I wish we were back at your flat right now," he says.

I turn and kiss him. "Me too."

"In your bed," he kisses me back.

"Or in the bath," I suggest.

"Anywhere," he growls into my ear and my stomach flips. I circle my arms around him and push my fingers in under his shirt, feeling his skin turns to goosebumps at my touch. It is his turn to shiver. "Are you OK?" I ask him.

"Yes," he says. "I've never been better."

"Come on," I say, and I loosen my grip, "I'll race you back to my place."

I run across the sand, my hair in my face and my breath becoming raw and ragged. I can't see if there are holes in the sand in the darkness, but I don't care. I keep on running. I can hear Sam just behind me and I pick up speed, knowing he will follow me. I feel alive, and free, and happier than I have in years. Grinning to myself, I am panting, and a stitch is developing in my side. There's no way I'll even make it to the top of the beach at this pace but I don't care. Right now, in this moment, I just can't stop.

Thank you very much for taking the time to read *A Second Chance Summer*. If you've enjoyed this book, a positive review on Amazon or Goodreads would be much appreciated.

Coming Soon...

Find out what happens next in **After the Sun**

Book Two of the *Coming Back to Cornwall* Series

Sam and Alice, only recently reunited, face separation when Sam's only option in order to continue his studies is to leave Cornwall while Alice is committed to her new job managing the Sail Loft Hotel in landlady Bea's absence.

Sam's visits see him split in his loyalties between his daughter Sophie, and spending time with Alice. Sophie's mother, Kate, seems to be doing her best to make things difficult.

Meanwhile, Alice's friend Julie faces a similar challenge as her new partner, and Sam's best friend, Luke, is working in London. Struggling to keep herself in work now the summer season has ended, Julie has some big decisions to make.

Can these fledgling relationships pass the long-distance test, and can Julie and Alice make life in Cornwall work for them now that the summer sun has gone?

Acknowledgements

This is my first crack at something a little more 'mainstream' and it was not planned at all. I was working my way through writing a younger readers' series but, on a family holiday in Cornwall, inspiration struck.

I owe huge thanks to my team of ace beta readers: Lucy Claire, Katie Copnall, Janet Evans, Stella Leach, Helen Smith, Claire Wells and Kate Williams.

A special mention to Jenny Armytage who, as well as also being a beta reader, is somebody whose friendship I have been lucky enough to have for twenty-five years now and with whom I spent one sunny week in St Ives in 2001. Although it wasn't a whole summer, I know we'd have had as much fun as Alice and Julie if it had been – although we would of course have been far better behaved.

Last, but of course never least, thanks to Catherine Clarke: another person whose friendship I am very fortunate to have, another lover of Kernow, and the artist and designer of yet another cracking cover.

Writing the Town Read

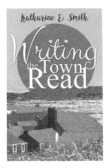

You can currently get an ebook of *Writing the Town Read* for FREE on Katharine's website: www.katharineesmith.com.

On July 7th 2005, terrorists attack London's transport network, striking Underground trains and a bus during the morning rush hour. In Cornwall, journalist Jamie Calder loses contact with her boyfriend Dave, in London that day for business.

The initial impact is followed by a slow but sure falling apart of the life Jamie believed was settled and secure. She finds she has to face a betrayal by her best friend, and the prospect of losing her job.

Writing the Town Read is full of intrigue, angst, excitement and humour. The evocative descriptions and convincing narrative voice instantly draw readers into Jamie's life as they experience her disappointments, emotions and triumphs alongside her.

Looking Past

Sarah Marchley is eleven years old when her mother dies. Completely unprepared and suffering an acute sense of loss, she and her father continue quietly, trying to live by the well-intentioned advice of friends, hoping that time really is a great healer and that they will, eventually, move on.

Life changes very little until Sarah leaves for university and begins her first serious relationship. Along with her new boyfriend comes his mother, the indomitable Hazel Poole. Despite some misgivings, Sarah finds herself drawn into the matriarchal Poole family and discovers that gaining a mother figure in her life brings mixed blessings.

Looking Past is a tale of family, friendship, love, life and death – not necessarily in that order.

Amongst Friends

Set in Bristol, *Amongst Friends* covers a period of over twenty years, from 2003 all the way back to 1981. The tone is set from the start, with a breathtaking act of revenge, and the story winds its way back through the key events which have led the characters to the end of an enduring friendship.

Both of Katharine's first two novels are written from a strong female first-person perspective. *Amongst Friends* takes her writing in a different direction, as the full range of characters' viewpoints are represented throughout the story.

How to Run a Free Kindle Promotion on a Budget

Written primarily for other indie authors, this is a great guide to making the most of your 'free days' in the Kindle Direct Publishing KDP Select programme.

With BookBub deals hard to come by, not to mention pricey, *How to Run a Free Kindle Promotion on a Budget* takes you step-by-step through the process, from planning to record-keeping. It also includes real examples to illustrate the success or otherwise of the techniques described.

Made in the USA
Monee, IL
01 April 2021